A Corner in Glory Land

"I want a future, Ivy, where I can be excited about what may come instead of worrying about finding a bunch of roughnecks pounding at our door with the intention of taking the law into their own hands. That might be *your* future, Ivy! James and Joseph were right to get out when they had the opportunity, and now I'm going do the same for myself. I'm leaving y'all to make your own choices about what your futures will be—no matter how dangerous or pathetic they may be."

"Oh…Eve! Please…I…" Her voice cracked, and she couldn't finish, so I finished the conversation for us.

"I'm tired now, Ivy—more than I've ever been in my life. And I've got to be back at the store in four hours. I need to get some sleep. So, please, let's not say anything else right now." And with the finality of that statement, I turned my back on her and my life in Silver Springs.

Also by Janie DeVos

Beneath a Thousand Apple Trees

The Art of Breathing

A Corner in Glory Land

Janie DeVos

LYRICAL PRESS
Kensington Publishing Corp.
www.kensingtonbooks.com

To the extent that the image or images on the cover of this book depict a person or persons, such person or persons are merely models, and are not intended to portray any character or characters featured in the book.

LYRICAL PRESS BOOKS are published by

Kensington Publishing Corp.
119 West 40th Street
New York, NY 10018

All Kensington titles, imprints, and distributed lines are available at special quantity discounts for bulk purchases for sales promotion, premiums, fund-raising, educational, or institutional use.

Special book excerpts or customized printings can also be created to fit specific needs. For details, write or phone the office of the Kensington Sales Manager: Kensington Publishing Corp., 119 West 40th Street, New York, NY 10018. Attn. Sales Department. Phone: 1-800-221-2647.

Lyrical Press and Lyrical Press logo Reg. U.S. Pat. & TM Off.

First Electronic Edition: December 2017
eISBN-13: 978-1-5161-0432-1
eISBN-10: 1-5161-0132-3

First Print Edition: December 2017
ISBN-13: 978-1-5161-0433-8
ISBN-10: 1-5161-0433-1

Printed in the United States of America

For Sammie Ellis, who's as warm and easy going as the Ocklawaha River. And for Elaine Percival, whose passion for all things good and right makes her a true force to be reckoned with.

This one's for you, friends, with love.

Acknowledgments

Writing a book is so much more than just coming up with an idea and using a whole lot of imagination to bring it to life. It takes a whole lot of people who are willing to share their own expertise, skills, and experience to make it happen. In doing research for the first book in the *Glory Land* series, I needed to rely on some wonderful people who could help me peel back time on an old part of Florida that was of great fascination to me: steam boating on the Ocklawaha River. It's a part of Florida's story that I tend to think is often overlooked, but one which I feel deserves to be remembered and appreciated for adding yet another layer of unique richness to the state's history.

First, I'd like to thank John Beale, education and volunteer coordinator for the Florida Maritime Museum, in Bradenton, Florida. His patience and willingness in providing me with information was vital in helping me to paint an accurate and respectful picture of steam boating down Florida's rivers.

And Astrid Drew, research and new media director of the Steamship Historical Society of America, in Warwick, Rhode Island, who was helpful in providing information on the larger vessels: steam*ships*. Yes, there is a difference, and because of her expertise, I was quickly educated about that.

I'm very grateful to Ron Mosby, Ft. King Board of Directors member and historian, in Ocala, Florida, for the wonderful tour he gave me of the fort and for providing answers, or contacting others for the answers, about Seminole Indian life and social practices.

I'd very much like to acknowledge and thank Mr. Fred W. Wood, author and longtime resident of Evinston, Florida, who invited me to sit down in his family's old post office/general store on a hot July afternoon and generously shared his time, memories, and stories about his family and the town that they founded.

And, many thanks to a very special lady, my sister, Kathy Johnson, who is a longtime resident and realtor in Ocala, Florida, for providing me with information on the rivers in central Florida, as well as for a personal tour of the Silver Springs area, including the Ocklawaha. *It was all extremely interesting and helpful, Sis, and the addition of the milkshake didn't hurt, either. Love to you always.*

And, finally, a deep and heartfelt thank you to my wonderful, sharp-eyed editor at Kensington Publishing, Alicia Condon, who took a chance on me. *To you, Alicia, I am forever grateful.*

Preface

The Ocklawaha River
Silver Springs area, Central Florida
July 1875

I didn't like the river when I first saw it. It scared me. Maybe it was because of its color, a dark greenish brown caused by the many trees that hung above and over it, staining the water with their sap, as well as shading it throughout much of the day. But, my father, Hap Stewart, saw things quite differently when we came upon it. He pulled our tired old horse to a stop on the road, which was nothing more than a sandy trail, and looked around from the wagon's seat, breathing the air in deeply. His bright blue eyes were as excited as they were at Christmas. Mama always said he was worse than the four of us kids about the holiday, though she smiled when she said it, and I think she actually thought it was kind of sweet. But his eyes were the only part of his face that was childlike that day at the river. The dust from the road had settled into the deep lines on his face, giving him a gray, worn look, even though he was just thirty-four years old. My thirty-six-year-old mother, sitting beside him, had fared no better. The only sign that there was any youth left to them was my father's still-bright auburn hair, a Scottish trait he was well proud of, and Mama's blond.

"Ceily, ol' girl," Papa said to her, "we didn't even have to die to do it."

"What in the world you talkin' about?" Mama distractedly asked. She was caught up in the sight of the enormous river before us. It curved and moved like a gigantic slithering snake, and its deep color only added to the illusion. It was a quiet river, though its flow was even and strong. Before Papa could answer Mama, my twelve-year-old brother interrupted them.

"Can we go swimming?" Joseph was already heading toward the back of the wagon, assuming the answer would be yes. He was two years older than our brother James, and three years older than my twin sister Ivy and me, and was, by far, the best swimmer out of the four of us. As we'd traveled down into Florida from Thomasville, Georgia, we'd often taken advantage of the many rivers, lakes, and ponds we'd come across, and Joseph didn't see any reason why this time would be different.

It had been three days since we'd last had a bath, and with the intense July heat bearing down on us, a swim sounded heavenly. But, before my anxious brother could work his way around a couple of pieces of our old furniture that blocked his way off the wagon, an enormous splash quickly turned everyone's attention back to the river and to an area of disturbed water. It was quite obvious that something heavy had just entered. Suddenly, a small, dark gray skull covered with rough hide broke the surface. As it rose a little higher, two small black eyes appeared above the water line, too. The alligator could obviously see our family for he swam along the bank of the river with his eyes firmly rooted on us. He was in no hurry as he went on the hunt for more accessible and familiar dinner choices than any of my family members offered.

"Still wanna go swimmin', son?" Papa smiled, amused.

"No, sir." Joseph shook his head, eyes wide.

"Let's go, Pa, 'fer it gets us," I urged. I stood behind Mama, ready to climb over the backboard of the seat which separated us and into the safety of her lap if necessary.

"No, now, that gator ain't gonna bother nothin' that ain't in that river with it."

"Still, let's go on," James said, not taking his eyes off the reptile and edging over a little closer to me, trying to get closer to Mama, too, and hoping Joseph wouldn't notice. James tried to emulate our older brother but most often fell short. It just wasn't in his nature. Even I knew that at my young age. Whereas Joseph was the leap-then-look sort, James was the mulling-things-over-before-taking-the-plunge kind. I was somewhere in between. Ivy, however, wasn't like any of the rest of us.

Though my sister and I had shared our mother's womb, there was nothing else about us that was twin-like. As a matter of fact, I looked more like my brothers than Ivy. She looked a good bit like Papa, even though she'd inherited Mama's nearly-white blond hair. But she had Papa's strong, sturdy build; his cornflower blue eyes, and his rounded facial structure. My brothers and I had Mama's leaner build, more angular facial features, and brown eyes, although James and I did have Papa's red hair while Joseph had somehow managed to get dark brown. Even though folks thought my sister and I were quieter in nature like Mama, Ivy acted more detached than anything else. I'd heard Mama say that Ivy's devil-may-care attitude was "either gonna save her or get her kilt, and should it be the latter, it's safe to say that it won't be in a very good way."

As the rest of us watched the gator as still as statues, Ivy reached down into a large wicker basket that contained some of the morning's leftover biscuits and threw one directly in front of the creature.

"Ivy! Don't waste our food!" Mama scolded while James told Ivy not to bring the thing's attention to us. But the biscuit sank, and the alligator swam on uninterrupted, obviously having larger victuals in mind.

"C'mon, Pa, let's get out of here. Let's find us somewheres safe to swim," Joseph urged.

"Can't." Papa hopped down from the wagon seat, placed his hands in the small of his back, and did a slight back bend, stretching his travel-weary body. "We've finally found it, and the amazing thing is we didn't even have to die."

"You back to that again?" Mama, sounding slightly annoyed, took her eyes off the gator to glance over at Papa before turning her attention back to the beast. "You're talkin' crazy. What in the world have we found?"

"This, m' darlin' sweet Ceily, is what we been waiting for, dreaming, saving, and sacrificing for. This is where we're callin' home. Just look at this place!" He swept his arms out wide, emphasizing the wilderness around us. "We can make anything grow in this sunshine and heat, and here's a great big beautiful river to help us do it. Family, welcome to our very own corner of Glory Land!"

"Not sure that's what I'd call it," Mama said, looking down at the ground by the wagon for any biting, stinging, or poisonous thing. "Lord, God, it's hotter 'n blazes!" She jumped down and lifted her hands to me to help me down. "C'mon, Eve, honey." But I was in no hurry to be on the ground. Instead, I took a step back, bracing myself against the inside of the wagon, shaking my head defiantly. I noticed no one else seemed to be eager to jump out of the wagon either.

Papa would have no part of squeamish women or children, however. Reaching over the side of the wagon, he lifted me up by my armpits and set me down on the ground by him. "Might as well get used to it, little girl, 'cuz this is where you'll be livin'. Jus' wait 'n see; we're all gonna love it!"

"Either that or die tryin' to," Mama grimly stated as she spotted just the tip of a scaly tail slither into a hole beneath a palmetto bush. "And from the looks of things, I'd be willin' to bet it's the latter, and sooner rather 'n later."

Chapter 1
Claimed by the River

Ocklawaha River
South of Palatka, Florida
October 1883

The snagboat had cleared most all the debris away except for one thick submerged branch. Though it was hardly visible, it was long enough to get caught in the stern's recessed paddlewheel and bring the riverboat *Jocelyn* to a jolting, shuddering stop. The wooden vessel creaked as if in pain. Hurrying down the steps from the pilot house, Captain Odell Franks muttered obscenities under his breath so as not to offend his high-paying winter clientele. These lily-white, overly dressed, strange-speaking northerners were responsible for half of his yearly income. He thanked the good Lord for them but also gave thanks that he only had to serve them for half the year. I'd once overheard him telling the landing master at the Lake Weir landing that they were "stuffier 'n an attic on an August afternoon. But, at the same time, they's chillier 'n a bass on a Janu'ry mornin'. Strange bunch, they are." He laughed, shaking his head.

Coming alongside my father, who was the boat's steward, I looked over the stern with him to see what was hanging us up. Captain Franks joined us. "Branch?" he inquired. When Papa confirmed that it was, the captain turned around and shouted up toward the pilot house. "Emmitt," he addressed his colored wheelman, who stood at the door to the pilot house, a small four-sided structure that made up the third level of the boat. "I'm gonna have ya move 'er a foot or so, but hang on 'til I tell ya. First, I want your boys jumpin' on in and havin' a looksee. If they can jostle that thing loose, at least a little bit, the wheel might spit 'er out."

Emmitt's two boys were the captain's usual deckhands. Moses Hailey was seventeen, though Papa had said more than once that he possessed the level-headedness and skills of someone much older. Louis, his brother, was a year older and different from Moses in every way. Whereas Moses was slender and quick—both in movement and mind—Louis was broad and slow. It was clear who was in charge, but Louis seemed happy enough to let Moses regularly take the lead. Moses hoped to follow in his father's footsteps as a pilot on a riverboat one day. It was one of the most prestigious and best paying jobs a colored man could have in Florida. I heard Papa say one time that he didn't know who was prouder of Emmitt's position; his sons, his wife Mayoma, or dear Emmitt himself, especially given the fact that some of his family had been slaves on an indigo plantation in south central Florida. The Haileys had reason to be proud of Emmitt, and I understood how they felt. My family and I were just as proud of Papa, and the job that he did.

My father had gone from being a dirt farmer to working on a steamboat in the well-respected position of steward. Papa said he'd come to realize that he belonged on the water all along, and not in some field. He'd started out on a smaller steamboat, the *Revere*, soon after we'd finished building our pine clapboard house, which was set back a ways from the bank of the Ocklawaha.

Our home was two-storied with a front porch, which was considered pretty fancy, but Papa said he wanted to build the house big enough and fine enough the first time so that we'd never have to build another. My parents had a bedroom downstairs, and Ivy and I shared one of the two rooms upstairs, while our brothers shared the other. Mama wanted to paint the place white, or at least white-wash it, but there wasn't enough money to do it after putting the window glass and screens in. Papa told Mama that Mother Nature would paint it just fine in time, and she had, only her color choice was the dull gray of constant exposure to the elements. In stark contrast to the washed-out color of our home was the color-infused cabbage palm and live oak hammock it sat in. Varying shades of green foliage were broken by the brightness of an ever-changing variety of flowers. Ancient live oaks, hung heavy with Spanish moss, swayed in gentle rhythm with the slightest breeze. And cabbage palms and sables were scattered throughout our yard, along with magnolia, sour orange, grapefruit, and tangerine trees. We figured that someone had started planting a citrus grove years before, but had given up for whatever reason. What was left were a variety of citrus trees that still looked beautiful with their white fragrant flowers in the spring. To our delight, we found that the fruit could be used in jams, jellies, and preserves as long as it was sweetened up with something, which was usually honey.

Our home was located several miles to the south of Silver Springs. It was convenient for Papa's work, and convenient for our family, as well. Silver Springs had a well-stocked general store, catering to patrons who knew everything about everyone in the area, including who was hiring at the moment. Such was the case one morning when Papa learned that the captain of a small steamboat was taking on men.

Papa happened to be at the store buying nails and lard when the notice was posted, and after reading that the job required no experience whatsoever, he hurried down to the dock and was immediately hired on as the *Revere's* new stoker. For the entire trip, he did nothing more than shovel coal into the firebox to fuel the boat's steam. Trip after trip, from Silver Springs to Palatka, that's all he did. It was hot, back-breaking work, but it kept the family fed, and allowed us to add eight more chickens to the four we'd brought from Thomasville, as well as a new milk cow, plus the materials needed to build a hen house and small corral for our horse and cow.

The *Revere's* captain was well-seasoned and knew a good man when he saw one. Early on, it was apparent to him that Papa was a good-natured, jovial fellow, who could be put to better use working alongside the passengers instead of being hidden away in the belly of the boat. Papa was only too glad to come up on deck. He said that "feeding that furnace in the month of August, in Florida, was near 'bout as hot as feeding the fires of hell." Mama scolded him for saying that, but she quieted down when Papa told her that she ought to go try it herself and then say whether or not he had a right to describe it so.

As the boat's steward, Papa's job was to make sure that every passenger was well taken care of and comfortable. Papa was good at his job, and every captain knew it, often trying to steal him away from whatever boat he was on at the time.

Papa took extra care with the passengers who seemed most vulnerable, like the elderly and the unescorted ladies. It was a rare thing to see a woman traveling alone, although Papa said that Yankee women did it more often than Southerners. When I asked him why that was so, he said, "Southern women are given a greater sense of modesty and decorum at birth, but Yankee gals are born with a bigger sense for adventure and bigger opinions about everything, too!" I told him it sounded to me like those northern women had more exciting lives than the southern ladies did.

The majority of travelers from the north came seeking relief from the harsh winters and to see the glories of central Florida's crystal-clear springs. By far the most popular was Silver Springs. The water had amazing clarity so its many mysterious caverns and caves could easily be seen, even those at great depths. And from those depths came many thousands of gallons of water bubbling up each day, so the spring remained full and cool and crystal clear all the time. The water filling the springs came from underground rivers, and the sandy spring bottoms, with their green ribbons of grass, filtered the water, giving it the clarity they became so famous for.

Some of the locals were none-too-pleased with the arrival of the Yankees in late autumn, especially those who brought contagious diseases, like tuberculosis, with them. Mama said it'd be bad enough to come down with one of those sicknesses living in a big city, but at least those folks had big-city doctors and big-city hospitals to tend to them. "Here, though, there ain't nothin' much to keep the ailin' goin' other than prayer and a pinch of pity," she complained. But fears and resentments could usually be tempered by the money the northerners readily spent.

"All right, boys." Captain Franks turned his attention from the snagged branch in the paddlewheel back to Moses and Louis, standing at the railing outside the pilot's house. "Y'all go ahead and jump on in, but stay outta the way while your daddy's tryin' to move 'er a tad. Then, when I say, y'all try dislodgin' that piece of shit—pardon me—" He quickly nodded to the fancy northern folks who stood around the promenade deck watching with great fascination. "You stay down here and watch them boys, Hap. I'll go up to the house," he said, referring to the pilot house.

Captain Franks knew that if any damage occurred, there would be less explaining to do and less hell to pay if he'd been at the helm at the time. When the captain started to mount the ladder-style steps, Moses and Louis ducked beneath the railing and dove into the foreboding water with practiced ease. Even though it was noon and the land was lit by the sun's strongest light, the rays barely penetrated the water, and with the darkness of the boys' skin, the two disappeared below the surface as if they'd been swallowed whole by some monstrous open mouth.

They surfaced and quickly swam toward the bank, well out of the way of the paddlewheel; then Emmitt tried to back the boat up a couple of feet. A terrible grinding noise accompanied the slight movement, and the boat was immediately stilled. "A'right, you boys," Captain Franks yelled down to them. "Give 'er a try. See if y'all can get that bastard—pardon me"—he nodded again at the northerners and turned back to the boys—"outta there. At least see if she'll budge any with a little encouragement."

Both boys took a deep lungful of air, then disappeared below the surface. Soon scraping and knocking sounds could be heard coming from beneath the boat. Suddenly, the branch—whose size had undoubtedly been reduced some by its interaction with the paddle wheel—popped up to the surface like a bobbing cork. The boys each grabbed an end and dogpaddled with it to the bank, where Moses dragged it up and well out of the way of any other unsuspecting vessels. The two swam back to the boat and climbed up a rope ladder that Papa dropped to them. As soon as they were back on board, my father gave the house the all clear signal, and the freed paddlewheel began to turn and churn the water into thick white foam as a resounding cheer went up from the passengers. The *Jocelyn* was underway once again toward her home port of Silver Springs.

Chapter 2
Bee Stings

"Only eighty-three seconds late." Satisfied with the boat's arrival time considering the hold up from the snag, Captain Franks snapped the cover on his gold pocket watch closed, tucked it back in his navy-blue vest pocket, then climbed down from the pilot house. As the steamboat's engine was shut down, allowing the boat to drift the last several feet toward the dock, Moses and Louis threw lines from the bow and stern to two men on the dock, who tossed the looped ends over vertical log pilings.

At Silver Springs landing and general store, folks were always milling around to see if any work might be available, and there was a constant flow of people coming and going on the boats. Many of those arriving needed to be driven somewhere, like the town of Ocala, which was just six miles to the east, or the Silver Springs Hotel, as well as a smattering of private dwellings. And waiting for the opportunity to serve them all were local drivers in buggies and wagons of all sorts and descriptions, lined up in the shade of a stand of oak trees just to the right of the white, two-storied building that was the store. With eagle eyes, the waiting drivers scanned the new arrivals as they made their way down the docks, watching for hands to shoot up in the air, hailing a ride. Then the first driver to spot the signal shot forward in his conveyance, making a mad dash to the dock before another driver could beat him out of a fare.

Since the general store was a stop on a stagecoach line, those needing transportation to towns farther away could find a list of times and destinations on a schedule posted above the ticket window next to the front door. Mr. Carmichael Brody owned the place, but also acted as ticket agent. He'd hurriedly step up to the window and don a visor whenever a customer was in need of a ticket. Brody was tall, big and bald, but if Mother Nature had short-changed him on a full head of hair, she made up for it with a thick, bushy mustache. The man loved peanuts and ate them throughout the day, snitching them from the large barrel that sat at the end of the counter. Because of that, Mr. Brody always had bits of peanut skins stuck in his mustache, and I wondered why his wife, Adele, didn't insist that he either shave the food-catcher off or at least run a mustache comb through it.

In big part, the flurry of activity at the landing was centered on outgoing and incoming cargo. Men off-loaded the shipments coming from the north, much of which were textiles and steel, and on-loaded cargo from our area, such as uncut logs, produce, and citrus. The freight would make the journey up the Ocklawaha, to the Welaka River, and finally the St. Johns, which would run to Jacksonville. Then the cargo was loaded onto trains from there.

Between the general store and the landing house, where the riverboats went for repair, hunters and trappers hung their freshly killed and dressed meats on racks. They were always ready to haggle over prices with anyone interested, but because they were a rough bunch, both in looks and in character, the asking price was most always paid without much negotiation. There was usually a variety of game available, as well as fish, alligator, and turtle. Some of it was fresh, but most was smoked, and though the fresh meat was by far the most desired, the smoked meats and fish lasted much longer.

There were also hides and furs to be purchased. Even though most of the passengers from the north had shed their heaviest coats of leather and fur once they crossed into the southern waters, there were still those who sought out the fine-quality skins. They shipped them to family back home or had them made into new winter clothing to be briefly worn in the south's short-lived winter. Though the majority of the time it was mild in central Florida, it wasn't uncommon for the temperature to drop well below freezing, and because the humidity was usually high, the cold could chill a body to the bone and kill vegetation overnight. It was a fear that the citrus grove owners and farmers dealt with from December through mid-February, for a deep freeze could wipe them out and turn a small Florida town into a ghost town.

Sitting on the porch in front of the general store were some of the local farmers, their wives and daughters, and widows and single women, selling live chickens, fresh eggs, and vegetables that were freshly picked, pickled, or canned. Mama and Ivy were often there. Mama always had eggs to sell, courtesy of the more than twenty-five chickens we owned by that time, as well as some of her canned goods. And Ivy brought to market honey that she harvested from the bees she'd started keeping. More sought-after than Ivy's honey, though, were the herbs she collected and the remedies and homemade medicines she made from them. Over the years, she'd learned the art of medicine making through the wonderful tutelage of Mayoma Hailey, Moses's and Louis's mother, and Emmitt's wife.

Mayoma had been born and raised in the area and had learned the skills of medicine making from her mother, who'd learned it from her mother, a full-blooded Seminole who died en route to Oklahoma during the forced march on the Trail of Tears. Mayoma's mother, Betty McIntosh, had been given to a colored family right before the government flushed the Seminoles out of the area, but because many colored people were part of the forced march, too, a small number of families moved deeper into the woods where they'd be harder to find. It was there that Betty grew up, eventually married, and had Mayoma, who then learned the ancient knowledge and skills needed to make vital medicines, elixirs, and tonics. Once there was no longer the fear of the government rounding up any more red- or brown-skinned people, Betty and Mayoma began bringing their medicines and herbs to the general store at Silver Springs. It didn't take long for the women's natural remedies to become highly sought after, especially since the area couldn't seem to keep a doctor for long, even though illnesses and injuries were as commonplace and plentiful as rat snakes in a barn.

Mayoma and Emmitt still lived in the house that they'd built eighteen years before, right after they'd gotten married. They were our closest neighbors, a mile away. Mayoma had started teaching my sister about the medicinal properties of the indigenous plants after Ivy had shown interest in an elixir the older woman had made from elderberries to help fight a hacking cough James had. We feared my brother was developing pneumonia, and I was sent to get Mayoma since Silver Springs was between doctors at the time. Within a couple of days of his taking the elderberry elixir, James's condition had greatly improved, impressing the whole family but especially Ivy. She decided then and there that medicine making was something she wanted to learn, and we saw a passion and excitement in her the likes of which we'd never witnessed before.

Most every day, except Sunday, Ivy went to the Haileys' home to be instructed by the patient and kind Mayoma, who accepted my sister's newborn passion without question, and painstakingly taught her which plants would cure and which ones would kill. Then she carefully oversaw

Ivy's selection and preparation of them until she was absolutely sure her fine young student wouldn't do someone in instead of fixing someone up. Even at the youthful age of seventeen, my sister was beginning to be regarded as a trusted medicine and herbal woman in her own right and was a regular fixture in front of the general store.

As soon as the boats docked, the steamboats' stewards and cooks, as well as the tourists, hurried over to the various foods and medicines that were available that day, carefully examining and selecting them. Papa did the selecting for the *Jocelyn*, alongside the boat's cook and Papa's close friend, Alfonso Kite.

While Papa and Alfonso selected the foods for the return trip to Palatka, the crew on the *Jocelyn* busied themselves with their own jobs, including making any necessary repairs to the vessel, as well as giving it a thorough washing down. Though Papa's job included overseeing the tidying up and changing of bed linens in all eight of the passengers' staterooms, which held two to four bunks each and were located on the first two of the three decks, the deckhands were expected to keep their own sleeping quarters below deck neat and clean, and the task was to be completed before the new passengers arrived.

The stokers were also busy loading the boat with enough coal to generate the steam needed to get it to the next port. The last thing anyone wanted, be it passenger or employee, was to run out of fuel in the middle of nowhere on the Ocklawaha River. In the day, it was sweltering hot; at night, there were swarms of bloodthirsty mosquitoes, deerflies, and chiggers. While the crew worked quickly readying the boat for the next trip, I looked around the cabin to make sure I'd packed up everything I'd bought, including cloth for the new dresses I would make for Ivy and me, as well as the material and batting I'd splurged on for a new quilt for my parents.

I was just finishing up the last of my schooling in the small, one-room schoolhouse in Silver Springs, but, before I would be through in the spring, I wanted to use the old sewing machine that was stored away in the back of the school's small coat closet. It was there that I could secretly work on the quilt I wanted to surprise my folks with at Christmas.

Aside from the material I'd bought, I also double-checked that I'd safely packed away a small parcel containing writing materials, envelopes, and stamps. While Ivy was honing her natural talents to become a healer, I hoped to follow a different path altogether: I wanted to become a journalist.

As often as I could, I wrote about the goings-on in the area. I supposed they might seem quite ordinary to some folks, but I hoped that those living in cities or larger towns might find my stories about life in the wilds of

Florida interesting. Compared to other places, especially northern cities, the state was sparsely populated, and I realized that I was writing about a subject that few people had experienced. Once my story was written, I'd usually take it to the general store to be mailed out, but there were also postal boxes that were nailed up on trees at the different landings, and I could always stick a letter in one of them. One of the arriving steamboats carrying mail would pick it up and deliver it to whomever was taking the mail on the next leg of the route. I sent my stories to various newspapers, including the larger ones, like the *New York Times*, the *Chicago Daily Journal*, and the *Jacksonville Times-Union*, and the smaller ones, like the *Marietta Journal* in Georgia, and the newly formed *West Hillsborough Times*, a weekly newspaper in Dunedin, Florida. So far, I'd only been published once, and it was with the *Marietta Journal*. I couldn't have been more pleased. I'd written about one of the local boys who'd been savagely attacked by a gator while a whole steamboat full of visiting northerners looked on in horror.

It had happened on a return trip from Palatka, just the year before. We were pretty close to home when the attack happened, and it was all on account of another snag. It wasn't a branch that caught the paddlewheel this time, however, but a piece of a roof that had blown off during one of the tremendous summer storms that were a regular occurrence.

The *Ashland* was a brand-new boat, owned by the well-respected Hart Line, and it was her maiden voyage. Ivy and I had gone up to Palatka in the hopes of selling a bunch of jars of her honey and several of my quilt throws so we'd have enough money to buy a pretty wall mirror from the Sears catalog as a birthday present for Mama. She'd been admiring it and because she was never one to want much for herself, we were determined to get her that mirror. We'd succeeded in earning the money and had promptly gone into Palatka's large general store and ordered the item, which Papa would pick up once it came in so it could be hidden away until Mama's birthday.

Ivy and I were in great spirits, having accomplished what we'd set out to do, and we were standing out on the promenade deck, enjoying the breeze and watching some sandhill cranes poking around for small fish at the river's edge when the *Ashland* hit the snag. Anyone not holding on to something was tossed about as we came to a dead stop. Immediately, the boat's captain ordered his deckhand to jump on in and try to free up the paddlewheel. The young man was Gene Pinder, and from what I was told afterward, both he and the captain were seasoned boatmen, but it was only the second time the two had run the Ocklawaha. No sooner had

Gene's splash smoothed out on the water's surface then a louder splash was heard, and though we couldn't see through the white foam, we knew there was something down there with him.

Suddenly, I spotted a line of bubbles making their way to the surface and a beeline straight for Gene, who was already removing the paddlewheel's snag. People started hollering for the man to get out of the water, but he didn't have time. With a violent tug, the deckhand was pulled completely underwater, and, within seconds, a bright red plume rose up, mixing with the dark green of the water. "Gator's got him," the steward yelled out. He pronounced it like a typical native Floridian, so that it sounded like "gay-tuh." But northerners and southerners alike knew exactly what he meant. The captain, who had seen the gator from the house, quickly grabbed his rifle. It only took him one shot to make the gator set Gene free, but when several of the men reached over to pull the man back on board, only one leg came up with him while the alligator swam off with the other.

Fortunately, we were close to the dock at Silver Springs, and Mayoma Hailey was there. Unfortunately, though, the man had lost an enormous amount of blood, and even though Mayoma worked on him for an hour, there was just no saving him. Finally, after whispering, "Mama!" to his long-dead mother, Gene Pinder closed his eyes on this world and moved on to serve a higher and mightier captain for all of eternity.

When I wrote the article, I wondered if city folks would think it was too wild and gory, but apparently it wasn't. The editor at the newspaper told me it was just the kind of thing they loved to put in their special Sunday edition and to send any more stories like it. Though I was plenty pleased he liked it, I thought it a bit strange that the readers in Marietta liked blood-and-guts tales on Sunday. And I wondered if they read them before or after church services.

Leaving all gruesome memories of poor Gene Pinder behind, I put on my wide-brim straw hat, smoothed down my green-and-white gingham dress, and left the stateroom. Walking out on the promenade deck, I was immediately startled by the sharp blast of a steamboat whistle. Looking off to the right, I watched the large *Cedar Queen* come around a bend in the river.

At eighty-two feet long and twenty-two feet wide, it was the largest steamboat on the narrow Ocklawaha. My brother, Joseph, was the boat's engineer. It was his job to make sure that the boiler was operating at the right temperature, for if it went past its limit, an explosion would likely occur.

I quickly scanned the porch in front of the general store to see if Mama was there. Spotting her, I headed in her direction to put my purchases in the wagon she always parked behind the store. Once I was rid of those, I would go see Joseph. He was working the run up the St. Johns River to Jacksonville. He'd been gone a long time because a new boiler had been installed while they were in port. I loved my older brother and missed him dearly when he was gone. I was getting used to his absences though, which was a good thing because come springtime, he and Regina Freeman were getting married and would build a home about twenty miles north of us near Eureka Springs. Not only was it closer to Regina's parents, but it was also closer to the St. Johns River, which would open greater opportunities for my brother. Since the St. Johns flowed into the Atlantic, far larger boats worked the St. Johns. Larger boats meant larger paychecks, and Joseph had his heart set on working for one of the big Atlantic steamship lines that ran north to New York and south to Savannah.

After placing my packages under the wagon's seat so that they were out of sight, especially from my parents, I started to make my way toward the *Cedar Queen*. I took my time so that I wasn't in the way of the flurry of activity going on around the large boat. As I walked along, I watched the comings and goings of a variety of different people. Some of the faces were familiar, while others were not. Some folks looked as if they knew exactly what they were doing, while others looked almost bewildered, as if they'd stepped off the boat onto the shores of another planet. Most of the newly landed tourists were polite, but there were a few who felt as if they were superior in every way to the people of Florida.

I couldn't help but smile when I overheard a man with a hard northern accent arrogantly arguing over the value of a deer skin with one of the area's best hunters, Max Harjo. If the Yankee didn't back off, I thought, then Max might take a notion to skin *him*. From what I'd been told, he was half Creek Indian and half something else, which made him big enough, and dangerous-looking enough, that people knew not to mess with him; at least the locals did.

Just as I started to look away from their argument, I spotted my sister sitting on a barrel tucked back by the side of the store, directly behind Max. From the look on her face, I could tell she was bemused by the men's heated negotiations. I started to go over to her, but something stopped me. I felt that she wouldn't necessarily be glad to be interrupted from watching the two men. Just then, the tourist threw his hands up in the air and stomped away. Max watched the man retreat with hard eyes before turning his attention to my sister. His expression immediately softened, and he grinned as he said something to her that made her laugh. She then extended a jar of honey to him. Taking it from her, he reached out and tugged a lock of her blond hair in a familiar and playful way. Feeling as though I was watching something I shouldn't, I turned away before she could see me.

I had never seen Ivy talk to Max before. In fact, other than knowing him by sight and reputation, I wasn't aware she was acquainted with him. However, there were probably a lot of things I didn't know or understand about her, even though I wanted to. Ivy had a way of shutting herself off from people, even those she was closest to.

There were times when she felt like a stranger to me or, if not a stranger, then just plain strange. I hated the distance between us, but I knew we both felt that way about each other sometimes. The truth was I loved her deeply, probably more so than anyone else on God's green Earth. However, James and I were much closer and much more alike. We were considered "reliable and hardworking," but we also shared a creative side. I loved writing, and he had a passion for drawings and designs.

James and I had been the only two of the four siblings who had wanted to finish school. His hope was that he could go to college to study structural engineering or architecture. To do that, he needed money for tuition and board, so he'd found work with one of the local timber companies. He spent long, hot days cutting scrub pine and oak trees. With each tree that fell, he envisioned himself going off to school at the University of Georgia next year. I promised to help him write his admission's letter once he was sure he had enough money together. I tried to help him with the financial part of it, too, with money I made from my sewing and quilting, as well as from any articles I sold. James refused my help at first but relented when I told him I was keeping a record of what he owed me and that I expected him to pay me back when he designed his first building. I kept no such record, of course, but I knew he wouldn't accept my help if I didn't assure him I was keeping track. He did refuse to take any money from our parents, though. He said that they'd already raised him to be a decent enough fellow and that they shouldn't have to see to it that he became a highly educated one, as well.

Joseph had dropped out of school at the end of eighth grade after hearing the call of the river, but he'd worked hard, and we were proud of what he'd accomplished so early in life.

Ivy had disliked school the most out of the four of us and had dropped out halfway through the seventh grade. She'd followed her own path, but sadly, my sister's road seemed to lead away from our family. Even though Ivy and I didn't spend a lot of time together anymore, or see eye to eye on a whole lot, we still shared an unquestionable bond, one I knew I'd never share with anyone else.

Maybe it had to do with the fact that we'd been side by side since the moment of conception and breathed our first breaths just seconds apart. Whatever the reason may be, there was an undeniable bond between us. However, I wouldn't lie to myself about the fact that there was also a gulf widening between us. As we became more aware of who we each were as individuals, with differences in opinions, tastes, attitudes, and interests, the chasm that those differences created was beginning to water down the fact that we were twins. And the truth of that stung me far worse than a whole hive of her beloved bees ever could.

Chapter 3
Mother River

I smoothed down the corners of the brown-and-white linen tablecloth over the long table made of pine planks set on top of several sawhorses. We didn't care that our tables were nothing fancy, just as long as the food was good and plentiful, and because it was Thanksgiving, it was bound to be.

It was our usual community Thanksgiving picnic, and every family in the area was bringing dishes that showed off their culinary skills. While much of the nation crammed into overheated and overcrowded dining rooms, many in Florida celebrated outside, taking advantage of its nicest season. The morning had actually been chilly. It was cold enough to necessitate keeping a small fire burning in the stove, even after all the cooking was done. But the southern sun had worked its magic and had warmed everything by the afternoon.

More and more people were arriving at William Moseley Park, which was named after the state's first governor. The park wasn't like the manicured ones I'd seen once in Savannah. There were no squares with statues, or meandering groomed pathways with iron benches. Instead, there were the typical white sandy trails, dotted with scrub pines, oaks, and palm trees, as well as one low-rising Indian burial mound that we stayed away from simply because it wasn't a flat enough area to erect our makeshift tables on. I, for one, though, thought it might be rude to be laughing, drinking, and eating on top of dead Ocklawaha and Seminole Indians, so staying away from it was just fine with me.

The south boundary of the park was the river, which continued her steady movement as though it was just another day. She was a constant, and the most important thing to our community. She was our life blood, and our crops' life line, and we loved her, yet feared her. She was like a strict mother who set down her own rhythm and rules. When the fish weren't biting so well, or when her banks overflowed, flooding the towns, which had happened many times in the past, though not while I'd lived by her, we still clung to her, waiting for her to find favor with us again. And she always did.

I walked over to the river to wash gravy off my hands after spilling some from an overly full bowl. Squatting down, I hiked up my new deep-blue wool dress, so as not to wet it, and smiled down at my old, dirty laced-up work boots poking out from underneath the red scrollwork I'd embroidered on the hem. The ground was muddy in places from a cold front that had come through the day before, bringing rain with it, and I wasn't about to get my only good pair of shoes muddy.

I was peering into the water to push back strands of my copper-colored hair, which had pulled loose from my long braid, when I saw a familiar reflection in the water. It was Ivy. Teasingly, she gripped my shoulders and gave me a slight shove forward. I grasped her wrists tightly. "If I go in, you go in!" I laughed. I let go of one of her wrists, and as she pulled me up by the other, I was disappointed to see that she was dressed in a pair of James's old overalls. Our father hated it when she wore them, which was nearly every day, and I knew he would be especially unhappy about it when she showed up at the Thanksgiving table in them.

"Where's your new dress? I thought you wanted to wear it today." I smiled, trying not to sound or look the way I felt. I'd finished it late the night before because she'd said she wanted to wear it, and I'd gladly obliged her to help prevent more friction between my father and her.

Papa was beyond frustrated with Ivy. He was unhappy she'd left school to become an herbal healer. It just didn't sit right with him, and he hated that she spent most of her time with the Haileys. Even though he thought a lot of them, he still thought of them as beneath us. They were colored, and we were white. Right or wrong, Papa felt that Negroes had a certain place in society, and whites had another. And it was only through work that the two groups should mix.

Ivy had tried to reason with him that what she was doing *was* work, not socializing, but Papa didn't see it that way. He felt that being a medicine woman was just short of practicing some form of witchcraft and something that only "Injun squaws, Voodoo Hoodoo women, and Negresses do," as he rather crudely put it.

To those on the outside, it might have seemed as if our father considered Ivy the black sheep of the family, but the truth of the matter was he had a soft spot in his heart for her because she was the spitting image of his mother, except for having our mother's blond hair. But as Ivy got older and continued to do exactly as she pleased, there had been many a ruckus in our household between the two of them. Mama tried to argue on behalf of Ivy, that at least my sister was doing something helpful for folks instead of making life harder for them, but the argument went in one of Papa's ears and out the other. I was absolutely convinced that there weren't two people more stubborn and hard-headed on the face of the good Earth than my father and my sister.

Ivy looked down at her overalls. "Mayoma and I were making an elixir using beets, and I didn't want to stain my new dress with the juice. I want it to stay green, not be purple and green." She laughed, though a bit awkwardly.

"I figured you were at the Haileys." I was irritated. Aside from the fact that I knew Papa would take one look at her and the sunny celebratory day would suddenly become overcast, it really bothered me that she hadn't been home to help Mama and me with the cooking. Though Mama had never said it, I felt there were times when her feelings were hurt because Ivy spent most of her waking hours with Mayoma, even when Mama needed help with something. Mama didn't say anything to Ivy, but I could see the hurt in her eyes at those times.

While I knew that learning the art of medicine making did involve many hours, I also knew that Ivy didn't feel that she had much to learn from our mother. My sister had told me once that she felt Mama should have done more with her life than to simply be someone's wife and the mother of his children. Stung by her prickly arrogance, I'd responded by saying that it had taken a special woman with enormous courage to travel hundreds of miles into an unknown wilderness with a large family to care for and that she'd made sure none of us had ever gone hungry or gone without, even when Mama probably had.

My sister changed the subject. "Mama said to come get you. Reverend Troxler is about ready to say the blessing. Lord, there's a mountain of food! Mayoma and I brought two chocolate pies and a coconut cake to add to it. Two of the tables are covered with desserts alone!"

"Ivy, would you do me a favor—'specially since it's Thanksgiving?"

"What?" She actually leaned slightly back from me, as if she was already getting defensive over what I might ask her to do.

"Stay home tomorrow. Just spend some time with us, with Mama."

"Well...I...maybe, Eve, but I've got things to do with Mayoma, and we—"

"And you hardly have anything to do with your family, Ivy." I could hear the anger creeping into my voice, but before I could say anything more that would send Ivy off in a huff, I took a breath and then her hand. "C'mon," I said, forcing my tone to be lighter. "Let's talk about it later. For now, let's go eat. We'll pass on the turkey and head straight for one of your pies." I smiled. Ivy laughingly agreed, obviously relieved that I'd changed the subject.

As we got closer to the picnic tables, we realized that everyone's head was bowed and only Reverend Troxler's voice could be heard, and he was just finishing the blessing. We quietly joined the gathering in time to add our own "Amen" and then walked over to where Mama had fallen into line at one of the buffet tables.

"Oh, good, there you are!" Mama said as she let us cut in.

"Where are Papa and Joseph?" Ivy asked, scanning the crowd.

"They're saving room for all of us at the table with Captain Franks and his daughter Ursula. It's been hard for 'em since Mrs. Franks died last year from that stomach abscess. Your father wanted to make sure we'd be sittin' together."

"Oh, wonderful," James said sarcastically as he cut in line with us after getting himself a glass of iced tea. "That'll make for fine dinner conversation. We'll be stuffing our guts while Ursula tells us for the hundredth time about her mother's rotting one."

"James, hush!" Mama looked around to see if anyone had overheard.

"Well, Mama, it's true." I laughed. "Bless Ursula's heart, but throughout the school year she's been telling anyone who'll listen about how 'God awful it was' and 'how bad the smell was' and—"

"Y'all are gonna go sit under that tree and eat if you don't hush your mouths. Lord, I thought I raised you better 'n that," Mama threatened, keeping her voice low so that no one else could hear.

"You did." Ivy laughed. "That's why we know better than to go spilling our guts to everyone who'll listen."

That was it. We all started laughing, Mama included. "All right, that's enough! Stop laughing. Think terrible thoughts," she suggested, which only made us keep laughing. Then she tried pinching us, which made us laugh harder.

I pulled myself together by the time I filled my plate and wound my way through the crowd toward my father, who was waving me over to his table. "Afternoon, everyone. Happy Thanksgiving," I said as I set my plate down next to Ursula, while Captain Franks, Papa, and Joseph all politely stood to greet me.

"You, too," Ursula mumbled, hardly glancing up. Instead, the large girl kept her eyes glued to her plate as she shoveled a forkful of corn pudding into her mouth.

Soon, Ivy, Mama, and James arrived at the table, and the look that Papa gave my sister was unmistakable. There was no question that he was unhappy with her overalls. There'd be a heated conversation between the two of them when we got home. But, for the time being, everyone was cordial with each other, including my father and sister.

After greetings were exchanged and remarks made about how nice the weather was and how much food had been brought, Papa returned to the conversation he'd been having with the captain. They were talking about the near certainty that Henry Flagler's railroad would work its way through Florida. Word had gotten around that he was eyeing the St. Augustine area and had decided to build a big hotel there. He saw great potential in developing Florida into an enormous tourist destination, but Flagler knew that there needed to be a solid transportation system in place first. His beloved railroad was the answer, and we knew it was just a matter of time before it arrived. It came to Ocala in 1881 and had taken away some of the steamboats' business. It was a subject that was constantly on the minds of those employed or impacted by the steamboats servicing the Ocklawaha River, and many people had great misgivings about the inevitability of the railroad crisscrossing all of North and Central Florida. There was no doubt that the prospect of the enormous progress that the railroad would bring to our area was exciting, but it would also mean that some of the old ways were bound to disappear, and that could mean some real hard times for a lot of people.

"Joseph, m' boy, you got the right idea about gettin' on with one of the big ships out o' the St. Johns port," Captain Franks said to my brother as he pushed his chair back from the table and pulled his pipe and a pouch of tobacco out of a breast pocket inside his navy-blue seaman's jacket.

Using his thumb, he tamped down a pinch into the pipe's bowl, then pulled a match from the same pocket, struck it on the sole of his left boot, and drew in long and hard, trying to coax the dark tobacco into taking the flame. "Yes, sir," he said, blowing out the match with a thick stream of smoke. "Them large ships ain't quite as dispensable as the smaller ones are. They'll still use the big ones to carry some cargo and fancy passengers on longer voyages. But the smaller ones—like our river ones—well, hell, you might's well chop 'em up and use 'em for firewood 'cause that's about all they'll be good for once the trains finish comin' through. Well, that and for carrying tourists who think it's big adventure roughin' it onboard a boat the size o' the ones we're runnin' now. Shoot, them Yankees see a raccoon walkin' along the bank, and they think they've been on some big safari." He laughed and his head bobbed. I liked Captain Franks. Even with his crabby and crusty old ways, one couldn't help but like him. Captain Franks was as consistent and reliable as a man could be and as seasoned and well respected as any captain on the river ever was.

I heard Papa laugh over something else the captain said, but I didn't hear what it was. I was thinking that if the rumors were true, these weathered and toughened old men of the river, who knew everything there was to know about the moods and temperament of the Ocklawaha, would soon be part of a quickly vanishing breed. And I wondered if the river would know when they weren't there anymore and would miss them riding on her, just as much as my father and his captain would miss being safely cradled between the banks of Mother Ocklawaha.

Chapter 4
Deer for a Tiger

Ivy stayed home until about noon the next day—at least her body did. Her mind was somewhere else, though, because we often had to ask her something twice. Finally, she'd had enough and said that she really needed to go because Mayoma was going to teach her how to make a new salve for lacerations. I heard Mama sigh when the screen door slammed behind her, though I wasn't sure if Mama did so because she was disappointed Ivy hadn't stayed any longer or if she was actually relieved she'd left. Mama was no fool. She knew her daughter and knew that Ivy had been itching to go all morning.

I finished shelling the walnuts that were going into Christmas cakes and cookies that we'd bake over the next several weeks. Some would be sent to friends and family in Georgia, while others would be given to our friends in the area. There was still another bowl of pecans to be shelled, but Mama knew that I wanted to get another story sent out in the afternoon mail, so she told me to go on. I tossed my apron on the counter, shook my light blue wool dress free of bits of shell, picked up my letters addressed to several magazines—this was a new avenue I was trying—and grabbed my straw hat off the rack by the front door. I knew the small riverboat the *Sun Fish* was picking the mail up about two o'clock, which only gave me about half an hour to get there. If I had to go on foot, I wouldn't make it, which meant that my letters would sit at the general store until the next mail pick up.

"Okay if I take the wagon, Mama?"

"Go ahead, honey," she said, after glancing back over her shoulder toward her closed bedroom door. "Your father's dead to the world right now. Nice he could go back to bed after breakfast, and even nicer he's got the whole weekend off. He's 'bout worked to death."

"I won't be gone too long. You need anything from the store?"

"Well..." She stopped shelling nuts to think for a moment. "No, I don't think so." I started for the door but she stopped me. "Tell you what; if any of them hunters has some fresh deer meat, get me some for stewin', would ya? I'm cravin' it after all of that turkey."

I screwed my face up at the thought of venison. It was too gamey for me, but Mama loved it and had eaten plenty of it growing up. She'd been raised by a father who was a mean drunk, and she, her two sisters, and her mother had suffered much because of it. He was out of work most of the time and took it out on them, sending them off to bed with welts, bruises, and empty stomachs on more nights than she cared to remember. Had it not been for wild game, Mama told us, they'd have surely starved to death. And much of that wild game had been killed by my mother, who had taught herself how to shoot to survive. I told her I'd see what I could find, then hurried out the screened door. Our old horse, Maggie, was eating some sweet feed out of a bucket inside of the corral. Apologizing for taking her away from her favorite treat, I quickly hitched her up to the wagon, and we started down the sandy trail toward Silver Springs.

It was nice to be alone. There were so few times when I was. I craved those moments and had to carve them out for myself when I needed to write without any interruptions or noise. I always headed deep into a hardwood hammock that was close enough to the river to catch a breeze but far enough away from the house to not catch my family's voices.

There was a place I usually went to, where three massive oaks created a thick arbor that shaded me on the hottest days. It almost felt like a spiritual place, and whenever I was there, words seemed to pour from me as if my guardian trees were dictating them to me. Today, however, instead of focusing inward, I enjoyed all that was going on around me. The woods, or "Big Scrub," as the locals called it, were busy. Critters argued and fought or played together in the sunlight and the shadows of the trees. Because the weather was cooler, animals were more active. Unlike the months of June through September, when the heat during the middle of the day could bring a grown man to his knees, the fall and winter months meant full days of busyness before comfortably curling up inside somewhere to sleep through the chilly evenings. Man and beast weren't too different, I thought, as I made my way down the trail.

Suddenly, the reins in my hands were pulled to the left as Maggie, startled, sidestepped. She tossed her head and snorted, then tried backing

Janie DeVos

up. "Whoa, Mags! Whoa, girl," I said, trying to calm her while getting a tighter grip on the reins. I stood up in the wagon to get a better look ahead and spotted the cottonmouth moccasin that had spooked her. It was curled up in the middle of the trail, where it had been enjoying the heat of the noonday sun, but now it was on alert. It stayed completely still, but its head was raised as it assessed the situation.

"Go on, now. Get!" I shouted, pulling a walnut out of the bag sitting on the floor by me, which Mama had asked me to deliver to Mrs. Brody for her holiday baking. I threw it at the snake but just missed the thing. However, the nut whizzed close enough by its head that the snake didn't wait for another. It slithered off the trail into a clump of palmetto bushes, obviously in no mood to mess with horse, rider, or walnuts. "It's okay, Mags. We're okay. C'mon, now." I gently slapped the reins and we lurched forward. We needed to get a move on because I didn't know how long the *Sun Fish* would be in port.

When we got into town it was unusually busy, especially for a holiday weekend. But, as long as the general store was open for business and boats were coming in and out, then I supposed folks would be coming in and out, too. I parked the wagon behind the store then grabbed my letters and the bag of nuts. I'd run out of stamps, so my first stop was the general store to buy some and deliver the walnuts to Mrs. Brody—and hopefully without Mr. Brody seeing or his wife's holiday baking wouldn't have many nuts in it.

As I came around from the back of the building, I saw that a few of the hunters were there with some fresh meat. Tom Bigalow had what looked to be alligator meat; and Rayne Longwood had a wild boar that was hanging from a rack. It looked as though it was asleep upside down, until you turned the animal around to face you and saw that it was fully gutted. And next to Rayne was Max Harjo, with nicely butchered sections of fresh deer meat. After delivering my mail to the *Sun Fish*, which was already in and loading cargo, I'd see what I could get from Max. It would have to be at a very decent price, however, because I only had thirty cents in my pocket, which I'd brought to cover stamps. Mama and I had forgotten about getting some money for the meat from the blue-and-white ginger jar she kept on the shelf next to her salt bowl. It held the cash she made from selling her goods at the general store. I decided to only get enough stamps to cover my outgoing mail and no extras. Hopefully, that would leave me enough to get the deer.

Fortunately, Mrs. Brody waited on me right away, so I was able to give her the nuts and get stamps quickly; then she checked the mail that an earlier boat had dropped off and handed me two letters. One was from

Mama's sister, Emma Jean, in Lexington, Kentucky, and the other was for me from the *Saturday Evening Post.* I had sent the magazine editor one of my stories just the month before so I was surprised to get a response that fast, if even one at all. After thanking Mrs. Brody, who made a remark about "getting a letter from such a fine magazine," I quickly left the store while tucking the letter safely away in the pocket of my dress. I was dying to read it but needed to drop off my outgoing mail first.

I boarded the *Sun Fish,* along with several other passengers, and once on board, I heard someone call my name. "Well, howdy, Miss Eve!" Lucas Knight was up at the pilot house. "You fixin' to ride along with us today?" "Oh, hey, Mr. Knight!" Lucas was one of my favorite people at the docks. He was a long-running steamboat pilot who had worked on practically every boat with every captain. But he was getting up in years now, and only ran the river as a fill-in when someone's regular pilot wasn't available. Holidays were one of those times.

"You got more letters goin' off to them big city papers 'n all?" he asked. Most of the people on the boats knew me through my father, but they also were constantly delivering mail to and from me.

"Yes, sir." I laughed. "And I just got one back from the *Saturday Evening Post,* though I haven't had a chance to read it yet."

"Well, don't let me stop ya!" I could hear the smile in his voice, if not see it on his face. He said nothing more as though he were waiting for me to pull the letter from my pocket so we could find out its contents together.

"Oh...well, I..." I really didn't want to open it then. I wanted to wait until I was by myself to either savor the good news or be disappointed in private. The truth was, though, that I was getting rather good at keeping my chin up over the disappointments. If there was one thing I was learning as a writer, it was that you got far more rejections than acceptances, and you learned to take it in stride. "I'm kind of in a hurry...and I have to get some deer meat for Mama," I quickly added. "If you don't mind, I..."

"You go on, Miss Eve." I could still hear the smile in his voice. "Sometimes a body jus' gotta be by itself when it's 'specting news. Might be he wants to shout to the heavens in happiness without nobody thinkin' he belongs in the crazy house or shed a few tears without worryin' someone's watchin'. You go on now—but do let me know how it turns out, all righty?"

"All righty!" I enthusiastically said. "Next time I see you. I promise! Bye, Mr. Knight." I started to leave but stopped and turned back to him. "And, thanks." The wise old man tipped his cap. And I knew he understood. Stepping inside the main level's salon, I found the steward immediately, gave him my letters, and climbed off the boat. Turning around on the dock,

I waved at Lucas Knight, who I knew would be watching me from the pilot house. His white teeth were in contrast to his dark skin, and I could see that he was smiling broadly and waving. *Lord, please make a few more like Lucas Knight if you're working the production line today*, I prayed as I walked away. Hurrying down the dock, I set my sights on the racks of deer meat. I wanted to be on my way as soon as possible.

Max Harjo was leaning against the side of the general store, smoking a thin cigar and wearing a broad-brimmed black felt hat that had a hawk's feather sewn at an angle on the right side. When he saw me stop at his rack, he pulled the cigar from the corner of his mouth. "You needing somethin'?" His voice was low and deep.

"Well, yes, but…"

"But what?" He dropped his cigar, crushed it with his boot, then pushed himself away from the wall, and walked up to the racks. He was even taller than I'd thought he was, now that I was standing directly in front of him.

"Mama needs some deer meat for stewin', but I don't have much money with me. How much is a pound of it?"

He looked me up and down, assessing me. I wasn't sure if he did so because he was trying to figure out if I was lying about how much money I had or if he was just being rude, as quite a few of the men in the area were known to be. Central Florida, which was sparsely inhabited but heavily wooded, was not an easy place for a woman to live. It attracted some pretty seedy characters who just needed to lay low for a while or for the rest of their lives. Max Harjo's eyes followed my body all the way up until he was looking me dead in the eye. I was surprised to see that his were a very dark blue, which was a sharp contrast to his very black hair and tan skin. "How much you got?"

"After buying my stamps, I've got twenty-four cents left."

With that declaration, the corner of Max Harjo's mouth lifted slightly into a half smile. "I get thirty cents a pound for it. But I'll tell ya what; you keep your twenty-four cents and tell Ivy she owes me some of her honey."

"Oh, well, I…I couldn't make a deal like that without asking her, Mr. Harjo. I mean it's her honey and…and I…Couldn't you just give me twenty-four cents worth of meat, and we'll be fair and square?"

"Naw. I'd rather have her honey."

His half-smile had spread into a full-blown one. He was obviously enjoying this, and it irritated me. "Never mind, Mr. Harjo. I don't need it that badly." I started to walk away.

"Hold on, *heruse hvmken!*"

I could hear him laughing, which infuriated me more than his blasted bartering, and he'd called me by some strange name, which was probably Indian and probably not good.

"What did you call me?" I turned around to face him, but he was no longer looking at me. Instead, he was standing at his butcher's table, slicing into a nice slab of meat. I walked over to him, hands on my hips. "What did you call me, Mr. Harjo? I want to know!"

"'Pretty one,'" he said as he rolled the meat into a sheet of newspaper. "But I should have called you *kaccv hokte!*" He tied a piece of twine around the package and held it out to me.

"I don't want your meat, Mr. Harjo!" I said, turning to go.

"Ahhh, but your mama does," he said without missing a beat while still holding the package out to me.

For a moment, I struggled over whether it was more important to refuse it and walk away, or swallow my pride so that Mama could have her deer meat for dinner. "Damn it," I softly exclaimed as I snatched the package from his hand.

Max was laughing again. "Tell Ivy she owes me honey, little *kaccv hokte!*" he reminded me as I furiously stomped away. "Oh, and, Eve..."

I stopped dead in my tracks, startled by hearing him say my name. How did he know it? Did my sister talk to him about our family, about our lives? I slowly turned around to look at him. He was no longer laughing, but softly smiling instead.

"That means 'tiger woman,' and it fits."

Chapter 5
Eruptions

I was still angry when I drove out of town. Though I was tempted to run Maggie as hard as I could to get away from Silver Springs—specifically Max Harjo—I needed some time to myself.

The nerve of that man, I thought. *And, how does he know Ivy so well? It would have been a simple purchase if I hadn't spent that money on those stamps for*—My letter! I'd forgotten all about it! Pulling on the reins, I stopped in the middle of the sandy trail, pulled it out of my pocket and ripped it open. When I unfolded the letter, a check fell out of it. Picking it up off the floor of the wagon, I saw that it was made out to me in the amount of ten dollars. Sticking it in my pocket, I began to read the letter. The editor of the *Saturday Evening Post* had loved my story and was going to publish it in the January issue. He also asked that I send stories as often as I could, and he thought my writing "painted a clear and vibrant picture of Florida."

Thoughts of arrogant Max Harjo were all but forgotten as I slapped the reins against Maggie's rump. I wanted to get home in a hurry now, and Maggie would get two sugar cubes for her efforts.

We were nearly home when we came to a place where the river cut further into the land, causing the trail to take a sharp bend. Making the spot even more difficult to navigate were the dense clumps of spiky palmettos that grew right at the edge of the trail, forcing me to stay in the middle of the road. There was so much heavy vegetation encroaching on both sides that it was hard to see or hear anyone coming, and because of that, we nearly ran into Mayoma's wagon. She pulled hard to her right, and I pulled hard to my right, narrowly missing each other but trampling some bushes on each side. Backing the horses up, we got our rigs back on the trail and took a moment to make sure everyone was all right.

"Lord, chil', you got the devil chasin' after ya?" she asked but not unkindly so. There wasn't an unkind bone in Mayoma's body.

"No, I... No." I was still a little shook up. "Whew! I nearly killed us all. I'm sorry, Mayoma."

"We're no worse for wear. But, what's gotcha goin' so?"

"I just got a letter from the *Saturday Evening Post*. They're publishing one of my stories."

"That *is* good news, now ain't it?" She was genuinely pleased for me. We had always liked each other.

"It is. Thanks. Are you going into town to sell today?" I noticed she had a crate filled with small bottles, as well various bundles of herbs in the back of the wagon. "I'm surprised Ivy didn't want to sell some of her medicines, too. Was she headed home?"

"Don't know." Mayoma's brows knitted together. "She didn't say."

"Well, if she's not home, then I bet she's playin' with her bees." I smiled.

"I bet that's right! She sure loves 'em good, don't she?" She laughed, shaking her head. "Well, better make hay while the sun's still shinin'. I'll see ya, honey." She slapped the reins against her horse. "Oh, and Eve, slow down some gettin' home," she said, almost as an afterthought. "I want you writin' them stories about the foolishness of us folks here in the scrub for a long time to come." She smiled.

"I will, Mayoma; thanks." I clucked at Maggie to get her moving again.

The sun's rays barely penetrated the trees' thick canopy overhead, but what light did get through was distorted, marking the trail with an abstract, speckled pattern. A soft breeze blew in across the river, and I turned my face toward its cooling touch. Near the far bank, standing half in and out of the water, were several cypress trees, whose long roots always reminded me of old men's skinny legs with knobby knees.

I inhaled deeply; the air was heavy with the smell of fish, heat, and sweetly pungent vegetation. Florida. It smelled like Florida. As wild and dangerous and threatening as the land could be, it had claimed me as one of its own many years before. The river was the land's heartbeat, and she often called me to her, especially when I was troubled, and, even with my good news from the magazine, I felt uneasy, but I couldn't put my finger on exactly why. Perhaps it was because of my confrontation with Max Harjo, though I didn't feel like that was really the cause. Whatever the reason was, though, I needed these last few minutes alone with the river to settle myself.

By the time I got home, Mama was about ready to head over to the chicken coop to chase down our supper. She'd pretty much given up on the deer meat and was getting ready to kill the old hen that constantly attacked some of our younger hens. I couldn't help but laugh over the fact that their society didn't seem so very different than ours, and if Mama had a hand in it, the feathered femme fatale was going to be given the harshest sentence of all.

"It's good and fresh," Mama said after taking the meat out of the newspaper and smelling it. "Half redskin or not, that man always has good meat."

"I'm surprised no one has run him out of town or killed him just for being half Indian," I remarked.

"Well, Max has enough white in him to keep him alive. And bein' that he's one of the best trackers 'round here, folks is happy enough he's got some red in him, too."

"Where'd he come from," I asked as I chewed on a fresh string bean while carrying the bowl of them over to the table to snap.

"Alabama, some say, though I've heard it said Lu'siana." She spooned a scoop of bacon grease from a small crock into a cast-iron Dutch oven on the stove. Once it started to sizzle, she added the deer meat, then moved to the kitchen sink, and started rinsing several carrots and onions in a bucket of water she'd brought in from the pump outside. "No one's sure where he hails from, though," she said, picking up the conversation again while she began cutting the vegetables into chunks. "He keeps pretty much to himself. Don't say too much to anyone."

I muttered something under my breath about him sure being talkative today, but when Mama asked me what I said, I responded with a question of my own.

"Has he got any family?"

"Not that anyone knows. Heard tell that he had a wife and babe that up and died a long while ago, before he got here. Some say it nearly killed him, while some say he killed them! Bottom line: no one knows, so they fill in the blanks to suit themselves. Why?"

"Oh, no reason, just askin'. I'd never talked to him before today, even though I'd seen him around. He's a little...well..."

"Savage-like?"

"No. I wouldn't say that. Not really. He was...just different, I guess. Not like the rest of the folks around here."

"And that's why you gotta stay away from him." She turned and pointed her knife at me to emphasize her point. "We stay with our own kind." She returned to the stove and added the vegetables.

"Then maybe we should have stayed in Georgia, Mama—with our own kind."

She was caught off guard by my response and turned to look at me. "What's gotten into you today, Eve? You havin' your monthly?" She wiped her hands on her apron, walked over to me, and placed a hand on my forehead.

"Mama, I don't run a fever when I'm having it." I laughed, turning my attention back to the beans. I was a little uncomfortable with the whole conversation. It was time to change it. "When's Ivy gonna be home?" I knew she'd have no more of an idea than I did, but at least we got onto a different topic.

"Lord only knows." She added salt from the salt bowl to the stew and then a couple of peppercorns, which she wacked open with a good smack of her meat mallet. After tasting it, she added a little more salt then put the lid on it and moved it to the back burner. "Couple of hours and we'll be eatin' good."

"Mama, I almost forgot! I got a letter from the *Saturday Evening Post*!" I pulled it out of my pocket, and she sat down at the table to read the letter. Just then, there was a knock at the door. It was Emmitt Hailey.

"Emmitt, come on in. Lord, you don't need to knock. Sit down. Can I get ya a cup o' coffee?" Mama was already heading for the pot on the stove while waving Emmitt toward the chair she vacated.

"No, no, Miss Ceily. Don't go botherin' yourself none. I'm fine." He stepped just inside the screen door and remained standing there with his cap in his hands. He smiled and nodded over at me. "Miss Eve."

The slender, middle-aged man never seemed to change from year to year. And he always seemed to be on an even keel. It was a rare occasion when I'd seen him mad, and it was usually on the boat with one of his sons when they weren't performing their duties to his level of perfection.

"I'm sorry to interrupt y'all, but I just got a note from Cap'n Franks, who heard from Cap'n Dial, on the *May Breeze*. Seems some of Dial's crew drank all through Thanksgivin' night and ain't in no shape for running the river today. Sent word to Cap'n Franks, wantin' to know if we can make the trip for 'em instead on the *Jocelyn*. They's some folks gotta get on up to Palatka tonight so's they can catch their connectin' ship on the St. Johns in the morning. Cap'n Franks told him he'd do it if'n he could get his crew together. So, that's why I come."

"Lord, even when y'all have the day off, you don't have the day off." She shook her head while wiping her hands on her apron. "Let me go rouse him. I wish you'd both say no, but I know you won't do it. Moses and Louis goin', too?"

"Just Louis. Moses ain't around, so we might find us another hand at the dock. Lord, I'd give my eye teeth to have a third of that boy's energy."

"And I'd give my eye teeth for the other two-thirds." Mama laughed as she opened the bedroom door and went in to wake Papa.

As dangerous as trips on the Ocklawaha could be at night, I still wished I could go with them. It was truly magical seeing the river and springs by firelight, which is what they used to navigate the narrow river. Metal washtub-style pots were set on the roof of the pilot house, and resinous pine knots were burned within them. Deckhands stood on the sides of the boats holding torches high and illuminating cypress, oaks, and palms, turning them into ghostly sentinels that stood in quiet communion as the boats passed by. Only the best pilots were able to run the river at night, and Emmitt Hailey was one of them.

Just before the sun went down, Mama and I sat down to supper by ourselves. Papa had left with Emmitt, Ivy wasn't home yet, Joseph had gone up to spend the remainder of the Thanksgiving weekend with Regina and her folks, and James was staying at the timber camp. Much of the time, the timber crews were working a good ways out, and it just made sense for James to stay in camp instead of making the long trek home in the evening and then back again before daybreak. About halfway through supper, Ivy came through the door.

"Lord, girl, what kept ya?" Mama got up to get Ivy a bowl of stew. "You been workin' with Mayoma all this time?"

"Yeah," she said, sitting down at the table. "We just finished up a batch of poison ivy soap. I'm worn out." Mama put a bowl of stew in front of her. She grabbed a wedge of cornbread from a plate on the table and crumbled it to pieces into her stew. "That woman works me hard," she said before shoving a large spoonful into her mouth.

I got up to start on the dishes. It was hard enough hearing her lie, but it was harder to look at her while she was doing it.

After dinner, I sat down on the porch to write. The night wasn't too chilly, and the oil lamp offered some warmth, but even had it been downright cold, I would have still preferred the chill outside to my sister's company inside. Finally, fatigue won out, and I gathered up my writing materials and went inside just as the clock on the mantle struck ten. Mama was sitting alone in the living room, working on a cross-stitch sampler.

"Ivy go on to bed?"

"Uh-huh," Mama said, removing her spectacles and rubbing her tired eyes. "I'm not long for this world either." She stood up and groaned as she placed her hands in the small of her back. She had some arthritis, which was only getting worse each year. "Your daddy won't be home tonight, so there's no use sittin' up. I'll see ya in the mornin', honey."

"Night, Mama."

She went into her bedroom but left the door ajar so she could hear any of us if we called out to her in the night, just as she'd done when we were little. Old habits die hard. I smiled. She was a good mother.

Taking one of the lamps, I headed upstairs to my bedroom. Ivy was in bed, facing the wall with her back to me. I wasn't sure if she was sleeping or not, so I quietly set the lamp down on my dresser. I washed up at my bowl and pitcher, slipped into my light flannel nightgown, and undid the braid in my hair. It was down to the middle of my back, so I'd have Mama trim it soon. Grabbing my brush, I walked over to the window to look outside while I worked the tangles out. The magnolia tree's waxy leaves looked black-green in the moonlight, as did the citrus trees beyond. Off in the distance, lightning lit the clouds, which had a yellow haze to them, indicating a strong storm approaching. It was unusual this time of year, though not unheard of. Thunder rolled, following the slash of lightning, and before the sound even stopped, another bolt lit the sky. After closing the window most of the way, I slipped into bed, silently said my prayers, and stared up at the ceiling. I heard Ivy roll over. Glancing at her, I could see in the fading moonlight that she was looking at me, as well.

"Ivy?" I said softly and turned back to stare at the ceiling again.

"Yeah?"

"Where were you this afternoon? Really."

I heard her let out a sigh. She waited several seconds before answering. "Sometimes it's better not to know too much, Eve. Let's leave it at that, okay?"

I rolled onto my side to face her. "Ivy, you can talk to me about anything. You *know* that. I onl—" Before I could finish, there was a loud pounding and shouting at the front door. Startled, Ivy and I froze for a second before jumping out of our beds. Grabbing my robe, and relighting the lamp, I hurried downstairs with Ivy close behind.

Mama was coming out of her room, trying to stuff her right arm through the sleeve of her robe, while holding a shotgun in her left. "You girls move off to the side!" She ordered. "Lord knows who's out there and what they want."

The pounding was actually causing the heavy door to shake. Walking up to it, she stated loudly, "Who's—"

"Miz Ceily, it's Emmitt Hailey! I got Mister Hap here, and he's bad hurt!" Mama threw the deadbolt and pulled the door open. Emmitt was standing in the pouring rain, and behind him was his wagon. A tarp was haphazardly thrown across the bed of it and a pair of feet was sticking out beneath it. "He's bleedin' bad! Moses has gone for Mayoma." He turned back to the wagon, stepped up into the bed, and pulled the tarp back, exposing my father. He was as pale as death.

"I'll get his feet," Mama said, handing me the gun, and ran down the porch steps to the back of the wagon. Emmitt slipped his arms beneath Papa's torso and, as gently as he could, pushed him toward Mama so that she could get a hold of his legs. "Girls, get some more lamps lit!"

I ran back into the house, grabbed the lamp on top of the couch's end table, and attempted to light the wick with a wooden match. My hands were shaking so badly that the match went out, but I finally got the lamp lit with a second one.

As I went for more lamps, I saw Ivy in the kitchen throwing wood in the stove to get the fire built up. We'd need it for warmth, as well as hot water to cleanse any wounds or sterilize any utensils we might use. I brought two more lamps into the living room and found Emmitt gently laying Papa down on top of the tarp that Mama finished spreading beneath him. My father's white steward shirt was completely drenched in blood, but because of the rain, it was washed out to a medium shade of pink. His navy-blue pants had been stained a dark purple color. Papa's skin was so white it almost had a blue hue to it.

"Bring me hot water, scissors, sharp knives, and lots of towels. Tear up a sheet, too," Mama said over her shoulder to us. Her voice was firm but calm.

"I'll get the linens," I told my sister as I started to run up the stairs to the closet where we kept them.

"What happened?" I heard Mama ask Emmitt in a flat voice.

"Damn boiler exploded," he answered.

I returned with the linens and saw Emmitt pulling off the one shoe Papa still had on. Only a sock remained on his other foot. Then Emmitt began to pull down his pants so that every inch of my father's battered body could be examined. Mama worked at cutting away his jacket so that she wouldn't have to move my father any more than necessary.

"Cut those towels into long lengths, girls."

Taking one of the knives, I began to slice through the material as I watched Mama pull away the remains of Papa's jacket. When she did, the room went completely quiet as the source of the massive bleeding was revealed: only a stump remained just below the shoulder where my father's right arm had once been. Tied around the stump was a blood-soaked cloth acting as a tourniquet, which Mama began to carefully cut away.

"Give me them strips of cloth, somebody! Quick! We got to stop this bleedin', or we'll lose him for sure. Emmitt, you say Moses went to fetch Mayoma?" She continued to work at removing the tourniquet but it seemed to be plastered to him because of the thick stickiness of the blood.

"Yes, 'm. He showed up on the dock right as we were pullin' out. We'd found us another hand, so he was bein' left behind. Glad he was. Least he's alive. Wish Louis had been late, too." His voice cracked.

Mama froze as she was reaching for cloth strips Ivy was handing to her. "You mean to tell me Louis was killed, Emmitt?"

Emmitt nodded his head but didn't look up from working Papa's pants off from around his feet.

"God in Heaven! What're you doin' here, then?"

"Ain't nothin' more I can do for him, Miz Ceily...or for Cap'n Franks, neither. Least I can try to help save Mister Hap."

He finally looked up at Mama, and we could see tears streaming down the gentle man's face. His anguish was obvious, but, somehow, he'd managed to keep it in check to try to help save a man he loved and deeply respected. I couldn't help but wonder if my father would have been as selfless if the situation were reversed.

Just then, there were two sharp raps on the door, and Myoma and Moses stepped in. I could see the rain was still coming down in torrents before Moses closed the door. Mayoma didn't say a word, but her eyes immediately fell to my father. Pushing the hood of her soaked dark gray cloak back off her head, she unbuttoned the one large button holding the garment closed, then pulled it from around her shoulders and handed it to Moses. Mayoma knelt by my father and began to gently probe him, assessing the situation. Ivy walked over, knelt behind Mayoma, and softly asked what she wanted her to do.

"Pray," Mayoma said over her shoulder. Then she looked around at all of us. "Pray harder 'n you ever prayed in your life, then start all over again." She turned her attention back to my father, and the whole room went quiet as the medicine woman bent over him and began to work.

Chapter 6
The Waning Light

I gently slapped the reins against Maggie's rump to encourage her to pick up the pace. The first few raindrops had started falling and I was glad I'd taken the time to spread the oil cloth over my wagon-load of supplies. Ten pounds each of wet flour and cornmeal would do little to help feed our family, and though times weren't dire, they were still leaner than they'd been before Papa had been so badly injured. The boiler explosion hadn't just taken Papa's arm from him, as well as the ability to make a decent living, it'd also taken his gusto for life, and the light that had once shone so brightly from his brilliant blue eyes had been dimmed by bitterness and pain.

The physical pain had finally eased but not the mental agony. My father now saw himself as a lesser man and one that had little to offer his family. There were days after Papa's physical strength had improved, when he'd quietly walk off by himself, and I wondered if he'd come back once darkness fell.

One afternoon, after spending several hours writing, I was walking the trail home when I spotted my father standing at the end of an old boat dock. He was staring down into the water and didn't hear me. I stood frozen in place on the road directly across from him. I waited, holding my breath, wondering if Papa was thinking about taking an eternal swim. Just as I started to call out to him, he awkwardly sat, hung his legs over the end of the dock, put his face in his one remaining hand, and cried like a baby. With tears streaming down my own face, I walked off the trail and into the woods, out of sight of my father. The last thing I wanted was for him to see me. I knew he wouldn't appreciate it if I witnessed him in this vulnerable state.

I pulled my shawl tighter. The rain was chilly. It was late February, and the winter had another round or two to go with us before the first warm spring breezes. Opening my umbrella, I held it over me with one hand while holding the reins in the other. Suddenly, I caught a movement off to my left. There, tending to her beehives, was Ivy in a pair of James's old blue overalls.

"Hello, Sister!" I was glad to see her. I was ready for some company to help pull me from my melancholy thoughts.

"Oh, Lord, Eve! You scared me!" she said, holding her hand to her heart. "Didn't anyone ever tell you it's not polite to sneak up on someone in the woods?" She laughed as she walked toward me, pulling her thick work gloves off.

"You about done there?" I asked.

"Yeah, I'm gettin' cold. Oh…wait a minute," she said, heading back in the direction of the hives. "Just let me grab the ducks Moses dropped off a little while ago." She reached down behind an enormous oak and picked up a burlap sack covered in small wine-colored stains. She threw it into the wagon's bed and climbed up by me. "He shot six today over at Lost Lake."

"Nice of him to share. Papa loves duck. That's one gift he might actually allow himself to enjoy." People had been so kind and generous, and while most of the family was grateful, my father was embarrassed and often refused to eat what was given to us. "Here," I said, handing Ivy the umbrella. I got Maggie going again and after talking about our day, the soft tapping sounds of the rain on the umbrella lulled us both into a comfortable quietness. After several minutes, Ivy broke the silence.

"I hate going home."

Her statement startled me, but I understood it. Ivy voiced things that I wouldn't admit. "I know," I sighed. "Maybe things will get a little better over time."

Ivy turned to face me. "Sometimes I wish Mayoma had just let Papa die that night. I'm sorry. Lord, I know that's a terrible thing to say. But, honest to God, Eve, I bet if we coulda asked him, he'd have said for us to give him a large glass of whiskey, to sing 'The Old Rugged Cross,' and to let him bleed himself dry. Sometimes I think that would have been the kinder thing to do."

I knew she was right. "I just wish he'd go back to work. Cap'n Dial has tried time 'n again to get him to work on the *May Breeze*. He told Papa that he needed a steward with one good head more than two good hands.

Papa won't do it, though, 'cause he thinks the only reason Dial is offering him the job is because he feels guilty. Emmitt keeps telling Papa that's not so, but there's no convincing him. Lord, it'd be good for him to be back on the water. And I'm going to say this, Ivy: James and Joseph need to get on with their own lives and stop trying to keep the rest of us going. Did you know that Mama was asked to help out with the laundry at the Silver Springs Hotel but had to turn it down?"

"Mama mentioned it but didn't seem to want to say much about it. I bet Papa put his foot down."

"Of course he did. The hotel's owner, Mrs. Landingham, was only trying to help, but Papa about had a fit. When Mama told him she wanted to do it, he told her that he'd never lifted a hand to her in his life, but if she tried to take that job, he'd use his one remaining hand to whip her. Then he had me drive him over there in the wagon. I begged him to just let it go, but he said he'd try riding over on Maggie or walk if need be. Well, I took him 'cause Mama asked me to do it. When we got there Mrs. Landingham was standing in the side yard of the hotel, and Papa goes marching over to her. Says, 'Don't ya know it ain't polite to ask a white woman to do wash for another white woman, and especially alongside a negress?' Poor ol' Mrs. Landingham was dumbfounded by it. Just behind her Miss Simone, the colored woman, was scrubbing a shirt on the washboard. I was watching her and the only sign she gave that she heard was that the rhythm of her scrubbing was interrupted for just a second—like she'd flinched. I was embarrassed for everyone, but mostly for Papa. It was rude and...well... it just wasn't right. Besides, Ivy, the money that colored woman makes and that Mama could make for helping her would be equally as green. So, instead of her bringing in a little money, Mama's havin' to tend to Papa's every need, making him that much more dependent and Mama that much more worn out."

"And it shows," Ivy added. "Seems like Mama moves a little slower every day. Well, we'll all just keep chippin' in some of what we each make and—"

"The money you and James and Joseph make needs to stay in your own pockets," I said, cutting her off. "James wants to go to school, and Joseph has a future with a wife and family. And you work hard for your money and ought to be able to do what you want with it. In the meantime, here I am, barely contributing when someone buys a story—which hardly pays enough to feed a flea on a diet. So, I spoke with Mrs. Brody at the general store today, and she said they could give me some part-time work."

"Are you sure, Eve? I know your writing is everything to you."

One thing I appreciated about Ivy was that she respected my writing. As little girls, she always wanted me to tell her stories. "My writing has to come second right now. Besides, I'll have time to write. I have to be practical, and I have to be fair. I have to pitch in. And to tell you the truth, if I don't get enough work at the store, I'm marching myself over to the hotel and takin' up Mrs. Landingham's offer to work beside Miss Simone."

"Papa would kill you."

"Well, at least we'll all be wearin' clean laundry for my funeral."

We both chuckled but were quiet the rest of the way home. When we got there, we could see oil lamps shining through the window in the last light of day. I felt like our strong and once-seemingly invincible family was just like the daylight, rapidly fading.

Chapter 7
As Wide as an Ocean

"Mrs. Levi, I don't set the prices. I just work here," I sighed, tired and frustrated after dealing with yet another customer who was none too pleased that the price of her purchase at Silver Springs General Store had gone up. In Mrs. Levi's case, the item was a bolt of cotton calico. According to Mrs. Brody, supplies and shipping costs had gone up, but nobody was fool enough not to equate the large new home she and Mr. Brody were building with the increased prices of the store's inventory.

It wasn't quite ten in the morning yet, and I'd been there since six. Somehow, my part-time job had turned into a full-time job, and though I was grateful for the money, I was tired most of the time from staying up late to write.

"Well," Mrs. Levi continued, "just give me ten yards instead of twelve, and I'll have to make do. Honestly! How's a body supposed to make a dress out of that amount of material!" she grumbled.

By that body losing a few pounds, I silently responded to the overweight woman as I reached for the measuring stick and scissors that were kept beneath the counter. When I stood up with them, the bells on the front door jingled, and Max and Ivy walked in.

"Hey, Ivy." I chose to ignore Max and set about measuring the length of material for Mrs. Levi. "If you need something, I'll be done here in a minute."

"No, you go on. I just need a couple of things, and I know where to find 'em." She headed down one of the aisles, leaving Max leaning against the far end of the counter. After finishing with Mrs. Levi, I had no choice but to address him.

"Mr. Harjo, is there something I can help you with?"

His black felt hat was pulled down low on his forehead, making his blue eyes appear darker and formidable. "Naw," he answered as he pulled a toothpick from the corner of his mouth. "I'm just waiting on Ivy. We're goin' huntin' for hogs."

"Ivy? Hog hunting?" I started to laugh but realized he was serious. I'd never known my sister to shoot anything, much less something as ferocious and deadly as wild hogs. Just then, Ivy rounded the end of the aisle and walked up to the counter with her items: a wide-brimmed brown suede hat, a pair of soft-soled Indian moccasins, and a bar of paraffin wax that would be used to waterproof them.

"Hunting, Ivy? I thought you hated it."

"Well, it's time I learned to do it, even if I don't like it. You've brought in small game, Eve, and James and Joseph have shot the bigger stuff. I've got to pitch in, too."

"If you wanted to learn how to shoot, why didn't you ask James or Joseph to teach you how? Or Mama? She's a better shot than any of us. She taught me."

"Well...Max offered, so we're goin'."

There was no mistaking the edge to her voice. I didn't look over at Max or say a word to him, and he said nothing, but I could feel him staring at me. I confirmed it when I turned to ring up my sister's purchases.

"That'll be three dollars even." But before Ivy could pull out any money, Max firmly placed three silver dollars on the counter. Not looking at him, I turned and put the money in the cash register and said over my shoulder, "When will you be back?"

"When we've bagged one," Max responded.

When I turned back around, they were already walking through the door. No one said anything more.

I worked the entire afternoon. By the time I got home, Mama had supper ready, but Ivy still hadn't returned. Not daring to tell my parents the truth about where she was, I lied. I was mad at myself for doing it but was even angrier with Ivy for putting me in the position of having to do it. I was vague about her absence, simply saying that I'd heard she'd gone hunting but wasn't sure about who all she'd gone with.

After dinner, as I was bringing in some firewood off the side porch, Ivy rode into the yard, with a medium-sized dead hog slung across the back of her horse, Sage.

"The huntress has returned!" she announced tiredly.

I hurried in the house with the firewood and came back out to help her. Walking into the yard, I could see that the animal had been completely gutted and bled dry. Where there had once been a right eye, there was now a hole the size of a walnut. It had obviously been a clean, quick kill.

"Did you shoot it?" I asked, as she handed me a bloodstained burlap sack and dismounted.

"Max did. I tried to get him to take most of it, but he wouldn't do it." She began untying the knot in a rope that had kept the hog securely in place. Suddenly, she stopped working the knot and turned to me. "He's a good man, Eve. I wish you'd give him a chance."

"What do you really know about him, Ivy? Do you know anything about where he's from, his family, his history?"

"Not really. He doesn't talk much."

"And why's that?" I was irritated with the man's reluctance to let anyone know him.

"Because it's not anybody's business," she countered, anger seeping into her voice.

"You're right, Ivy! But the only problem with that is when you go off in the woods with someone you know nothing about, you stand the chance of not coming back out of those woods the same way you went in!"

"That's ridiculous, Eve!" She gave up trying to loosen the knot. Instead, she pulled out her hunting knife and sliced through the taut ropes. "I'll tell you this much," she said, shaking her knife at me to emphasize her point. "He's been a damn good friend when I've needed one. And I can't say that about everyone I know." Her eyes said what she would not. I knew she was accusing me of not understanding her, and perhaps she was right. Or perhaps we'd just drifted so far apart that seeing each other's side of things was difficult.

"Now, let's get this hog dressed and inside before some animal comes along and figures it'll make a good meal," Ivy said. And with that, she angrily yanked on the ropes at the hog's back feet, pulling him off of her horse and down to the grass below. Then she stomped off to the house to get James, who was between jobs with the timber companies.

As I waited for them, I picked up the burlap sack that I'd set down on the ground next to me, and peering inside, I saw that it contained the hog's innards. At the moment, mine felt about as torn up.

Chapter 8
Shattered Pieces

March of '84 was more than just the usual transition time between the end of winter and the birth of spring; it was also the time that Ivy and I transitioned from being girls to young women.

Some of the other changes that month were Joseph's wedding to Regina and his subsequent move upriver to Eureka Springs. But there were others changes that could not have been predicted had a whole room full of seers been carefully studying their crystal balls. For one thing, James was not only accepted to the college of engineering at the University of Georgia; he was given a partial scholarship, as well.

His excellent grades had paid off, and it seemed as though his dream of becoming a structural engineer was likely to become a reality. While I couldn't have been prouder of him, the day he waved goodbye from the promenade deck of the *Tansy Jane* to begin his journey was one of the saddest days of my life. I put on a brave and cheerful face for my brother, of course, but he obviously saw through it for he held me the longest and hardest of our family. When the steamboat's shrill whistle blasted, giving its final call for all departing passengers, I started to pull away from him, but he pulled me close and told me not to let my dreams fade into the narrow confines of everyday life at Silver Springs. Then, after kissing me hard on my cheek, he climbed on board.

The great joy and pride that our family felt for my brothers were doused by my father's constant moodiness, which was fueled by the fact that his only interest was the bottle. His good-natured personality seemed to be lost, only to be replaced with the tendency to verbally lash out at us. One afternoon, however, it came very close to a physical confrontation.

Mama had been gone all morning, and though she'd told Papa that she'd be back after dropping off a baked chicken and biscuits to a sick church friend and a stop at the general store, she didn't get home until midafternoon. I made my father dinner, but he refused to eat until Mama returned. As he grew hungrier, he grew angrier. I prayed that nothing bad had happened to my mother to delay her so and, if she did come through the door unscathed, that her reason for being so late would sit right with Papa.

Finally, she drove the wagon into the yard, and before the horse had come to a full stop, Papa went out the door to demand her explanation. I followed him but continued on down the steps to get Maggie unhitched and to quietly warn Mama that Papa was fit to be tied.

"Ceily! Where the devil have you been?" my father bellowed.

Mama took a deep breath. "I stopped by the Silver Springs Hotel. Let's go on in, Hap. It's startin' to sprinkle. I'll tell ya about it inside."

Sensing that what she had to tell him was not good news, he remained on the porch as she climbed the steps and then walked past him. "What were ya doin' there?" he demanded.

"Talkin'." She went through the screened door and Papa followed her in. I quickly put Maggie into the corral and hurried inside.

"Did you eat? Did Eve fix ya somethin'?" She was obviously putting off having to answer him.

"I didn't want nothin'!" His voice was growing louder as his patience grew thinner. "Answer me! What were you doin' there?"

Mama walked around the other side of the kitchen table so that it was between her and my father. "I took that job helpin' with the laundry."

The room went deathly quiet. No one moved. It was the first time I'd ever known my mother to completely defy something my father decreed. They stared each other down. Papa's eyes flashed cold blue fire.

Finally, Papa spoke low and flat. "I'm tellin' you now: No wife of mine is gonna be workin' beside no darky." As he said the last vile word, he slammed his fist down on the table, making everything on it jump.

"And I'm telling *you*, Hap, I'll work beside the devil himself to keep food on our table and a solid roof over our heads," Mama countered. "We need the money. The boys are gone now, and they need every dime of the money they make. And the money that Eve and Ivy contribute just isn't enough to keep all of us goin'. And it ain't their responsibility! We've got to do something! *I've* got to do somethin' more than just sitting around here watching you drink yourself to death."

"Don't you do it, Cecelia. I'm warnin' ya. Don't you do it."

I couldn't remember the last time I'd heard my father call Mama by her full Christian name, but I would bet there was a heated disagreement going on then, too. It probably didn't come close to anything of this magnitude, though.

"Well, I am, and that's—"

Before my mother could finish her sentence, my father pushed aside our kitchen table to get to her, sending plates and utensils crashing to the floor. Mama turned to get away, but Papa got a hold of her upper arm and jerked her back to him. He squeezed her arm hard enough to make his knuckles turn white and her skin turn a bright pink.

Papa brought his face so close to hers they were nearly touching. "I swear to God, woman, I'll beat you 'til there ain't a part of you that's not black 'n blue. Now, I'm gonna say it again," he continued, almost as if talking to a small child. "You ain't gonna do any lau—"

"Let her go, Papa!" I interrupted, wedging myself between them. I placed my hands firmly in the middle of his chest and pushed him hard.

Papa stumbled back, nearly falling, but he stopped himself by grabbing the edge of the kitchen table. Stunned, he glared at me for a moment as if trying to decide what to do; then, swearing under his breath, he grabbed his half empty bottle of whiskey and walked out the door and down the trail, out of sight.

"You all right, Mama?" I asked as I turned away from the window after making sure he was gone. She nodded, but she rubbed the indentations left by Papa's fingers. She'd have bruises. "Where you think he's goin'?" I asked, looking out of the window again.

"I don't know, Eve. I just don't know. But I wouldn't mind him stayin' gone—for a while, anyway."

I figured that the heat of the moment had made her say that and that she'd feel different in a few hours or a few days. I had gotten to the point where I felt the same way and highly doubted that I'd feel any different. The sad truth was that the man I held most dear in life, the one I'd always counted on, who gave me the greatest sense of security, had now taken that security away. By example, my own father had taught me a most valuable lesson: If you allowed your heart to love and trust someone fully and freely, the odds were that your heart would be shattered into a thousand tiny pieces, and there were no directions for putting it back together again.

Chapter 9
New Roles

Papa didn't come home for three days. Mama wanted to search for him, but I told her not to. I figured he'd come home when he was ready, and until that time, he probably didn't want to be found. And I just wasn't ready for him to come home yet. There was a sense of relief in the house and a quiet peace that hadn't been there in a long while. Although, some of that quiet was caused by the fact that we were worried about Papa, what the future might bring, and how Papa figured in to our future. On the morning of the fourth day, he walked into the house looking the worse for wear, and without saying a thing, he went straight into my parents' bedroom and slammed the door behind him. He slept through the night, but I was fairly certain no one else in the house did.

Papa said nothing about the episode, other than that he had stayed with his good friend Alfonso Kite, who'd been the cook on the *Jocelyn* before it exploded. He neither apologized nor tried to explain his violent behavior. However, something seemed to have humbled him, and I wondered if he could remember what had taken place and was ashamed of it. Whether that was it or not, something in him began to change. He started busying himself with little projects around the house, such as working in the garden or tending to the horses. These were things the rest of us usually did, but because we were often away at our jobs, Papa took it upon himself to take over those chores. And, in time, he seemed to go back to normal; his old self flickered alive in him. As a result, we didn't dread returning home from work as much, wondering what might set off another round of fireworks and send us scurrying for cover.

While the situation with Papa seemed to be improving, the situation with Ivy was not.

There were many times when my sister came home very late in the evening, and when asked what had kept her, she couldn't quite look any of us in the eye as she answered. According to Ivy, she was working extra-long hours with Mayoma or hunting and fishing with "friends," and as if to prove that was where she'd really been, she'd lay a freshly killed turkey on the table or put a nice string of bass in the sink.

My folks didn't ask too many questions about her activities, and I figured that Mama just wanted our home to remain peaceful and not revert to the battleground that it had been. Papa, though better, remained detached and less interested in family life than he'd been prior to the accident. I felt that was because my father finally accepted that the roles had changed in our family, and that he needed us to help keep food on the table and a roof over our heads. I also wondered if my father didn't quite trust the way he might react to us, or overreact to us, so it was just easier for him to turn a deaf ear and a blind eye to our goings-on. There was no doubt about it: Papa was still a broken man, and the result was a seemingly apathetic tolerance to what his wife and children were doing or *might* be doing.

Easter was in mid-April that year, and we were looking forward to the holiday. The town was having a parade on Saturday. It was really nothing more than the women and girls walking down Main Street wearing their Easter bonnets and the men riding their horses dressed in their best finery. Afterward, there was to be an egg hunt and a picnic. I'd gotten up early so that I could be at the store to help color eggs for the hunt. Mama and I had boiled dozens of them the night before to add to those being contributed by families in the area, and I was loading them into the wagon when Ivy walked out of the shed with her saddle. It was just starting to get light; beautiful wisps of purple, orange, and gold highlighted against the soft gray of the sky, heralding another beautiful spring day to come.

"Will you be in town later?" I asked.

"Probably." Ivy threw her saddle over Sage. "I have a bunch of jars of honey to sell, but I have a couple of things I have to get done at Mayoma's first."

"Well, if I don't see you in town, I'll see you later at home," I said, settling myself on the wagon's seat. Then I flicked the reins and drove Maggie out through the corral gate and onto the trail to town.

By the time I got to the store, Mrs. Brody had already wrapped three dozen hard-boiled eggs with different colors of yarn. The dye in the yarn would bleed out in the boiling water, which was laced with vinegar, coloring the eggs a softer shade of the yarn's color. The work left our hands and nails stained dark brown from the mixture of colors, but I didn't mind; the price was small in comparison to the pleasure. Grabbing more yarn, I joined Mrs. Brody in the tedious process.

About midmorning, I walked outside for some fresh air. My eyes stung from the vinegar water, and from the onions I'd been peeling. We'd use the skins as another method of staining. The eggs dyed from them would be a brown color, but before we dyed them, we'd mark each egg with a cross made from a stick of beeswax. The dye wouldn't color the beeswax, leaving the mark of the cross to stand out boldly against the brown. We'd run into a problem, though: We were nearly out of wax.

Aside from needing fresh air, I wanted to see if my sister was around. Chances were, she'd have some beeswax with her. Scanning the different people who were selling things on the porch and under trees, I didn't see my sister, but I spotted Mayoma sitting under one of the massive oak trees off to the right. I hurried down the steps and over to her.

"Morning, Mayoma. Is Ivy around?"

"Morning to you, too, Miss Eve. I ain't seen Ivy in a couple of days. Coulda used her yesterday, too. I was pickin' bull nettles, and four hands woulda made these two hands a lot less sore." She smiled good-naturedly.

"I thought she was... Never mind. If you do see her, would you tell her I'm lookin' for her?"

"Will do, Miss Eve. Though don't know when that'll be—tomorrow maybe."

"Thanks, Mayoma." I turned and walked away. The tears that had been brought on by the vinegar and onions were being replaced by ones brought on by anger and frustration. My sister had lied to me again. I was both angry and afraid for her. I knew that whatever she was doing couldn't be good or she wouldn't have to lie about it. Keeping my head down so that I wouldn't have to talk to anyone as I fought back the tears, I came around the front porch of the store heading for the steps when I suddenly slammed into something solid and broad: Max Harjo. I stumbled backward, but before I could fall, Max grabbed my upper arm and steadied me.

"Whoa there, *kaccv hokte*! You're gonna hurt yourself."

Startled by his sudden appearance and embarrassed at being so clumsy, I was at a loss for words. All I could get out was, "Sorry...I...sorry." I couldn't look at him, so I smoothed down my apron instead. Then, mumbling for him to please excuse me, I started to walk around him but immediately stopped. "Mr. Harjo, you haven't seen my sister, have you?"

"Un-uh." He shook his head, watching me closely. "Saw her yesterday, but not today. She'll turn up, though."

There was almost the hint of a smile at the corners of his mouth, as if there was some joke I wasn't privy to. He irritated me beyond measure. "Well, I know she'll turn up! I just wondered...I...Never mind!" I walked around him and up the steps. I entered the store, and when I turned to close the door behind me, I could see that Max was leaning against the railing watching me and still smiling.

Chapter 10
In Black and White

I worked until late in the afternoon and though I was tired, I knew it would be a while before I could get home. I wanted nothing more than a hot bath and my warm bed. Also, I was curious whether Ivy was back; if she was, I was going to confront her. I wanted to know what was really going on. However, I had one more job to do before heading home, and it required me to go to the old school house. I was going to put the final touches on the quilt that I had been making for my parents for last Christmas but hadn't had the chance to finish until now. The long hours of caring for my father during his convalescence, plus the many hours I'd put into work at the store, not to mention my writing, had prevented me from spending much time on the piece. But I was determined to give it to them for Easter; so, tired or not, I would burn the midnight oil finishing the quilt.

There was just one more task I needed to do before leaving the store, and that was to sort the mail into the receivers' mail slots. Fortunately, there wasn't much mail, so I hoped to be able to get the job done quickly, before Mrs. Brody could find something else to hold me up. With just a few letters left, I came to a card addressed to Mama from Aunt Emma Jean, in Lexington, and a letter for me. The return address on it was the *Florida Times-Union*, a newspaper based in Jacksonville. Wanting to be out of the store as quickly as possible, I stashed both pieces of correspondence in my apron pocket, finished sorting, grabbed my straw hat, and called out to Mrs. Brody that I was leaving. She bade me a good night, and I hurried out.

It was even later than I'd realized. The sun was beginning to go down, so I set Maggie at a good pace down the trail. I didn't like being on the trail in the dark, though I knew that'd be the case after working on the quilt.

There were many nocturnal hunters, and I'd not thought about bringing the shotgun with me. About thirty minutes later, I reached the schoolhouse. As I approached, I saw a soft light glowing in the back room. It was the room that was available for any teacher who might need housing, especially if he or she was single and wasn't concerned with finding a place big enough for a spouse and children. The new teacher was a young woman from Kansas, and though Miss Langford seemed nice enough, I hadn't known her long enough to feel as though I could barge in on her unannounced. I slowed Maggie down, debating whether I should intrude upon her or just go on home, but it was early in the evening, so I hoped that she wouldn't mind my working for an hour or two on the old sewing machine.

I pulled the wagon to the side of the building; then, after grabbing the large satchel that held the quilt and materials, I walked toward the back to knock on the door. Before I reached it, I came to a low window, and as I passed it, I glanced in and some movement caught my eye. I started to turn away, so that it wouldn't seem as if I was spying on the woman, but then recognition stopped me. Immediately, I looked back through the glass and there, on the bed, was my sister Ivy, lying naked and pale in the light from the candle burning softly on the nightstand. Her skin looked as fair as fine porcelain, especially compared to the much darker body that moved against hers, rhythmically and urgently. It was hard for my head to comprehend what my eyes saw. But there it was, flesh on flesh, as my sister moved in perfect unison with Moses Hailey.

For several seconds, I couldn't move. I stood there just long enough that my sister caught sight of me watching her. The look of absolute shock and horror on her face must have reflected my own. Moses turned to see what she was reacting to, and as he did, my sister's hands moved from their tight grip around his buttocks to his chest to push him off.

Stunned at seeing me, and unbalanced by my sister's push, Moses half fell out of bed, but he immediately scrambled up, snatching his britches off the bedpost as he did, and then he ran out of my line of vision.

Ivy reached for her clothing on the floor by the bed. As she moved, I was finally able to do what I hadn't been able to just seconds before: I ran—and ran fast. I got back to the wagon, grabbed the reins, and slapped them hard against Maggie. The sting of the leather startled her, and she shot out of the school yard as though a swarm of bees was after her. Darkened woods or not, I had to be away from there fast, and the faster I could put the two of them behind me, the better off I'd be. Finally, about a mile down the road, I had to pull off. Standing up in the wagon, rather than stepping down onto the trail, I leaned over and threw up in a clump of palmetto bushes. After nothing more could be purged, I wiped my mouth and took in great gulps of fresh air, all the while listening for the sounds of Ivy and Moses coming after me. Above all, I didn't want to see them. So, taking in one last deep, steadying breath, I urged Maggie on, and we made our way home by the light of the full moon.

Chapter 11
Dreams and Nightmares

When I got home, my parents were just sitting down to supper. Mama was plating pork chops. "Good timin'!" Mama smiled over her shoulder as I immediately went to the sink and began washing my face. "I set a place for you even though you said you'd be kinda late today."

I kept my head hanging over the sink. "No thanks, Mama. I can't eat. I've got a splitting headache. I'm just goin' to bed."

"You runnin' a fever, Eve?" She immediately put the skillet back on the stove, then came over and placed a hand on my forehead while I was trying to dry my face. "Lord, but your eyes are red, honey! And your face is flushed as all get out. Maybe I ought to run and get Mayoma since Ivy isn't—"

"No!" My emphatic reaction startled her.

"I just thought she might have some—"

"All I need is sleep, Mama. I just spent too much time hanging over pots of boiling vinegar and peeled too many onions. I just need to go to bed." We said goodnight, and as I climbed the stairs, I felt as though I weighed twice as much as I did; each step made me feel heavier than the last. I had the weight of the world on my shoulders, and I couldn't think of any way to lift it off me.

I walked into my empty bedroom and noticed that Ivy's bed was made. I wondered if she'd come home that night and whether I wanted her to or not. I untied my soiled apron, tossed it over the back of a chair in the corner, and walked over to the window to look out at the moonlit yard below as I worked at the buttons on the front of my dress. A large opossum walked across the sandy driveway; then, spotting something in the magnolia tree that interested him, he rapidly climbed up the trunk and was quickly hidden by the dark waxy leaves. Finally, I pulled the dress over my head, threw it on top of my apron, and crawled into bed. I hadn't been lying when I'd said I had a headache. My temples throbbed like a thousand bass drums manically keeping rhythm to some nameless tune. Sleep wasn't going to come easily, even though I was exhausted.

The image of Ivy and Moses entwined kept playing over and over again in my head. And my list of questions grew and grew, along with my anger. How many times had she told me she'd been somewhere, doing something with someone else, when she'd actually been with Moses? How long had their affair been going on, and how did it come to be? Did they actually think they could plan a future together, and if so, where? Surely not here in the South! And with that realization came the bone-chilling fear that if they were ever found out, they'd both pay dearly for their liaison.

Moses would be beaten or lashed thoroughly, at best, and perhaps even killed. It wasn't too far-fetched to imagine that some of the men in the area would torture him and then string him up. Just the year before, at Moss Bluff, a young colored man, had been caught stealing some money from his employer at a feed store and the poor man had been flogged and *then* put on trial. Of course, he was found guilty, then pulled out of the courthouse, and viciously flogged again. There wasn't much left of his back other than shredded muscle and bone. Afterward, they threw him in the Ocklawaha, and that was the last anyone saw of him. No one knew if he'd made it out alive and run off somewhere. The odds were high he'd never reached the far bank but had drowned at the bottom of the slow-moving river instead.

As to what would happen to Ivy, that would depend on how tolerant and forgiving the people in the area were. On one hand, my father was a respected member of the community. Actually, our entire family was, and because we were white, chances were that Ivy wouldn't be driven out of town. She might go unscathed physically, but psychologically, she'd be severely punished. Without question, she'd be ostracized by everyone and, in all likelihood, our entire family would, too. And then what? Would I ever become the journ—

Suddenly, I remembered my letter from the *Florida Times-Union*! It was still in the pocket of my apron.

I hurried across the room and dug into the apron's front pocket; then I lit the lamp on my nightstand. In the letterhead, the name of the newspaper was printed in bold block lettering. Looking down at the salutation to see whom it was from, I was shocked to see that it was not written by a department head, but the editor in charge, Charles H. Jones. Quickly, I began to read:

April 2, 1884

Dear Miss Stewart;

Let me begin by telling you how much I have enjoyed your colorful essays on life in the wilds of central Florida. I have read each one of them, and, I must confess, I have eagerly awaited each new adventure and experience that you so skillfully describe for your readers.

Due to the recent acquisition of the Florida Union, and subsequent merger with my daily paper, the Florida Daily Times, it is imperative that I expand my staff to appeal to a larger, more varied readership. As editor in charge, I would be quite remiss if I did not include an excellent writer who specializes in feature articles of the most entertaining kind to encompass all areas of reading enjoyment, and my hope is that you will be agreeable to fill that post.

If you are interested in this position, I would be delighted to discuss the required duties, as well as the bimonthly salary, and would be available to meet with you as your schedule permits. Please be assured that should you accept this position, our company would be most helpful in providing a generous allowance for moving expenses to the Jacksonville area, for that would be a necessary requirement.

I do hope you'll give great consideration to this excellent opportunity, Miss Stewart, but I also ask that you contact me as soon as you are able so that I may plan and move forward accordingly.

With warmest regards,

Charles H. Jones
Editor-in-Charge
Florida Times-Union

My hands were shaking as I folded the letter, replaced it in the envelope, and then stuck it under my pillow. I would sleep on it, though I was quite sure my head and heart were already heading down the St. Johns River into Jacksonville, and it was just a matter of getting my feet prepared to follow.

As I lay on my side, with my hand beneath my pillow touching the letter, I thought about how people's lives could change so drastically and in just a matter of seconds. There was no doubt about it—the day had been an amalgam of lightness and darkness, a day during which both nightmares and dreams had come true.

I heard Ivy come into our room a little after the living room clock struck three. I was lying with my back toward her, but I could hear her undressing and then heard the squeaking of the bedsprings as she lay down. I wondered if she'd call over to me, and she finally did.

"Eve, are you asleep?" she whispered.

"No."

"Eve, I'm sorry. I didn't mean...I'm sorry. I'd give anything if you hadn't—"

"If I hadn't what, Ivy? Seen you and Moses?" I turned over to find she was on her side facing me.

"I wasn't going to say that. I'm sorry you had to see us...you know... like that."

"Do you know what would happen had it been someone else who saw you? Dear God, Ivy! You're playing with fire!" I hissed. "And you're both going to get badly burned." She didn't say anything. "How did this start?"

"I don't know. It just did. I spend a lot of time over at the Haileys' place. Sometimes, when Mayoma couldn't go with me to gather the plants we needed, Moses would go. We'd talk about things, you know? And we got to know each other better, and we got to where we wanted to spend more time together. Sometimes, we'd go swimming, or fishin'. Then, after time, one thing just kind of led to another. You know what I mean?"

She sought confirmation that I understood, that it made sense to me. Only it didn't. I knew the boundaries that society had set up and it never occurred to me to step over them. "How long has this been goin' on, Ivy? And don't you dare lie to me."

"About six months, I suppose."

"And didn't you suppose this could get you and Moses killed?"

"We knew it, so we've been real careful."

"Oh, Lord, Ivy!"

We both lay there saying nothing. Then my sister asked me the question that I knew had to be foremost on her mind.

"Are you going to tell Mama and Papa?"

"You really don't know me anymore, do you, Ivy! And after tonight, I can promise you that I don't know who you are anymore, either! Of course, I'm not going to tell them. It's taken months for things to simmer down around here, and the last thing I want to do is stir everyone up again. This would make things a thousand times worse."

"I'm sorry, Eve. I know it's gonna to be hard on you to act like everything's okay—between you and me, I mean."

"No, it's not."

"Really, Eve?" Ivy, sounding both surprised and hopeful, propped herself up on her elbow.

"I'm leaving, Ivy. I got a job offer from the *Florida Times-Union*. It's a paper in Jacksonville, and I've been offered a full-time position as a staff writer. If I take it, I have to move there, and I can't think of a better time to go."

"Oh, Eve, please don't go because of me. Can't we just go on like noth—"

"Stop, Ivy! Just stop. Don't say another word! If you cared so much about me, or this family, you wouldn't have started this mess with Moses. But, to answer your question, no, I can't pretend I didn't see what I saw or know what I know. But I'll tell you this: I'm not going because of you. I'm going because of me. I'm going to a place where I don't have to stand between Mama and Papa anymore when they're fighting or boil onions in vinegar water until my eyes are nearly swollen shut because our father feels too sorry for himself to get out and get a job. And I'm going so that I won't have to worry about seeing something so disturbing when I innocently glance through a window.

"I want a future, Ivy, where I can be excited about what may come instead of worrying about finding a bunch of roughnecks pounding at our door with the intention of taking the law into their own hands. That might be *your* future, Ivy! James and Joseph were right to get out when they had the opportunity, and now I'm going do the same for myself. I'm leaving y'all to make your own choices about what your futures will be—no matter how dangerous or pathetic they may be."

"Oh…Eve! Please…I…"

Her voice cracked, and she couldn't finish, so I finished the conversation for us. "I'm tired now, Ivy—more than I've ever been in my life. And I've got to be back at the store in four hours to get ready for that egg hunt. I need to get some sleep. So, please, let's not say anything else right now."

And with the finality of that statement, I turned my back on her and my life in Silver Springs.

Chapter 12
A New River

St. Johns River
Outside of Jacksonville, Florida
April 14, 1884

I leaned against the railing of the elegant steamboat the *Chattahoochee* as I admired the size and grandeur of the St. Johns River. It dwarfed the Ocklawaha in width and length. Though I missed the protective confines of the narrow Ocklawaha, to feel the openness of the expansive river, and the wind that blew wildly across it was exhilarating. Even though I'd ridden it before, the St. Johns took on a whole new persona now that it belonged to me, just as the Ocklawaha had belonged to me days ago.

Joseph joined me at the railing, leaning over it and allowing the wind to wash away the stench of the coal that covered him like a second skin from long hours spent down in the boiler room. My brother breathed in the fresh air deeply. "Sure is a long cry from the Ocklawaha, isn't it? Makes it look more like a stream." He turned to me, smiling. "You must be excited, landing that job at the paper 'n all."

"I am." I nodded enthusiastically. "It's hard to believe I'm actually a journalist." I shook my head at the amazing turn my life had taken in such a short time, when just the week before, I'd been listening to complaints about the prices of Mrs. Brody's merchandise and stocking shelves with cans of lard and gunpowder. But, as of four o'clock the previous afternoon, I'd become officially employed at the *Florida Times-Union,* when the editor in charge and owner of the paper, Mr. Charles Jones, and I had agreed to a starting salary and my duties as a new staff writer. I was then given the tour of the enormous building, introduced to other employees, and shown to my very own desk. Though it was one of many in a large room, the three by four-foot oak desk belonged to me, and it would act as the starting gate for me to become the kind of journalist that I always dreamed I could be.

It was decided that my articles would be printed several times a week and would cover more than just the weddings and coming-out parties of the various debutantes in the city. I would also write feature stories on a wide range of subjects, lending creative flair to the writing instead of just hard facts. Mr. Jones wanted the newspaper to be a consistent source of current news as well as delightful entertainment for its subscribers. And if that wasn't enough to keep me busy, I could always help out with the writing of obituaries or ads for the classifieds.

After I had completed my interview and a tour of the paper, I was driven in Mr. Charles Jones's own elegant conveyance to Mrs. Sikes's "boardinghouse for proper young women," where I was whisked upstairs to the Victorian home's third floor and a tiny corner room I would be sharing with two other young women. Both were nurses at the hospital, and their schedules varied. Because it was the only available bed, I assured Mrs. Sikes the girls' odd hours would not disturb me and immediately told her I'd take it. Thus, by six thirty that evening, I had an oak desk and a twin-sized iron bed and a future I could call my very own. And, because of that, the air on the St. Johns River smelled even sweeter than the familiar pungent air of the vegetation-infused Ocklawaha.

"So, how long before you'll be back to Jacksonville for good?" Joseph asked.

"I'll start a week from Monday, so ten days from now. It'd be nice if I'm on the *Chattahoochee* with you again."

"You might well be," my brother said. "Well, I'd best get back to my post. Don't want those stokers slackin' on their jobs, and I don't want 'em blowing us sky high either. I'll see you for dinner."

I watched him walk down the promenade deck and back into the main cabin. I was proud of him. He was building a fine reputation, as well as a new home so that he and Regina could start to fill it with the large family they hoped to have. They were obviously happy, and I was happy for them.

I was also happy for James. I'd had a letter from him already, and it seemed as though he was quickly falling into his own rhythm at the University of Georgia. Because he was on a partial scholarship, he'd needed to find employment and he had but not with a timber company. Instead, he'd found work as a cook in one of the student dining halls. He said he qualified for it because he'd cooked plenty for the men in the timber camps, and the manager of the dining hall figured if James could keep a camp full of lumberjacks happy, he could keep a bunch of students happy, too. His classes were interesting, for the most part, and his dorm was comfortable and reasonably priced, so he was making it just fine, he said.

And then there was Ivy.

She and I had not said too much before I left to interview with the paper. Actually, we hadn't seen each other much either because she stayed away even later than she usually did. She gave Mama and Papa all kinds of excuses, and because it was just easier to believe her than argue with her, they accepted them. There would have been a time when Papa would have put his foot down about her gallivanting around at "ungodly hours and with God-only-knows who," but those days were all but forgotten. Everyone in the family was changing or moving in their own direction.

I went over a mental checklist of what all I needed to do for my move to Jacksonville. Of course, there was the packing to be done, but that wouldn't be much of a chore. I didn't have an abundance of anything. I would work at the general store for a few more days for the extra money, but it was more of a favor for Mr. and Mrs. Brody, than out of necessity. And I'd try to spend a little time with Ivy.

As angry as I was with her, she was still my sister, and I loved her. I realized that most of my anger was fear-based and that nothing was going to change that. Her relationship with Moses was a hopeless and reckless one. At best, they'd part ways after coming to the conclusion that the road they were on would lead to disaster. At worst, they'd be forced apart, and the different ways that could happen were too awful to think about. I prayed that the two young lovers would come to their senses before someone knocked sense into them, and I prayed that if that should happen, they'd both live through it.

A white seagull landed on the railing just several feet from me. I guessed he'd done this before and been rewarded by finding a bit of food on the deck, or even in the hand of a passenger. "Sorry little one," I softly said. "I don't have a thing to offer you." As if the bird understood, it immediately flew off, catching the current of the river's stiff breeze. It gracefully lifted higher and banked off to the left and out of sight as it flew across the ship's bow. I felt like the bird in some ways: I was now free to fly wherever I chose and to land where I wanted to. I just prayed that the ground beneath me would be a little more solid than it had been in a long, long while.

Chapter 13
When the Sun Goes Down

I settled into my job at the newspaper easily. I felt like it was something I'd been destined to do. In just the three months I'd been there, I'd become friends with my roommates and enjoyed spending time with them, though it didn't happen very often. We were all busy with our careers but made a point of getting together whenever our schedules allowed. At work, however, female journalists were well outnumbered by men. There were a few women who were secretaries and friendly enough, but they were busy with husbands and children and had little time for anyone or anything else. But one young woman, Colleen Hannigan, who wrote a column about food and included her "tried-and-true" recipes in her articles, had been friendly with me from the very first.

Colleen and I enjoyed dining together, especially in any new restaurant that the paper paid her to review. She was considered royalty in the area's eating establishments and was treated as such. Colleen even looked the part, standing nearly six feet tall, with a full-figure and bright red hair. It wasn't hard to imagine her lording it over the masses at a jousting match in medieval Scotland. I admired her greatly and enjoyed being with her, never minding that I often felt quite invisible next to her.

Another person I'd met through work, though he didn't work for the *Florida Times-Union*, was David Perlow. He worked for Henry M. Flagler, the oil tycoon who had become interested in developing Florida. David was a land developer who scouted different locations as possible sites for Flagler's future hotels in the St. Augustine and Jacksonville areas. After visiting the area on his honeymoon, Mr. Flagler had seen a wealth of opportunities awaiting those willing to risk investing in the undeveloped, sparsely populated state. Once railroad tracks were laid and the iron horse started opening Florida in ways that steamboats and mule-pulled wagons never could, the need for more lavish hotels, restaurants, and other amenities would immediately follow. I'd interviewed David Perlow for one of the articles I was doing on how the economic growth of Florida would mean the demise of certain long-running businesses, which, undoubtedly, would include the steamboat industry.

We met on a Wednesday afternoon at the St. James Hotel. He was only in town for two days, and one and a half of those days were completely booked, but he agreed to see me while having dinner, although the Philadelphian referred to it as "lunch." *"We'll kill two birds with one stone, so to speak,"* he'd written in response to my request for a meeting with him. *"Meet me on Wednesday, in the St. James Hotel's dining room at 12:30."* I immediately sent a response back to him via our paper's messenger boy, agreeing to the time and place.

The day of our meeting, I arrived a minute or two before twelve thirty. As I hurried down the sidewalk in front of the enormous multistoried hotel, I didn't stop to admire the façade of the imposing structure's exquisite wraparound verandas and fine Victorian woodwork, which never failed to impress society's most well-seasoned traveler. Nor did I take a moment to admire the St. James Park, which was directly across the street and one of my favorite places in town. The park, with its natural, simple beauty, perfectly balanced the grand opulence of the hotel. Once in a while, if time permitted, I ate my dinner there, just to escape the confines and noise of the newspaper.

Two of the hotel's doormen opened the massive front doors for me. As I hurried into the lobby, I was once again awestruck by the elegance of the room. Its dark wood appointments had been polished until they glowed, and magnificent materials and tapestries adorned both the furniture and the walls. Beautiful carvings, from cherubs to Greek goddesses, peered down from pedestals and balustrades throughout the room, and rugs that looked as though they'd been inspired by the world's great gardens graced the inlaid wood floor throughout the massive room.

Off to the left and next to the elevator—which was a testament to the modern conveniences of the hotel—was the Bougainvillea dining room. Standing in front of the etched glass door was the formally attired maître d, complete with well-waxed handlebar moustache and well-oiled slicked-back hair.

"Good afternoon," I said as I walked up to his podium.

"Madam." He bowed slightly. "Will you be dining with us this afternoon?"

"Yes. Actually, I'm meeting someone who is probably here already. Mr. David Perlow?"

The maître d' scanned the reservation sheet on his podium, and I watched his gaze go from the top to the bottom and back again before he shook his head. "I have the reservation, though I don't have the party—well, at least not the full party. I'm afraid he hasn't arrived yet. I'd be happy to seat you, though. We have quite an exquisite wine list, and I'm sure—"

"That'll be fine," I abruptly interrupted. I was irritated that David Perlow was late, but then the thought crossed my mind that perhaps I was being stood up. "If you don't mind seating me, I'm sure my party will be here soon."

With an affected bow, the man asked me to please follow him and led me through the dining room and out to a corner table on the veranda, where a soft breeze carrying the slightest hint of roses wafted in from the open expanse of the park across the road. As soon as I was seated, the maître d' snapped his fingers, and a waiter appeared at his side. After ordering a sweet iced tea, I sat back and tried to relax. My new light-yellow suit, complete with brown trim on the cuffs and collar, also had a bustle, and though it was smaller than previous fashions, the yards of bunched-up material were uncomfortable to sit on. But even more annoying than the bustle was the little matching hat that sat at a jaunty angle in front of my bun. Though it was pinned in place, I felt as if it would fall off at any moment. A straw hat was much more my style, for it fit well on the head, and, more important, it had a purpose. This decorative headpiece was nothing more than that, and I'd had enough of it. Fashionable or not, I removed it and sighed audibly.

"That bad, eh?" someone said just beyond the veranda railing, startling me.

A tall young man, perhaps in his late twenties, smiled mischievously at me from the sidewalk. Caught off guard, I said nothing but smiled in return as the man walked past me at a good clip. Not two minutes later, the same fellow was shown to my table.

"Ah, Miss Stewart! I thought that might be you—at least I hoped it was," he boldly declared in a northeastern accent. "I must admit you looked uncomfortable—and impatient."

"Oh...well...uh, I'm not used to these little hats, I'm afraid." I smiled, lifting my discarded hat from the table.

"Please accept my apologies for my tardiness. I was finishing up a meeting with a realtor, and, well, to be honest, I'm afraid I lost track of time."

His brown eyes twinkled, and the dimple in the middle of his chin deepened as he smiled. I also noticed that he had chipped one of his front teeth. It didn't take away from his good looks; rather, it just added a boyish charm. I found that little defect endearing and, for some odd reason, I suddenly felt at ease. I'd tossed and turned throughout the night, wondering if I'd forgotten anything of great importance on my list of questions to ask Mr. Perlow, and I worried that he'd see my lack of experience and not take our interview seriously. Even though not five minutes had passed since meeting him, I felt he would answer my questions kindly, without condescension or judgment. And I also felt that I could be honest with him.

"If the truth be known, Mr. Perlow, I was nearly late myself. And that's not the first or the last time, I'm sure." I smiled.

"So, we're going to have a bare-all/tell-all interview here. I like it!"

His statement made me blush, as if I'd been too forthcoming about my personal shortcomings. And he noticed.

"Why, Miss Stewart, I do believe I've brought a nice glow to your cheeks!"

He was obviously amused. Saving me from having to respond with some clever quip, which I didn't have at the moment anyway, the waiter arrived and took Mr. Perlow's drink order, explained the day's specials, asked if we had any questions about the menu, and then hurried away.

Mr. Perlow casually rested his arms on the table and leaned in toward me. "So, before you begin with your questions, I have one of my own. Do you mind?"

"Not at all." Though this was the biggest interview I'd done with someone of his importance and influence, it was not my first, and in the past, I'd found that interviewees often asked about as many questions as the interviewer.

"In no way do I mean this disrespectfully, but I was quite surprised to get a request for an interview from a female journalist rather than the usual boring, dry male reporter. How is it that you ended up here and writing about business rather than how to bake bread?"

I couldn't help but smile at his candid question. And the fact that he asked it, rather than just thought it, made me feel that much more comfortable with him. "I'm a feature writer, Mr. Perlow, but I also have a…well, vested interest, you might say, in what you and Mr. Flagler are planning to do here in Florida. On one hand, I can't say that I blame y'all for wanting to bring the railroad throughout the state to service more territory than the St. Johns railroad does, or even the JP and M lines do. Mule-pulled trains do not a railroad make." I smiled.

"So, I can certainly see the appeal and the opportunities that present themselves to y'all. On the other hand," I said, taking in a deep breath, "my family has been involved in the steamboat business for a long time now, and for those of us who've relied on that line of work to keep food on the table and a roof over our heads, the thought of Henry Flagler coming in here is…well, pretty daunting, to tell you the truth."

"I can certainly understand why you'd feel that way." David's response seemed genuine. "But the railroad will bring in a lot of jobs for a lot of people. Granted, some of the old ways of the old days will be rendered obsolete, but there'll be a lot of different opportunities and doors opening. And it's not just the railroad that will provide jobs, Miss Stewart. There'll be hotels built—and lavish ones at that. And as trains access more and more of the state, there'll be the need for more hotels, housing, restaurants, hospitals, et cetera, et cetera. The list is endless. To be sure, some of the doors will certainly close on antiquated services, but many new doors will open, as well. No one will go hungry if they're willing to work."

I was busy scribbling notes as he was talking and when he finished, I looked up at him thoughtfully and asked, "Have you ever been on a steamboat, Mr. Perlow?" When he started to answer, I held up my index finger, and he waited. "I don't mean a steam*ship*, but a steam*boat*?"

"I didn't realize there was a difference," he answered.

"There's a world of difference." I smiled. "A steamboat can show you a whole different world than a steamship can. Have you ever seen any of the blue-green springs in central Florida? They're mystical. They're magical. At least the Indians have always thought so, and I have to say, I agree with them. Most people would, once they've seen them.

"Or have you ever steamed down a narrow river in the dark?" I continued. "Navigated by pine knot torches that illuminate flowers that only bloom after the sun goes down? And in that same ghostly light, seen critters whose eyes glow red like the devil's own as they peek out from cypress trees or out of palmetto bushes silently watching you pass? It's a world unto itself, Mr. Perlow, and once the trains come plowin' through, all of that beauty, all of those seemingly unimportant things will be lost or, at the very least, go unnoticed. Oh, don't get me wrong; I can appreciate the opportunities that will come to the state, but I'll also mourn those things that my family and I will have loved and lost, and all in the name of progress. They may not mean much to a lot of other folks, but they sure mean somethin' to us."

David Perlow's brows were slightly pinched together as he listened intently, but when I was finished, he smiled his dimpled smile at me. "Miss

Stewart, you ought to be a politician, instead of a journalist—or at least a speech writer for one."

"Well, Mr. Perlow, one never knows where that beloved train of Mr. Flagler's might lead, does one?"

He softly laughed, and I could see a hint of admiration in his eyes. "No, Miss Stewart, one certainly does not. But I do know one thing with certainty."

"Oh, and what's that?"

"I'd like to take you to dinner tonight."

"We're having dinner right now," I teased.

"Okay, then the meal eaten after dark," he countered.

"Well…" I hesitated for a moment, but only for a moment. "All right. Pick me up at the paper when the sun goes down. And Mr. Perlow," I added as an afterthought, "don't be late."

Chapter 14
Signed, Sealed, and Delivered

David and I began seeing each other on a regular basis. He courted me with an energetic perseverance that was typical of his self-confidence and sure-footedness. He seemed to know exactly what he wanted from life, which was power and the wealth that comes along with it, and exactly how to go about reaching the lofty goals he set for himself. David's enthusiasm for his work wasn't solely based on his strong work ethic and deep abiding loyalty toward Flagler, but also on the fact that if the oil tycoon did well with his Florida real estate holdings, then so would David. Part of their agreement was that David got a small interest in each property Flagler developed, which would bring some handsome dividends to Flagler's handsome right-hand man.

David came and went frequently, returning to his home in Philadelphia when needed and coming to Florida as necessary to oversee Flagler's burgeoning developments. On a couple of different occasions, I was allowed to accompany him when he was on one of his scouting trips. At those times, I wrote pieces for the paper about awakening parts of Florida that had seen little, if any, development and probably looked much as they had when the Timucua, Ais, or Jeaga Indian tribes occupied those areas.

The near-virginal land of Florida's coastline was primitive and wild, and its beauty awed anyone who saw it, including the well-traveled David Perlow. And while his excitement about the future was somewhat infectious, I still felt a deep sadness that so much progress was going to change the feel of the Florida I knew and loved. Without a doubt, its quiet natural beauty was being changed, and Florida would never be the same again.

My feelings toward David were also changing. I found that he was not only charming and very attractive but also a kind and thoughtful man, who made me feel cared for and appreciated, even though his business required an enormous amount of his time. Sometimes, we went to the St. James Hotel for an evening of music, dancing, and dining. Other times, we did something more casual, like go on a picnic or simply stroll along the banks of the St. Johns River discussing our dreams of the future. As we walked hand in hand along the river one evening, our light banter took a more serious turn.

"Eve, we've been seeing each other for—what, about three months now?"

"Nearly," I confirmed. "We started courting in spring, and next weekend is the Fourth of July."

"I want you to come home with me next time I go." He stopped and gently tugged on my hand so that I turned to face him. "I want my parents to meet you."

"I'd like that," I said softly, and David leaned in to kiss me. It was deep and long, and though it wasn't the first time, our relationship had just shifted to a new level. We both felt it, and we showed each other in the depth and passion of our kiss.

Finally, we pulled apart, and I laid my head against David's chest as he continued to hold me.

"They'll love you," he whispered.

"I hope so."

"They will, because I do."

An awkward silence followed, and though I knew he was waiting for a response from me, hoping I'd say I felt the same way, I'd been caught off guard. As the months had passed, I realized we were growing closer, but I hadn't realized he'd fallen in love with me, and I didn't know what to say. I knew I cared deeply for him, but I wasn't sure my heart was quite ready to be given away. True to his character, however, David was able to voice what I couldn't at the moment.

"Am I hurrying you along too quickly, Eve?"

I could hear the smile in his voice as I remained wrapped in his arms. "Well, maybe a tad." I smiled as I gently pulled away from his embrace so that I could look at him. "I know I think about you all of the time and want to be with you all of the time, too. But so much has happened in the last year of my life that I sometimes feel as if I can't catch my breath."

David smiled at me with understanding in his eyes. I had no doubt that this man standing before me was the perfect one to give my heart to once I was ready to commit myself.

I wondered if I was holding myself back from loving him. I'd suffered such heartache in the last year, watching my parents' marriage implode, while witnessing Ivy and Moses's relationship, which could be nothing short of disastrous. David knew nothing about Ivy's relationship and little about my parents', other than the fact that my father had been badly injured and hadn't been the same since. I just wasn't quite ready to put all the skeletons in my family's closet on display yet, not even for David. At the moment, it just felt good to be free from all family ties and from those I loved but who had broken my heart. As I thought about it, I realized the barrier I'd erected to protect myself from any more pain was only going to prevent me from knowing happiness or the joy of a healthy love with a kind and wonderful man.

"Will you give me some time, David? I know I feel more for you than I've ever felt for any man before, but…I—"

"You take all the time you need, Eve," he said as he searched my eyes and brushed some wayward strands of my hair back from my face. "You catch your breath and when you're ready, I'll be here."

He gently pulled me to him again and we quietly stayed that way for a moment. I heard the wake from a passing boat lap against the seawall, and off in the distance, perhaps along one of the moonlit savannahs, a coyote raised its head, calling out to its mate. It was a lonesome, forlorn sound, making me hold on to David more tightly, grateful for his love.

As we walked back toward my boardinghouse, I suddenly had a thought, and I turned to David. "Before we go north to see your folks, could I convince you to come home with me? It's my father's birthday in two weeks, and I haven't been home since I moved here. I thought it'd be a good chance to see everyone. Besides, I promised Mr. Jones that I'd write a story at some point about the turpentine camps around my area that are destroying the pine forests by harvesting the trees' gum."

"I'll have to check my calendar, Eve, but I believe I can squeeze it in before I have to be back in St. Augustine. I won't be able to stay but a day or two, though." But that was fine with me. I needed a couple of days to really gauge the temperature at home, and I wouldn't be able to do that while David was there and my family was—hopefully—on their best behavior.

When I got back to the boardinghouse, I planned to write a letter right away to let Mama know we were coming home. However, as I checked the table in the foyer for any mail that might have come for me, I found that a letter had just arrived from her. She wrote on a regular basis, and I was always happy to hear from her, though nothing much had changed since I'd left. And the fact that there was a lack of information about Ivy's doings made me believe that Mama didn't see a whole lot of her, and that, in and of itself, worried me deeply. I'd only heard from Ivy once, soon after I'd left home. It was an apology letter of sorts, telling me how sorry she was that I'd found out about her and Moses that way and that she hoped even something so serious wouldn't get in the way of our feelings for each other. What exactly had she meant by saying "something so serious"? Did she mean it was a serious matter that I'd caught her in such a compromising position, or did she mean that her relationship with Moses had grown into a serious one? But considering that the two had been having relations, I figured she meant it both ways.

Sighing, I lit a lamp on the desk in the corner of the bedroom and began to read Mama's neat writing.

> *Dear Eve,*
>
> *I hope you're doing alright and still enjoying your life and job in Jacksonville. Everything at home is real good. I'm happy to let you know that your daddy is the new steward on the May Breeze. He was nervous at first, but he settled into it in no time and everything is going fine. He's been back to work for three weeks now, and he's pretty much like his old self. Still gets crabbier than he used to, but is a bunch better than he was the last time you seen him, and far more than when he first got hurt. It's good seeing him smile a lot again. I sure missed that during all that time he wasn't working. I think I missed that more than anything else, paychecks included!*
>
> *Ivy's doing ok, too, I guess. We don't hardly see her cause she works such long days, but she seems fine enough.*
>
> *Well, I guess that'll do for now. I need to write Joseph and James to let them know about your daddy's job. I know they'll be tickled.*
>
> *By the way, I don't suppose you could come home for Hap's birthday on the 15th, could you? I know that'd be his favorite birthday present.*
>
> *Your loving mother.*

Putting pen to paper and laughing as I did so, I wrote:

> *Dear Mama,*
>
> *You must have read my mind!! I'll be home for Papa's*

birthday, and, if it suits you both alright, I'll be bringing a
gentleman friend home with me. His name is David Perlow, and
I'm anxious for you all to meet him.

   Your loving daughter,
   Eve

   The next morning, I put the letter in the outgoing mail at work. Somehow, I felt that once the letter was actually signed, sealed, and delivered, my future was well on its way to being so, too.

Chapter 15
Going Home

David and I traveled down the Ocklawaha on the *May Breeze*. Though I was excited to show him where I'd come from, I was pleased to see that it was Papa who constantly pointed out various things on the river or talked about the river itself, almost as if it had a soul. I knew exactly how my father felt, but I wondered if David would see it as we did or think we made far too much of a river that was, at times, not much wider than a large creek. But I underestimated how deeply David felt about land—*all* land—as well as the rivers that ran through them. He seemed to be as spellbound with the interior of Florida as he was with the coastal areas. And just as much as David seemed to love our part of Florida, my father seemed to love him.

David was truly interested in what Papa showed him and didn't treat my father as some silly Florida cracker who hadn't ventured much beyond the state lines of Florida or Georgia. One of the things that made David Perlow an excellent business man was the fact that he was an inquisitive listener and an attentive audience.

Mama met us at Silver Springs Landing, where the *May Breeze* offloaded us before continuing its journey downriver twelve miles to Grahamville Landing. Because Grahamville was the first port built in the area, it had become one of the busiest ones and had seen a huge increase in tourists recently.

"Mrs. Stewart?" David said, leaning out past me so that he could see my mother on the other side of the wagon seat. "If I bring Mr. Flagler here, would you and Mr. Stewart give him a tour of the area? I'm sure he'd be most impressed."

"Why, sure," Mama wryly drawled. "But let's be certain to ask the alligators to behave themselves before we do. We don't want some Yankee bein' chomped on while tryin' to impress that man. These are southern gators, Mr. Perlow. They're still a might touchy we lost the war, ya know." David wasn't sure how to take that, but when she began to laugh, he laughed, too. Somehow, I got the feeling that David felt as though he'd entered a strange new world, and his footing wasn't quite as sure as it was when he was at his old stomping grounds in Philadelphia.

Ivy not only joined us for supper that night but was actually at the stove cooking it when we walked through the screen door. The summer air was thick and heavy, and the smell of fresh bass frying in the skillet added to it. Fat hushpuppies bleeding excess grease onto an old newspaper sat on a plate at the back of the stove, and next to the sink was a large mound of shredded cabbage that was going to be made into coleslaw.

When she heard us come in, she shouted that she couldn't leave the stove, so we went into the kitchen to see her. As soon as she flipped the fish, she walked over to greet us. She quickly said a soft hello to David, then turned, and embraced me before saying anything to anyone else. She held me tighter than I ever remembered her doing; Ivy had never been a demonstrative person in any way. As she hugged me, she whispered, "I've missed you so." I could hear the sorrow and regret in her words and tone, and I knew exactly how my twin felt.

Thankfully, the evening went smoothly. For one thing, Papa didn't drink anything hard, though he was a thoughtful host and asked David if he cared for something a little stronger than Mama's sweet tea. David, seeing that no one else imbibed, courteously passed, and again, I was struck with his innate ability to fit in no matter where he was, or who he was with. We talked well into the evening until Henry Childers came to the door, requesting that Ivy come with him because his wife was having a hard time giving birth and Mayoma wasn't at home. As soon as Ivy hurried down the road on Sage, the rest of us headed up to bed. It was very late when I heard Ivy come into the room.

I rolled over to face her. "How'd it go?" My voice was thick after several hours of sleep.

"Fine. She had a girl. Named her Charlotte Rose. Both are doin' all right."

"That's good, Ivy. I'm proud of you." She uttered a soft "thanks" but said nothing else, and I could see how tired she was, the darkened silhouette of her slumping shoulders giving her away as she walked over to the closet to hang up her clothes. "Get some sleep, Sister," I said as I rolled back over.

A moment later, I heard her bed springs squeak, followed by an exhausted sigh. Not five more minutes passed before I heard my sister softly snoring. I smiled. For as long as I could remember, Ivy had snored. The sound of it had often annoyed me, and I claimed it kept me awake. That night, however, the familiarity of the sound comforted me, and I easily fell back to sleep.

Mama planned Papa's party for the following afternoon. It had actually turned into a bigger affair than I thought it would be, and I wondered if one of the reasons was that Mama wanted to show off her daughter's successful northern beau to all of their friends. I also wondered if Mama was trying to keep Papa on an emotional upswing after being in such a dark place for so long. But whatever her reasons for having the party, both she and Papa seemed excited about the fuss everyone was making over it, and I was grateful to see some joy returning to our home at long last.

The party was going to take place at the picnic tables in the side yard of the newly built Cross Springs United Methodist Church, and because my parents had taken such an active role in helping build the church, they were as proud of it as they were of their own home. Maybe more so. The church was something that the community had planned and prayed for a great deal, and with the help of many of the town's residents, as well as folks from surrounding areas, the church was finally completed. Papa's birthday party was the first big social event to take place there, and it pleased him beyond measure.

The next morning, Papa and David set off on horseback for a sightseeing trip of the area. Papa had acquired another horse so that he could get to work while allowing Mama to come and go as she pleased on Maggie. Mama still worked at the hotel doing laundry, and Papa still hated it, but Mama had stood her ground, saying that with all her babies out of the nest, she needed something to fill her time and it might as well be something that made her some money, too. What helped to smooth Papa's ruffled feathers, though, was the fact that Mama spent as much time working inside the hotel, as she did outside doing the laundry. Mrs. Landingham, the hotel's owner, had suffered a mild stroke, so Mama regularly stepped in to do some of the ailing woman's work.

While Papa and David were off exploring the wonders of Florida, all the women gathered at the church at noon to begin setting up for the party. The white A-framed wooden structure had a two-story square tower centered over the black front door. Fixed on the top of the tower was a large cross. The church was nestled in among tall pine trees, and the yard was a mixture of pine needles, white sand, and blotchy grass. In the heat of the summer, the shade that the trees offered was truly a blessing from

God, and the picnic tables under the trees offered a cool place to gather on a hot July afternoon. But the ever-present Ocklawaha, which bordered the east side of the property, offered the most thorough way of cooling off for those adventurous few willing to jump in. The massive amount of food rivaled our community Thanksgiving dinner, and the festive mood equaled it, too. Papa was well liked, and the fact that he was back at work and interacting with longtime friends pleased everyone. Because of that, Papa's party would be more than just a birthday party; it was a rebirth party.

By the time David and Papa showed up, most of our friends were already there, so Papa's and David's entrance was quite grand. True to David's thoughtful nature, he hung back a ways after the two dismounted, allowing Papa to bask in the limelight alone for a few minutes. As I watched David humbly standing aside, I could honestly say that I loved him, and the realization of that was both frightening and exciting. And it made me happier than I'd been in a very long time. I felt as though I could let go of the past and finally move forward.

Papa finished thanking everyone for turning out for his birthday celebration and then, as if remembering that David was there with him, Papa motioned him forward and introduced him to the waiting crowd as "Eve's northern gentleman friend, who's quickly coming around to our southern way of life." A great cheer went up, and some of the men standing closest to David either shook his hand or patted him on the back. If my father gave him the okay, then that was good enough for everyone. As I stood there scanning the crowd, enjoying seeing so many familiar faces, I spotted the Haileys standing well off to the side. I was somewhat surprised they were there. Usually, colored folks stayed with their own, and whites did the same, but our families were entwined with each other in so many ways, and they'd come as a show of respect for my father.

Mayoma and Emmitt were talking to Reverend Troxler's wife, Margaret, but Moses was staring off in the distance. Turning to see what he was looking at, I saw Ivy filling glasses of iced tea at the drinks table. I turned back to see Moses say something to Margaret; then he walked off toward Ivy. And I quickly walked over to her, too.

"Miss Eve." Moses somberly nodded to me as we arrived at the table about the same time. "It's good havin' ya home."

"I can help her with this," I said, ignoring his words of welcome and quickly grabbing a glass and a pitcher of unsweetened tea.

We stared at each other for a moment before he nodded; said, "Fair 'nough"; and walked away.

"He just came over to help me, Eve." Ivy sounded tired.

"He's done enough with you, Ivy. Can't y'all just stay away from each other? God A'mighty, Ivy! I swear you're just givin' people a reason to talk. I know if he's willing to help you pour tea today, he's been helping you do other things, and folks will notice things like that, too. They'll see how y'all look at each other, Ivy. Honestly, it's pretty hard to miss. People aren't dumb—or blind!"

"I'm too tired to argue with you today, Eve. Can't we just put our differences aside today and try to get along?"

I was amazed at how easily my much-too-stubborn sister backed down. It was so out of character for her, and I was instantly concerned. "You okay, Ivy? You had such a late night last night, and you look pretty tired. Are you doin' too much?"

"I have been lately, that's for sure," she conceded. "But I'm all right.

"Last week, I lost the beehive's queen," she continued. "I've been workin' to save some of my bees while tryin' to get another queen. And I've been helpin' Mayoma treat folks night and day lately. Two got shot up at one of the turpentine farms a couple of weeks ago; then we birthed twin babies earlier in the week. I swear, they just didn't want to be born. I thought we'd never get 'em out. We about lost them both, as well as their mother. Plus, pneumonia's been a problem lately. Don't know why, but it has been. Sometimes it feels like I'll never feel rested again."

"Ivy, you can't keep up a pace like that. You'll drop dead while trying to keep others alive. Mayoma's got to slow down some, too. She's no spring chicken, you know."

"Oh, I know, and that's why I try to be there with her as much as I can. For one thing, I've got to learn as much as possible before she's not around to teach me anymore. She hasn't been real well lately. She's got bad arthritis, and it about kills her with the pain. Besides, her hands aren't as nimble and able as they once were. So she needs me about as much as I need her." We were both quiet for a moment as we continued filling glasses; then Ivy stopped pouring and turned toward me. "Eve, let's take a walk later, after everyone's through eating. Just us. Okay?"

"Let's do." I smiled, nodding. "That'd be good. We'll walk along the river."

After I finished helping her with the drinks, I walked over to Papa and David at the fire pit, where a wild hog was slowly turning on a spit. The man tending the meat was squatting down with his back to me, though I saw that he wore a black felt hat with a hawk's feather on the side of it. It looked familiar. When the man heard my father and David greet me, he turned to look at me. I found myself looking into the dark blue eyes of Max Harjo. Seeing him again startled me. I wasn't expecting he would be here. As if reading my mind, or at least the expression on my face, my father said, "Max was good enough to shoot us a pig."

"Miss Stewart." Max touched the brim of his hat and stood, and as he did so, he looked me up and down as if assessing me. "It looks like city life agrees with you."

"Uh, yes...yes, it does. I'm enjoying Jacksonville. Are you doing well, Mr. Harjo?" Our conversation sounded forced, as if we were practicing the social graces because we were being observed.

"Why sure," he responded with a slight smile, as if he found the charade rather amusing.

Not knowing what else to say, I excused myself and hurried to the other side of the pit to join David and Papa. Where they stood, they were directly across from Max. Feeling as though he was watching me, I extended my hand to David, who immediately took it and hooked my arm through his. For some reason, I wanted it to be understood that David and I were a couple, but the fact that I felt the need to make that clear irritated me. As Max basted the hog, I could see him glancing up at us from beneath the brim of his hat, and it gave me a strange sense of satisfaction that he should find me so interesting. As I stood there with a small smile, it suddenly occurred to me that he was just as interesting, and instantly, my smile was gone.

Chapter 16
Sealing the Deal

Ivy and I never got to take our walk. Halfway through eating Papa's birthday cake, dark clouds gathered, followed by a tremendous thunder storm. Everyone scattered like ants when lightning struck one of the pine trees behind the church, splintering it into a thousand burning pieces. Mothers snatched up their children while everyone else made a mad dash into the church with food, tables, and chairs. The storm didn't last more than a few minutes, but it was long enough to signal the end of a fine afternoon, and soon thereafter, everyone headed back down the church's white sand driveway toward home.

The rest of the weekend went quickly, and on Monday morning, we rose early because David needed to catch the steamer, the *Shanahan*, north. He needed to be in Jacksonville to meet Henry Flagler, and, from there, the two would head to St. Augustine to complete the land deal for Flagler's new hotel. Before driving David to Silver Springs Landing, he suggested we take a short walk. The sun had only been up for a short time, but already the soft purple and orange streaks coloring the sky had faded from deep hues to soft watercolor pastels.

"Florida sure has beautiful skies," David said. "They're different in the north. I don't think they're as brilliant and certainly not as wide open." Immediately switching gears, he said, "Did your father enjoy his party? It seemed like he did. He sure had a nice turnout," David said nervously.

"Somethin' on your mind, David? You seemed a little fidgety at breakfast—a little anxious. You're not worried about the meeting with Flagler, are you? I'm sure you're well past prepared."

"Oh, yes. I mean, no. I…" He stopped walking, took a deep breath, and turned to me. "I mean I'm not nervous about the meeting."

Beads of sweat had broken out across his forehead and his upper lip. I had a feeling I knew where the conversation was going, but watching David squirm, when he was always so cool under pressure, was a rarity I found both amusing and endearing.

"Go on." I was trying not to laugh.

"I spoke to your father last night, and he's given us his blessing. I want to marry you, Eve." He gently grasped me by my upper arms. "I want you to be my wife." He hurriedly went on as if he felt he needed to convince me. "We can have a wonderful life together. We complement each other, in our goals, in our beliefs, in our visions of the future. And I know you'd be a wonderful mother. You can take care of our home—I'll build you a beautiful one, Eve. And I know under your guidance and tutelage, our children would thrive."

"You have it all planned out, don't you?" I laughed. But, in truth, I was feeling a bit uneasy. "What about my job at the newspaper, David? I don't know that I'd want to give it up. And I think this is one of those things we need to discuss before we go any further."

"Eve, if working for the newspaper is something you're set on doing, then I wouldn't think of stopping you. However, I think you'd find that it'd be overwhelming to try to keep your job, as well as keep up with a busy social life—which my job would require—and raise our children. You do want to have children, don't you?" When I confirmed that I did, he went on. "You could try to do it all, but I think you'd find it's just too much. I think you'll need to decide what your priorities are. I know I can't speak for your employer, but I can tell you that most men expect their female employees to follow the dictates of their husbands, and you might find that he encourages you to step down. Employers understand that most husbands don't want their wives working outside the home. Think how your father reacted when your mother went to work."

"Yes, but that was different," I objected.

"How so? Because they really needed the money? I'm sure you'd agree that your father didn't want your mother working at that job because he felt it was beneath her. Most husbands are going to feel that *all* jobs are beneath their wives—other than child rearing and taking care of their home, of course."

I knew he was right, but I didn't like it. It was a man's world, and to fit into it, women had to conform to their likes, dislikes, and demands. I didn't say anything, but a look of defiance must have shown on my face.

"Listen, Eve, you could become a novelist—like Harriet Beecher Stowe!" David knew exactly how to turn a difficult conversation into a more mutually appealing one. He knew that the highly respected author of *Uncle Tom's Cabin* had been a great influence on me. "You could write at home. I'll buy you the finest typewriter." He looked delighted, as if he'd just come up with the perfect solution to a problem that could have easily impeded his plans.

"All right." I laughed.

"All right, what?"

"All right, I'll marry you, David." I tried to stop myself from laughing, but he looked like an excited little boy at the moment. "But I *am* going to keep my job—at least for now. And I'll always write."

"I've no doubt you will, Miss Stewart. I've no doubt at all," he said as he lifted me high and swung me around. When he lowered me gently to the ground, I cupped his smiling face between my hands and pulled him to me, sealing the deal with a kiss.

Chapter 17
A Family No More

After seeing David off at the docks, I sent a wire to Charles Jones, asking him to allow me to stay for a few extra days to get wedding plans underway, and write the turpentine story. He immediately sent word back that he was exceedingly happy for me but disappointed that I would be leaving my position after our nuptials took place, if not before. I promptly replied that I fully intended on keeping my job, that simply because I took a man's name didn't mean that I took his identity, too, and that I expected my desk to be waiting for me after returning from Silver Springs, and again following my honeymoon. The fourth and final wire from Mr. Jones simply stated that he would have a permanent name plate attached to my desk. I was very humbled by his response, which made me all the more determined to keep my job.

Early the following morning, Papa and I took the wagon to the turpentine camp outside of Sharpe's Ferry landing. He needed to buy some pitch, which was made from turpentine, to seal some newly formed cracks on the *May Breeze*. I was happy Papa and I had a few hours to spend alone.

We took the trail at a slow pace. It was already hot even though it was still early, and we didn't want to tire Maggie needlessly. Besides, the trip gave us a chance to talk about the turpentine business. Papa knew far more than I did, but I did know that the farming of the resin or "gum" from the pines was slowly but surely erasing them from the land. As soon as the trees were no longer giving sap, the timber companies came in and cut them down. The greed of both industries was changing the landscape of Florida in the most destructive way, and the more my father told me about how extreme the situation had gotten, the madder I got. I certainly understood that people needed to live off the bounty of the land, but there was no excuse for rendering the land useless for decades to come. I couldn't help but think of James, and how he'd been put into the uncomfortable position of having to take part in that destruction to earn enough money to go to college. I was glad he was away from it now. I also thought of dear David, who had large dreams and plans for the future—a future that now included me. While I understood that people had all kinds of justifiable reasons for using the land, it didn't always sit well with me. However, I also understood that nothing was going to stop progress, especially in a place that was a virtual blank canvas just waiting for developers, architects, and industries to apply their brushes to it.

By the week's end, I'd finished gathering all my information for the turpentine story, and I'd also taken care of the one very important wedding detail I needed to deal with while I was home, and that was my dress. Even with all the fine dress makers in Jacksonville, I wanted Mama to sew the most important gown I would ever wear. She was a highly skilled seamstress, mainly because she loved it so, and spent many an hour perfecting her handiwork. She'd made countless pieces of clothing for everyone in the family, and I'd inherited the love of sewing from her.

Though I hated the fact that we couldn't work on it together, I was grateful that she was willing to do all the work on the fine satin and lace we'd ordered through Mrs. Brody. I knew that the elegant but simple pattern we'd designed together would turn out to be a beautiful creation. But while the dress would come from Silver Springs, the wedding and the reception would take place in Jacksonville.

When I'd driven David to the Silver Springs landing to catch his steamboat home, we'd discussed some preliminary plans for our wedding. Both he and I had agreed that it would be easiest to be married in Jacksonville, and in October, so we picked October 16. Because his work schedule was so tight, and the accommodations were far better than they were in Silver Springs, Jacksonville seemed like the best place for the wedding. It would also be more convenient for his parents to make a train trip there and not have to continue to Silver Springs by boat. My parents could easily travel on one of the steamers up to the city and would be excited to do so. It seemed like the most reasonable rendezvous point for everyone. Once I returned to Jacksonville, David and I would visit with the pastor of the First United Methodist Church about holding our wedding there, and then we'd work on arrangements for our reception at the elegant St. James Hotel. It was the perfect place, not just because of its opulence and beauty but also because it was the place where we'd met and it would always hold a special spot in our hearts.

The one thing that diluted my joy was the far-from-perfect situation with Ivy.

My sister hadn't shown up at the general store the day before to help pick out the material for her maid-of-honor dress, and I was more irritated than worried. It was Sunday morning, and I'd volunteered to wash up the breakfast dishes so that Mama and Papa could get on to church. My boat departed a little after two o'clock, and I still needed to bathe and pack before leaving, so I'd excused myself from going to the morning's service. As I finished putting away the plates, I could hear Ivy moving around upstairs. She was finally awake.

I'd heard her come in during the middle of the night, and I knew that she'd been down at the docks helping Mayoma fix one of the worker's hands, which had been caught between a piling and a steamboat as it docked. Making matters worse was the fact that the man's arm had been badly cut, too, and they were having trouble stopping the bleeding from one of his arteries. Papa had returned from a late run and had come upon the scene. He hadn't stayed long enough to see how things had worked out for the man, but at least I didn't have to wonder if my sister was off with Moses again. By the time Ivy got home, everyone was asleep, including me, and she'd been quiet as a church mouse so as not to disturb me. Either that or she didn't want to wake me and then have to explain what had been more important than meeting Mama and me at the general store. I hated to be so doubtful of the fact that she might, in fact, have been quiet out of consideration, but it was hard for me to judge Ivy's motives and actions. And more and more, I felt I knew her less and less.

Ivy walked into the kitchen as I finished washing the skillet. "Morning," she said. "Is there any coffee left?"

"There's some. It's still hot." I handed her a freshly washed cup.

"Eve." Her back was to me as she poured her coffee from the pot at the back of the stove. "I'm sorry I didn't meet you at the store yesterday." She still wouldn't meet my eyes when she went to sit at the table. I didn't join her. Instead, I turned my back to her and started wiping down the counter.

"Ivy, why is it you always come running when a stranger needs you, but you're never there when it's important to someone in your own family?"

"Lord, Eve, a man was bleeding to death last night. Of course, I had to go tend to him!"

"I understand that, Ivy, but we were supposed to meet in the afternoon, hours before that man got hurt. You've always got somewhere else to go and someone else to see about. I wanted you with me yesterday. This is a special time for me, and I wanted you there. Besides, I needed you to look at those material samples for your dress. They had a nice blue, and a green—"

"I can't be there—at the wedding, Eve." I quickly turned to face her, but she still wouldn't look at me. Instead, she kept her eyes averted, staring down at her cup. I could see that her hands were shaking, so much so that some of her coffee sloshed out of the cup.

"I don't understand! Why, Ivy? Of course, you've got—"

"I *can't* be there, Eve! I can't be!" She finally looked up at me, and I could see that she was fighting back tears. "I'm having a baby, Eve. Moses and I have to go away."

"Oh, God. Oh, my God, Ivy. How long have you known? Why didn't you tell me before now?"

"I've known for a couple of weeks. I wanted to tell you, Eve. I was gonna tell you at Papa's party, but then the storm came up. I couldn't send you a wire before that. Can you imagine me telling Mrs. Brody to please send you a wire saying that I was having Moses's baby and needed to leave?"

"*You white trash whore!*" The deep voice came from behind me, and I quickly spun around to see my parents standing at the kitchen window. Mama was as white as a sheet, but Papa's face was bright red, and his eyes bulged from anger.

Horrified, Ivy and I couldn't even begin to move, but my father could. He yanked open the screened door, breaking it off the top hinge. Ivy jumped up from her chair, spilling her coffee all over as she pushed herself away from the table. But before she could turn to run, our father backhanded her with enough force that it sent her flying into the pantry door, cracking it from top to bottom. Stunned, she began to slide down the fractured door, but I pulled her up, placing myself between her and Papa, who was coming for her again. By then, Mama had hold of Papa's arm and held him back while pleading with him to stop.

"Ivy, go!" I said as I pulled her toward the screened door. "Get out, now!"

"I swear to God I'm gonna beat that bastard baby outta ya!"

Papa threw off Mama's hold on him and started to go after my sister. But just as he charged by me, I stuck my foot out, tripping him and sending him sprawling across the threshold of the door. Throwing myself across him, I pinned him down as Ivy ran into the corral to get Sage. The horse wasn't saddled, but there was no time to put one on. Instead, my sister grabbed the horse's mane, pulled herself onto its back, and flew down the trail. For several seconds, no one said a word, and then my father pushed himself up and me off him. He brushed himself off, walked over to the cabinet, and pulled out a bottle of whiskey. He poured a long shot, threw it back, then turned, and pinned Mama and me with a look that dared us to move or say anything. He didn't have to worry; we were frozen in place. The wickedest expression played across his face, one that I'd never seen before on anyone, much less my own father. Then he said in a voice that matched the look, "I'm gonna hunt down that girl, and I'm gonna find her. And when I do, I'm gonna kill her and that little brown bastard baby of hers. Then I'm gonna do things to her little darkie boyfriend that'll make him sorry he ever laid eyes on a white girl, much less his hands, until he begs me to kill him, too."

Chapter 18
Choosing Sides

After Papa took another shot of whiskey, he calmly walked into his bedroom. Mama followed him, trying to talk some sense into him. I heard drawers opening and closing as I waited in the living room. Several minutes later, he came out, followed by Mama. Over his shoulder was a full canvas bag. He walked past me without saying a word, picked the whiskey bottle up off the counter, stored it in his bag, and walked out the broken kitchen door.

"He's goin' after her," Mama softly said as we both stared out the window. "He's packed clothes, and he's got two handguns with him. He means business, Eve. He means to take 'em all down." We watched Papa saddle his new horse, Zeus, one-handedly, and secure his bag to the animal. Finally, he hoisted himself up and rode off without looking back.

"Where's he goin', Mama? Did he give you any idea?"

"He said he's gonna track her down. And I know your father ain't no great tracker, so I'd be willin' to bet he's gone in search of one. Didn't that cook friend of his—Alfonso Kite—used to do some trackin'? I could swear I've heard your father say somethin' about that; Alfonso was a tracker for the North in the war, maybe? I dunno. I can't remember right now. Truthfully, I can't remember much about nothin' at the moment. Lord, God, what has Ivy gone and gotten herself into?" Mama was actually wringing her hands. I'd only seen her do that when she was extremely upset or worried. At the moment, she was a whole lot of both.

"Mama," I said, turning from the window that now looked out at an empty yard. "I'm gonna find her—hopefully before Papa does."

"What? How, Eve? How in the world you gonna do that? She may go to Mayoma's first to warn Moses, but then she'll move out fast, knowin' that's the first place your daddy'll go, too. Lord only knows where she'll go. But I'd be willing to bet one thing, and that's that Moses will be with her. You ain't gonna find 'em, Eve."

"I've got to try. I've got to find her before Papa does. I don't know if Ivy'll think that after some time he'll cool off, and she can come on back. But after what he said to us, there'll be no time when it's safe for her to come home, especially if he keeps drinkin'. I've got to let her and Moses know to stay gone. And if I can't talk some sense into them, then maybe I can with Papa. If I can't convince her to stay gone, then maybe I can convince him to just let her go."

"What about your boat to Jacksonville, Eve?

"Right now, Ivy's my main concern. She's my twin sister. I've got to try to find her before blood is spilled." I started up the stairs with Mama close on my heels.

"But, Eve, if your father needs help trackin' her, then how you think you're gonna find her?"

"I'm gonna get some help, too." Dumping out the few things I'd already packed in my satchel, I quickly got out of the cotton dress I'd thrown on before breakfast, then hurried into my brothers' room, and riffled through their closet and drawers, pulling out the things I needed. After donning a pair of James's old denim work pants and a canvas shirt and stuffing more of his clothing into my satchel, I hurried back to my closet and found Ivy's hunting moccasins. On one hand, I wished she had them. On the other, I was glad for them. Finally, I had all that I needed and hurried downstairs. Opening the drawer of the desk that sat in the corner of the living room, I took a box of rifle shells, then reached up and retrieved the shotgun from over the doorway. Papa never used it. It was too difficult to handle with one hand, but he was a sure shot with his handguns.

"I'm takin' Maggie, Mama. I'm sorry to leave you without a horse—or a gun." I smiled weakly at her.

"Eve, don't you go! You're gonna get yourself kilt before you can ever find her!" She'd followed me outside. "You can't track that girl alone!"

"I know it, Mama."

"But, who you think is gonna help you?"

"Max Harjo—at least I pray he will," I said as I walked out to Maggie.

Chapter 19
In the Beginning

When I got to the Silver Springs landing, the steamboat *Athens* was just pulling in. It was the boat I was supposed to take out of there. My heart was divided. I knew what had to be done, but it didn't help the ache inside, knowing that my plans for the future were presently on hold. Before going in search of Max, I needed to leave a note asking Mrs. Brody to please send a wire first thing Monday morning to my boss, Charles Jones, and to David's office in Jacksonville, telling them that I was delayed because of a family emergency and would be in touch as soon as possible. I knew I owed more of an explanation to David, but I couldn't say any more in my wire without the whole town talking. I stuck the note beneath the door of the general store, along with a dollar to pay for the wires, and headed over to the hunters' meat racks. Because it was Sunday, fewer people were around, but because the boats came in and out seven days a week and needed to resupply, some of the hunters could always be found there with fresh kills.

I spotted Tom Bigelow and Rayne Longwood by the racks and walked over to them. There was no disguising the look of surprise on their faces as they both assessed my unusual outfit. "Why, Miss Eve," Tom drawled, "you plannin' on doin' some huntin' with us today?" He smiled, displaying a mouthful of tobacco-stained teeth. "I'd be happy to show you how to pull my trigger." His laugh was as ugly as his teeth.

I had no time to waste, especially not on his vulgar jokes. "Mr. Bigelow, have you seen my father or Max Harjo"?

"Can't say that I have. You, Rayne?"

"Not since yesterday," the quieter man of the two answered. "Max never comes on Sunday, 'less he's got a real big kill."

"Where would I find him?" I asked, looking from man to man.

"Why, I can't rightly say," Tom replied. "But I'd try his place, I guess. Wouldn't you say, Rayne?"

"Yeah, I s'pose. He stays over near the Silver River—just a few miles from here."

"You know, little lady, they's lots o' things that can get ya—goin' into them woods." Tom grinned. "He's pretty far back, ya know. But I'd be happy to show ya, if you'd—"

"It's not necessary, Mr. Bigelow. I'll find my way." Wasting no more time, I turned to leave.

Tom spat a wad of tobacco juice, then asked as an afterthought. "Why ya huntin' him anyway, if ya don't mind my askin'."

"I mind," I called over my shoulder, and the sound of their laughter followed me as I remounted Maggie and headed out of town.

Silver River was fed by Silver Springs, and it connected the spring to the Ocklawaha River. What the Silver River lacked in length, it made up for in beauty. As I made my way west along the river, the low vegetation grew thicker around me, forcing me to slow my pace. I needed to watch for snakes and alligators resting in the shade. Another threat was the shrubbery itself. It was made up of sharp-edged scrub and saw palmettos. The low growing plants cut like a fine-toothed saw, so I worked my way through them carefully to avoid tearing Maggie's legs to shreds.

After fifteen minutes of fighting my way through the vegetation, I finally came to a large clearing. Sitting in the center of it, within a circle of sunlight, was a small, neatly built log cabin. All the pine needles had been carefully swept away, leaving room for a good-sized and well-tended garden on one side of the cabin. Because it was the hottest time of the year, only some okra and hot peppers were growing in a small section of it while the remainder of the garden looked as though it had already been prepared for the fall planting.

I rode to the other side of the cabin. Beyond the yard was a small, well-cared-for citrus grove. It looked like there were grapefruit and tangerines growing, but because it was the middle of summer, the fruits were very young and hard to distinguish from one another. A smokehouse stood at the edge of the yard, though I didn't see any smoke coming from the pipe on the roof. To the left of the smokehouse was a large drying rack with large pieces of meat hanging from it and a large wooden bloodstained table that was obviously used for butchering. There was no sign of life at the moment, and I didn't know if the cabin even belonged to Max, but I'd seen no other homesteads thus far. Whether it belonged to him or not,

I needed to make my presence known before I found myself face to face with the wrong end of a shotgun.

"Hello, in the cabin! Is anyone home?" I shouted. I waited a moment, then rode around to the back. Again, I shouted a greeting, but there was no response. Just as I was pulling the reins to turn Maggie back toward the west to continue traveling along the river, I heard a deep, familiar voice.

"Well, well. Little *kaccv hokte*." It was Max, and he was cresting the bank of the Silver carrying a string of bass. He wore no shirt but had on a pair of cut-off canvas breeches, and his shoulder-length black hair was not covered with the usual black felt hat but was tied back instead. Seeing him half-undressed and looking relaxed was strange and made me feel awkward, stopping me from saying anything for a moment. He walked toward me until he was close enough that I could see the water droplets clinging to his bronze skin and the amusement on his face as he took in my boyish outfit.

"Why are you here?" He walked past me toward the racks and smokehouse.

"I need your help," I said as I reined Maggie around to follow him.

"To do what?" He didn't look at me but threw his fish onto the butchering table and began cleaning them.

"To find Ivy."

His knife stopped in mid-stroke for a second before he continued. "Where's she gone?"

"Mr. Harjo, if I knew that, I wouldn't be asking for your help, now would I?"

"And with a smartass answer like that, you're not going to get it, now will you?" he replied without taking his eyes off the fish.

I knew he was right. I took a deep breath. "I'm sorry, Mr. Harjo. I'm just worried about her. I don't mean to be rude, but I've got to find her, and I've got to hurry about doing it, or she'll be killed."

Max stopped cutting and looked at me. "Who wants her dead?"

"Our father."

This time, Max set the knife down, then turned and walked toward the cabin. "Come with me," he said over his shoulder. "You can tell me what's happened while I grab some gear."

"Oh, thank God," I softly said. "Oh, and thank *you*, Mr. Harjo!" I said more loudly.

Max grunted a reply and walked into his cabin. After I dismounted from Maggie, I followed him in. His cabin was sparsely furnished but as well kept as his grounds were. On one side of the cabin was the kitchen, with a wood-burning stove and a small but beautifully made oak table with two chairs. On the other side of the cabin was his sleeping area. His neatly made bed sat next to a large window, and a thick dark brown animal hide lay across a quilt rack in the corner, obviously waiting for the return of colder weather. I could feel him watching me. Embarrassed, I quickly turned around to face him as he grabbed a bar of soap from the kitchen counter and began washing his hands in a large bowl of water.

"Sit down," he said, jerking his head toward the table. "And start at the beginning."

Chapter 20
The Journey Begins

The first thing we did after leaving Max's place was head for the Haileys' home. Unfortunately, we had to backtrack to get to their place, but we did so by using a well-worn trail that Max had cut over the years. Though it ran parallel to the route I'd taken to his cabin, I'd not seen it through all the dense underbrush, and I was relieved to find that the going was much less difficult and faster.

When we rode into the Haileys' yard, Emmitt immediately came out on the porch, and his worried expression told us that he knew what was going on.

"Emmitt, Ivy was here, wasn't she." It was a statement, not a question.

He nodded. "Guess 'bout an hour and a half ago. Said Hap's crazy mad. Said he knows about the baby. Hell, he knew before Mayoma and I did. We didn't know nothin' about nothin' until then. Moses grabbed some things, then got on Flint—his horse—and off they flew. It was a good thing they did, too, 'cause not an hour after that, your daddy come ridin' in here with Alfonso Kite. Hap says, 'Emmitt, don't try to protect 'em. They done wrong, and there ain't no denyin' that.' Said, 'As Ivy's daddy, I got to do the right thing now, and you're gonna do right by tellin' me where they've gone. And if you don't know, then you tell me which way they headed.' And I told your daddy that they headed east, even though I knew they headed west. He stared at me real hard for a minute, like he was gaugin' whether or not to believe me. When he saw I wasn't budgin' on tellin' him anything more, he and Alfonso headed out, goin' east. With all the tracks from my family comin' and goin' east to the docks, that'll keep 'em busy for a while. But it won't throw them off forever. That Kite fella knows somethin' about trackin', and he'll put 'em on the right track before too long."

"Where's Mayoma, Emmitt?" I felt like I was playing a mental game of chess, and I needed to know where all the pieces were on the board.

"In Ocala. After church, she drove her wagon over to tend to a sick friend who lives there. 'Sposed to be back later today. I'm glad she wasn't here to witness this. I know she'd do somethin' to try and stop it, but your daddy is lookin' for blood. He can't see straight right now, but I know damn well he can shoot straight, and I wouldn't want her in the line of fire."

"Emmitt, would Moses know how to get to where Mayoma is?" Max asked.

"Naw. Moses ain't never been to Judith's house before. He wouldn't have any idea how to get there, and he sure as hell ain't gonna stop folks and ask for directions."

"I want you to think hard, Emmitt. Where might he go that would be a good place to hide out for a while—especially with a woman expecting a baby?" Max pressed him.

Emmitt squinted, which knitted his eyebrows together, and gazed off in the distance as he took a moment to think long and hard. Max and I waited.

"Don't rightly know," he finally answered, focusing his eyes back on us. "He's got an aunt up at Orange Springs, but I don't believe that'd be far enough away to make him feel like he could breathe."

"What about rivers, Emmitt? Does he know any of them well enough that he'd be comfortable navigating them?" Max spoke calmly enough but there was no disguising the urgency in his tone.

"He knows a bunch of the rivers pretty good, but none of 'em real good—not like the Ocklawaha."

"Okay. Does he have a boat stashed somewhere? Say a canoe?"

"I know he had one. And if he doesn't still, he sure knows how to make one. He's got Seminole blood in him."

"Why would they need a canoe when they've got two good horses?" I looked at Max, and then Emmitt.

"Because two sets of horse tracks show up a whole lot better than no tracks left from canoeing down a river," Max replied.

I turned to Emmitt. "Where's the first place you'd look for them?"

"Wouldn't surprise me if they tried to put some miles behind 'em before tryin' to pick up a river somewheres. Everyone knows 'em on the Ocklawaha, so maybe they'd head for the Suwannee River to the north and take it to the Okefenokee Swamp. That swamp can shore hide a person who wants to drop outta sight. Ain't no one in their right mind gonna try to track anyone into that gator- and snake-infested black-water hellhole."

"My father's not in his right mind, Emmitt," I grimly reminded him.

"Let's go," Max said, reining his horse around.

"Sweet Jesus," Emmitt said under his breath, "protect these children."

"Amen," I whispered as I reined Maggie around, too. "Amen."

Chapter 21
Making Tracks

Max and I followed their trail west; then contrary to what Emmitt had told us, we headed south. "He tried to throw us off, too," Max said, crouching over the fresh tracks leading south instead of north, where Emmitt had said they'd most likely go.

"Why do you think they changed their minds about going north?" I asked.

"I don't think they did," he said, standing up and looking off to the south. "I think Emmitt told them to go south but is tellin' everyone else they're going north. He's not about to help anyone find them, including us. At this point, Emmitt doesn't trust anyone. Not a soul." He placed his black felt hat back on his head and instructed me to ride behind him rather than beside him so that we didn't disturb any more of the ground than we had to.

It was important we be as quiet as possible, which was not a hard thing for me to do. I was wrapped up in my thoughts, upset about the fact that Emmitt didn't feel as though he could trust Max and me enough to tell us the truth about where my sister and Moses might go. I realized that deep friendships and family ties had been severed. It hurt me to see the ease with which relationships could be shattered because it was taboo for two people from different races to fall in love.

The Haileys and the Stewarts had been friends for many years. It was a given that the families could count on each other, and the Haileys had been there for the Stewarts too many times to count. And, to a certain degree, the Stewarts had been there for the Haileys, as well. I had to admit that they had helped my family far more than we had helped them. However, in the south, where white folks depended on black folks for so much, it wasn't surprising.

What was surprising was that the Haileys seemed to hold no bitterness toward us, and seemed to love us without judgment or resentment. There was no doubt about the fact that they took a far higher road than we did, and I had to ask myself if I would have walked that same higher ground. At the moment, I couldn't answer. In the eighteen years of life that I'd lived, I'd accepted things the way they'd always been. Though I didn't always think it was fair, it was just the way it was, and I'd never objected to the status quo—not aloud, anyway.

We'd traveled approximately fifteen miles by sundown. It was too dark to follow any tracks, and too dangerous to continue moving through land filled with deadly creatures when we couldn't see, so we set up camp. The sky was clear so Max decided that we didn't need anything more substantial than a blanket lean-to. After lashing a cross pole between two large pines, he attached two smaller saplings to each end of the cross pole. The simple framework was all that was needed to tie his horse blanket to it, providing a slanted roof of sorts.

If it did begin to rain, we could quickly lay thatching materials, like palmetto fronds, on top of the blanket to keep us from getting drenched. Both dry weather and wet weather had their pros and cons. Obviously, the dry weather was more comfortable to travel in, but had the ground been damp, it would have been far easier to follow the tracks. However, Max was a well-seasoned hunter and able to read the dried, broken pine needles that covered much of the ground, as well as the broken branches.

From those alone, he was able to tell that riders had come through and stayed the course. We could only hope that the riders were Ivy and Moses. Max was fairly confident it was the fugitives, though, because the route didn't lead to much of anything, so there was little, if any, traffic. And so far, we'd only seen the two sets of tracks. If my father had determined that Ivy and Moses were actually headed south, then at least he was behind us.

We didn't dare light a fire after we finished setting up the lean-to. Though it would have been a comfort in the blackness of the thick piney woods, and a hot meal would have been welcome, we didn't want to give our position away. Fortunately, Max had brought a small supply of deer jerky and smoked fish. I was too worried to feel hungry, but the weariness I'd begun to feel since the sun set reminded me that to keep going, I needed to refuel my body.

"How far until we reach the Withlacoochee River?" I swatted at another mosquito, thinking that the night was going to seem endless. Once the biting insects had discovered us, they went after us with a vengeance.

We'd moved into the lean-to, but there was nothing to stop them from following us in.

Max ducked back into the lean-to after checking on the horses. "Probably about ten miles or so." He removed his hat, slapped at a mosquito on the side of his neck, and leaned back against one of the pine trees that supported our lean-to. I was resting against the other. "We'll break camp as soon as there's daylight, so we'll be there before noon—if we actually get that far."

"Why? What do you mean?" A mosquito flew into my mouth. Pushing myself up, I stuck my head out of the lean-to and spat. "Excuse me," I said, humiliated. As I settled back against the tree, I realized that the normal rules of etiquette did not apply right now. My greatest concern was not whether Max Harjo thought I was a lady but whether we could reach Ivy and Moses before Papa and Alfonso did. I *had* to warn Ivy and Moses not to come back. But I had no idea where they could go that would be safe enough for them. A colored man with a white woman would stand out no matter where they went. It was a dangerous world they'd created for themselves, and I had absolutely no idea where they would have a chance of surviving together.

"My gut tells me they'll ride the Withlacoochee all the way down to the Green Swamp, and maybe beyond that," Max said, shifting his weight so that he was lying on his right side facing me, propped up on his forearm. "The two of them might survive for a while in the swamp but not a newborn. My guess is that they'll travel all the way to the south end of the swamp, then continue on to the 'Glades."

"The Everglades?" I was confused. From what I knew, it was a no-man's-land—as bad as the Green Swamp. No one I knew would willingly live in that river of grass—appropriately named because of the saw grass. It could cut you to ribbons, and was worse than the saw palmettos. It was a place of endless grassy waters, intense heat, numerous kinds of biting insects, and just as many biting reptiles and mammals. It was certainly the perfect place to get lost in, if that was one's intention, but it was also a very easy place to get killed.

"Why in the world would they go to that godforsaken place?"

All the light of the day had vanished, leaving an inky and dangerous darkness in its place. It was impossible to see much detail on Max's face when he answered me, but I could tell by the tone of his voice that he was a little amused by my ignorance.

"Because, little *kaccv hokte*, the Seminoles are there. Do you know what the name *Seminole* means?" He didn't give me time to answer. He figured I didn't know, and he was right. "It means 'runaway,' so your white sister and her Negro boyfriend will be in good company. Besides, they're gonna need to go to the ends of the Earth if they plan on spending a long time on it. And the best place to do that is where a whole bunch of different people from different places and of different colors accept each other. They don't ask a whole lot of questions because none of them want to have to answer any. So that's why I think they'll head that way. But the big question is whether or not they'll be able to actually make it. If I were a betting man, I wouldn't put a dime down that they will. Hell, not even a penny."

Obviously realizing that his statement was not what I wanted to hear, he added, "But if I did have to place a bet, I'd put my money on Moses for being as capable as anyone I can think of to make it through that wasteland of a swamp that he's probably headed for." When I said nothing in response, he rolled onto his back, covered his face with his felt hat, and told me to get some sleep. But that, I thought as I swatted at a mosquito attempting to fly into my ear, was going to be an absolute impossibility. Daylight seemed like a very long way off, indeed.

Chapter 22
Crazy Brave

We arose at daybreak, but unlike the day before, the sky was overcast and a cool breeze hinted at the threat of approaching rain. We needed to get moving, and we also needed to find water. Though Max had brought water in a pouch that was made from the stomach of a boar, we'd finished that and some jerky for our meager breakfast. It was vital to rehydrate ourselves, as well as our horses, and we knew that Ivy and Moses would need to do the same. None of us could keep riding if thirst became a crucial issue. We hoped that their tracks might lead us to water. However, the chance was good that they could easily miss a small source simply by not knowing the lay of the land. So, while Max kept us on their tracks, I kept an eye out for a small creek or spring.

Most of the time, Max and I were quiet, only talking when we had to. It was far more important that we listen for any sound that might reveal my sister's position ahead of us or my father's behind us. After traveling for about an hour, I spotted a seep spring about fifty yards off to my right.

"You've got a good eye," he said softly as he dismounted by it. "Better than your sister or Moses. They didn't stop here, and they would have, had they seen it."

We allowed our horses to drink their fill then eat whatever they could find near us, which gave Max and me a few minutes to refresh ourselves, and refill the water pouch. Squatting at the edge of the spring, I loosened my tied-back hair and splashed the cooling water over my face and head, finger-combing it through my hair. It was exactly what I needed to clean some of the grit off me, as well as clear my head. Retying my hair, I walked over to Max. He'd rounded up our horses and was patiently waiting for me.

"You know, Mr. Harjo, I was thinking about the fact that my father is drinking again."

"Okay." He looked at me askance, unsure where the conversation was going.

"He grabbed a bottle of whiskey when he stormed out yesterday to go after Ivy. There are two things that whiskey does to him: It makes him angry, and it makes him sleepy. Do you know if Alfonso Kite likes the stuff? I was just thinking that, well, maybe if—"

Smiling, he finished my sentence. "That maybe they've slept a little longer than we did, and you can bet they're not thinking as clearly as we are. That's good, little *kaccv hokte*. That's real good. We're going to make a fine tracker out of you yet."

"I don't know about that, Mr. Harjo. Just the mosquitoes alone are enough to make me reconsider this as a lifelong occupation."

Smiling, he said, "Well, I'll say this much then, you're *hadcho*."

"Now, what does *that* mean?" Somehow, it didn't irritate me to be called by an Indian name the way it had that day at the docks, when he'd bestowed the title of *kaccv hokte*—tiger woman—upon me. This man was helping me, and asking nothing in return, so it was hard to get as irritated with him as I was before.

"*Hadcho* means 'crazy brave,' Or, 'you're so brave, you're almost crazy.'"

"I don't know whether to feel insulted or flattered," I said as I mounted my horse. "But it sounds a lot like your own name, to tell you the truth."

"Aside from a good eye, little *kaccv hokte*, you've got a good ear," he replied, mounting Sampson. "That's the meaning of my name."

"So, you're calling us both crazy and brave, then; is that it?" I asked, falling in behind him as he picked up the trail again.

"Yes," he replied.

"Well, you're only half right about that, Mr. Harjo. I'll agree that I'm crazy to be out here doing this, but there's nothing brave about it. I'm scared to death."

"And that makes you even braver, *kaccv hokte*."

We followed their dry trail for hours before a light, steady rain began. We kept moving though, and Max was still able to follow the broken needles and branches all the way to Withlacoochee. When we finally spotted the river from a good distance away, my immediate thought was how much it looked like the Ocklawaha. It was about as wide, and it was just as primitive looking. An abundance of foliage hugged her banks, including trees that hung out over the water and branches that submissively bowed down toward it.

Max dismounted and walked along the shoreline for several minutes, trying to figure out what my sister and Moses had done once they'd reached this point. I needed to stay out of his way so as not to disturb any clues they'd left. I waited out of the rain beneath a massive oak and watched Max retrace his steps, as though looking for something he hadn't yet found. After several minutes, he joined me under the tree. "They're still riding," he said as he climbed onto Sampson and urged the massive horse on.

"Why do you think they decided to do that?" I fell into step behind him again. It had only seemed logical that they would travel by water since they'd headed for the river.

"My guess is that Moses didn't have a boat here, and didn't want to take the time to build one—if he's even capable of doing that. Emmitt seems to think he can, but working with someone on a canoe is a whole lot different from building one on your own, at least one that's safe enough to travel a distance, especially with a pregnant woman. There'd be no point in giving up their horses if traveling on the river wasn't a better option. One thing's for sure, though; it's going to be a lot faster tracking them now. Their horses' prints are going to show up real clearly on this wet ground."

"That's good!" My spirits rose with the confidence that we'd find them soon.

"Not necessarily." Max shook his head. "If we can follow them more easily, then your daddy can, too. He's not gonna give up. And on that, I'd be willing to bet every dollar I have."

We rode late into the day and had just started to discuss the fact that we'd need to build a more substantial shelter when Max spotted an old cabin set back from the trail a ways. Though the windows were dark, and we couldn't see any tracks leading up to it, we were still cautious as we approached. Simply because we didn't see signs of life, that didn't mean someone wasn't holed up in the cabin.

As Max very quietly reminded me, Ivy and Moses weren't the only ones on the run in these parts. Most of Florida was still uninhabited, making it a likely destination for those seeking freedom. And if living a life of isolation in a harsh and unforgiving land seemed like a steep price to pay, those fleeing the law—or an enraged father—might consider it a real bargain.

"Let's ride out of view from that window. If anyone's watching, I want 'em to think we didn't see the place and rode on." After we'd gotten to the point where it was difficult to see the cabin any longer, Max stopped us. "Wait here while I take a look around the place. Then I'll come get you," he said in a low voice. "But, if something should happen—"

"Like what?" I whispered.

"I'm not saying something will! But, if it should, then you take off as fast as you can. Don't slow down, and don't look back. I'll catch up to you if I can."

I started to object, to suggest we just keep moving south, but he told me to hush and do as he said. Then he climbed off Sampson, and as quietly and stealthily as a thief in the night, he angled back through the rain-drenched woods to the cabin beyond. He stayed low and approached the cabin from the side, so that if someone should look out, it would be harder to see him. Slowly, he made his way around to the front window and cautiously raised himself up high enough to peek inside. Then he quietly moved to the back of the building. After a moment or two, he appeared on the trail again where I could see him, and just from the relaxed way he walked, I knew that there was no one home. I grabbed Sampson's reins, and we walked back to meet him.

"We'll stay here tonight. Everyone's got to sleep, and that includes us. We might as well be as comfortable as possible."

We secured the horses behind the cabin; then I followed Max up the rickety steps and through the unlocked door. Reaching into his pocket, Max produced a box of matches, lit one on the edge of his boot and quickly used the weak light to look for a candle or lamp. Sitting on a makeshift counter that was nothing more than several roughly hewn logs placed end to end was an oil lamp, and Max quickly lit the wick. Taking the lamp, he moved around the single room, assessing what was in it and what we might use. From the looks of things, it was an old fishing cabin. There were cane poles, and other items used by a serious fisherman, including an old net that Max retrieved from a nail in the wall.

"Now, this we can use. It's seen better days, but it'll still work. Rummage around and see if you can find anything else we might need. I'm going to try to catch us some dinner before the light is completely gone. Be careful about reaching into dark corners and cabinets—places like that. We aren't the only critters who prefer staying dry and sleeping under a roof." Then he walked out the door, leaving me to find things we might need, and, perhaps, a few other things we didn't.

Chapter 23
Muddy Mistakes

Max returned about thirty minutes later with supper. It was nearly dark now, but he'd still had enough daylight to make his trip to the river's edge very productive. In just a few attempts at casting the net, he'd caught two fat catfish. I'd already started a fire in the wood-burning stove so that we could dry our clothes, and I immediately set the fish to fry in an old iron skillet that was hanging from a hook on the wall. It would have been wonderful to have some bacon grease to cook them in, as well as a few potatoes to throw in, but I was grateful for what we had. It was certainly better than having another meal of jerky, or no meal at all.

"Eve," Max began as he pulled off his wet boots and socks. Hearing him call me by my Christian name startled me. I'd rarely heard him use it, so I knew he was about to say something important. "Other than nets and cane poles, what's something else every respectable fisherman uses—at least one that doesn't want to just limit his fishing to what he can catch from the bank?"

"A boat," I replied.

"Yep. And down near the bank, not fifty yards up the trail from here, there's one sitting there, tied to a tree, just waiting to be used. Had you and I gotten that far before we turned back to hole up here for the night, there's no way we would have missed it."

"Okay," I said, anxious for him to get to the point.

"I walked over to take a look at it—to see if it was still usable—and it is. It looks completely watertight. But you know what else was there?" I was afraid to ask, so I just shook my head. "Horse tracks on the bank," he continued, "and they're the same ones we've been following. Even though it's been raining hard, the horses are heavy, as if they're carrying a load, and the mud is soft. Their tracks were deep enough that I could still make them out."

"So? Maybe they let their horses drink!" I was tired, hungry, dirty, worried, and in no mood for games.

"Maybe so, but there are no tracks leading back up the bank. They crossed the river."

"That makes no sense! Why would they cross the river with their horses and leave a perfectly good canoe behind?"

"Because they didn't want to leave their horses behind. They intend on staying on the land—at least for now. But they're getting sloppy, careless. When you hurry or you're tired, you start making mistakes, and Moses is starting to make them. He tried to cover the tracks but left two that were still visible. I covered them, though. I don't want your father to figure out they crossed the river, at least not yet. Hopefully, he'll think the rain has washed out their tracks and that they're still heading south, on this side of the river, especially once he sees that boat. He'll figure they either didn't see it, or didn't want to use it. Eventually, he'll figure out they've crossed, though, and I'm afraid it might be sooner rather than later."

"Why do you say that?"

"Because those two tracks weren't the only thing I saw out there. In the distance, back to the north of us, I saw two flashes of light, but just briefly. Someone was trying to light somethin'. I watched for a while but didn't see anything else. Honestly, it's surprised me that we haven't seen any sign of your father yet. I think something delayed him for a little while. Either that or he's hittin' the bottle, like you said. There's always the possibility that it's someone other than your father and Kite, and they're intentionally stayin' behind us to let us do all the hard work that will lead the way to your sister and Moses. No matter, that little speck of light told me we're not alone out here."

"It's good you've got excellent eyesight, Mr. Harjo."

"One thing's for sure," Max said, stretching his damp feet toward the fire, "we don't need to run into anyone else. In the morning, you and I are going to take a swim. You do know how to swim, don't you?"

"I was brought up on the Ocklawaha. I can swim like a fish," I assured him, but I wasn't sure so about his plan. And I couldn't imagine what Ivy's strategy was. Were they just moving along aimlessly, or did they have some destination in mind? Because of their change in direction, I tended to believe they'd changed their minds about something.

"I'm glad you're a strong swimmer," Max continued, "because God only knows what else will be swimming along with us and our horses. Let's just hope our head count remains the same on the other side of the river as it is on this side."

Suddenly, the aroma of the cooking fish got his attention. "Are those about ready?" Seeing that they were, I carried the skillet over to the table, along with two forks and a couple of tin plates. I gave him a full fish and half of the other.

"Have you lost your appetite?" he asked before shoving a large bite into his mouth.

"That, and my confidence about Ivy getting across that river. She's not the greatest swimmer, but neither is my father since he only has the one arm now."

"Your father's physical limitations work in our favor. Ivy'll be all right. She's got Moses with her, and he's a strong swimmer. I'd be willing to bet that their head count was still four, including their horses, when they climbed up that east bank."

"You know, Mr. Harjo, for someone who says he's not a gambling man, you sure are willing to place a lot of bets."

"Only those I'm sure I'll win, *kaccv hokte*. And you can bet on *that*."

Chapter 24
Bitterness like Guilt

After finishing our supper, Max remained at the table, repairing a couple of holes in the net using some twine he'd found in a box with other fishing gear. While he worked, I made some coffee I'd found in one of the cabinets. Though there was nothing fresh about it, it was still coffee, and it would taste like heaven after a long day of riding in the rain. When it was ready, I brought him a tin cup of it and sat across from him.

"So, what happens once we make the crossing tomorrow, Mr. Harjo?"

He didn't look up to answer me, but kept his eyes focused on the net. "Dunno," he honestly replied. "But we'll know when we get there. We should be able to see some sign telling us which direction they're going. One of their horses has a good-sized nick in its hoof. It's making it a lot easier to be certain the tracks are theirs. And if the ground is as muddy over there as I think it'll be, then it's going to be as easy as following Hansel and Gretel's breadcrumb trail."

I was surprised to hear this tough, backwoods man use a children's fairy tale as an analogy. "What do you know about Hazel and Gretel?" I laughed.

He glanced up at me with a smile and turned his attention back to the net. "I was a little fella at one time, ya know."

"Where're you from, Mr. Harjo, if you don't mind my asking?"

"Huntsville, Alabama. And when are you going to quit calling me 'Mr. Harjo'?" He glanced up again.

I wasn't comfortable being on such casual terms with him, even though we were the only two together in a cabin in the middle of nowhere. Still... "Do you have any family there?" I knew I was prying, but I wanted to learn something about this man. All I knew was that he was a hunter, an excellent tracker, and a friend of Ivy's.

"Other than some distant relatives, everyone else is gone. My mother died when I was twelve. She was a Creek Indian and not used to the white man's world, but she learned to live in it when she married my father. He was a Scot, who'd come over here in the hopes of acquiring a land claim."

"If your father was a Scot, why do you have an Indian last name?"

"Creeks live in a matrilineal society. Children always take their mother's last name. My father allowed her to continue that tradition, so I was given his last name for my middle name. My full name is Max McCarty Harjo."

I was surprised he was willing to tell me so much, so I kept asking questions. "Whatever happened with the land claim your father was hoping to acquire? Did he receive one?

"Yes, but the land wasn't worth working. Instead, he became a hunter, met some of my mother's people as a result of it, and then married my mother. She died of cholera, and so did my two siblings, an older sister and a younger brother."

So the rumors that he had lost a wife and child turned out to be overspun gossip, which was usually the case when people talked about things they knew little of. Max had lost a mother and siblings, not a wife and baby. Either way, though, it was terribly tragic.

"I'm sorry, Mr. Harjo," I said softly.

"It was a long time ago," he replied, not taking his eyes off the net.

"What happened to your father?"

"He stayed around for a while longer, but I guess it was too hard for him to remain in a place where he'd lost so much. Eventually, he took off for parts unknown."

"And you haven't seen him since?" I was amazed that a father could so cruelly turn his back on his young son, especially when that young son had lost his mother and siblings.

"I saw him once more before he died. He had a bad heart. I guess it literally broke when he lost my mother, Adele, and Robby. Anyway, our paths crossed one time when we were both hunting up in the Florida panhandle. It was good to see him."

"You weren't angry at him?"

"Not really. I didn't hold any bad feelings toward him."

"You're a better person than I am, I'm afraid. I don't think I could have ever forgiven him."

"What's the point of hanging on to bitterness, *kaccv hokte*? It doesn't change the past, only the future."

I didn't say anything for a moment as I digested his last statement. This man, who had the reputation of being a tough, ruthless hunter, was nothing like that. It was amazing how wrong everyone had been—including me.

"So." He glanced up and smiled. "Ivy tells me you're a big-shot journalist now." He was obviously ready to change the subject.

"Well, I don't know about being a big shot, but I'm writing for the *Florida Times-Union* in Jacksonville now. I've always wanted to be a journalist."

"She also tells me there's a man back there that you're very fond of. I guess he's the one your father introduced at his party."

I was a little taken aback. I once wondered how much Ivy had divulged to Max about our family, and I was getting the picture that it was quite a lot. On one hand, it irritated me that she would so openly discuss my life. On the other hand, I was both touched and surprised that the goings-on in my life mattered so much to her. I was obviously on her mind more than I thought I was.

However, I didn't want to discuss David with Max. And for some reason, I didn't want to offer up the fact that we were now engaged. It was a very intimate and personal part of my life. Oddly enough, I felt I'd be put in the position of having to defend David's character. Perhaps it was because he was a land developer whereas Max was a lover of the land. There was also the possibility that Max, who hadn't lived the privileged life that David had, might view him as weak and soft. And though Max's opinion shouldn't have mattered to me, for some strange reason, it did. I needed to change the subject.

"Mr. Harjo, can I ask you something? How is it that you and my sister became such good friends? I mean, obviously she talks to you quite a bit about our family."

"We spend a lot of time together at the landing. You can learn a lot about people while standing around waiting to sell deer meat and medicines. It's a way of passing the time, I s'pose. And I guess we kind of both feel like outsiders—like we really don't quite fit in anywhere."

I dropped my eyes so that I was looking at my coffee cup. I was ashamed. As hard as it was to admit to myself, I knew I'd helped to make my sister feel that way, as if she was the black sheep in the Stewart family. After a moment, I looked up at Max. "Did you know about her and Moses?"

"I had an idea." He glanced up at me to weigh my reaction to his admission.

"Just an idea?"

"Listen," Max said, setting the net aside and resting his forearms on the table. "Not everyone in this white world of yours thinks that Ivy and

Moses being together is such a terrible thing. I've known quite a few white men who are considered pillars in their community, and they go home and beat the hell out of their wives a couple times a week just because. And they also prefer sleeping with anyone other than their wives—men and young girls included. Moses is a good man—Negro or not—who treats your sister with the kindness and respect that she deserves."

He was judging me, and I didn't like it one bit. "That may be, Mr. Harjo, but it's still not right!"

"So says the white lady."

"The white lady who is trying to chase down her sister before their father murders her, her colored boyfriend, *and* their baby!"

"Why are you getting so riled up, Eve? Have I hit a nerve?"

"Of course not! I'm not like my father!"

"Is that so? Then let me ask you this: How do you feel about Moses? Honestly."

"I hate him." I could hear the venom in my voice, but that was the way I felt at the moment.

"Why?"

"Because he's ruined my sister. He's ruined our family!"

"No, he hasn't, Eve! Your father has!"

"Go to hell!"

"I'm sure I will in the end, but for now, I'm going to sleep." Picking up his horse blanket and rifle, he walked out to sleep on the front porch, giving us both a little room to breathe, as well as giving me some privacy and the one cot in the cabin.

Though I was bone-tired, I knew I'd lie awake for a long time. I stood a better chance of getting some sleep with a swarm of mosquitoes swirling around my head than with Max's words swirling inside it.

In many ways he was right. My family often judged folks on the color of their skin and the kind of blood that ran through their veins instead of on the kind of thoughts that ran through their minds or on what was truly in their hearts. To Papa, especially, it was far better to be white-skinned and blackhearted than to be black-skinned and kindhearted. I was afraid that the apples hadn't fallen far from that bigoted tree. It shamed me to think that my brothers and I had gone along with that sort of thinking all our lives, never stopping to think about the fact that it was so terribly hurtful, and could even turn deadly.

I had failed Ivy. No matter what, I should have stood by her through the years, respecting the type of work she chose to do, and in her choices of friends...and lover. I realized I didn't have to always agree with her, but, as her sister—especially her twin—I should have always stood by her. *Always.*

Sometime in the middle of the night, the storm picked up in intensity. Lightning streaked across the sky like electric fingers reaching down from the heavens, followed by booms that sounded as though a canon had been shot off. The blowing rain and the possibility of being struck were enough to chase Max back inside. When the darkness was interrupted by another flash, I saw that he had settled down on the other side of the tiny cabin, closer to the nearly cold wood stove.

"I've truly been my father's daughter, haven't I?" I said to him. It was easier to do so in the blackness of the room than to have to watch Max's deep blue eyes judging me. "I'm ashamed."

"Hanging on to guilt is like hanging on to bitterness, *kaccv hokte*. It doesn't change the past, only the future."

His response wasn't judgmental or chastising. *This is a kind man,* I thought, *and a very wise one, too.* I said a silent thank-you to God that Max had been a friend to Ivy. And I suddenly realized that I wanted him to be one to me, as well.

"Good night…Max," I whispered, not thinking he'd hear me.

"Good night, Eve," he softly responded.

He not only had excellent eyesight; he had excellent hearing too.

Chapter 25
Crossings

Max gently nudged me awake before dawn. We needed to get moving as soon as it was light. I was immediately greeted by the smell of coffee and fried fish. Max had gotten up earlier to light the stove and put coffee on, and then he went outside to cast the net a few times while scanning the area around us for any other glimpses of someone's campfire or lantern.

Considering the size of the cabin, I was amazed his activities hadn't woken me. I asked him why he didn't get me up so that I could help him. Assessing me from head to toe, he wryly answered that from the looks of things, he should have let me sleep until noon. I knew I must have looked like something chewed up and spit out because my aching body told me so. I wasn't used to riding all day while living off jerky and fish like Max was.

"Other than the fact that you're tracking two-footed animals instead of the four-footed kind, this is just like another workday for you, isn't it?" I asked him while stuffing yesterday's dried-out clothes into my satchel.

"Yes, but I've done this before. I was a bounty hunter for a while in Louisiana."

I was surprised. "You've done a lot in not a lot of years, haven't you?"

"When you have to fend for yourself, and especially when you're young, you have to do a lot of things you don't like doing before you're big enough and smart enough to do the things you want to." He took a last swallow of coffee, then walked over to the door and opened it. "You ready?" He was anxious to get going.

"As I'll ever be." I grabbed my satchel and walked outside.

The dawn sky was the color of cement, but at least the rain had stopped. I scanned the land around us, looking for any sign of my father. I never thought there'd come a day when I prayed that my father was still drinking, but that day had arrived. That alone would slow him down. So, it was just a matter of whether he wanted Ivy and her baby dead worse than he wanted a drink. If the former was the case, then he'd try to stay away from the bottle. But if the cravings got to be too much, then the whiskey would win out, hands down.

"Eve, let's ride down the trail a little ways and see if there isn't an easier place to cross. The river's gotten higher and faster from all this rain," he said, taking Sampson's reins and mounting him. Looking out at the swiftly moving current, I realized that the river had become a much stronger opponent than it had been the night before.

We went about a half mile before coming to a narrower place in the river. Though it was still wide enough to be very dangerous, it was better than the spot where Ivy and Moses had crossed. Undoubtedly, the river had been slower moving and lower then. Either that or something had forced them to cross it at that point.

"How experienced are you at crossing rivers?" Max asked.

I told him I'd only ridden Maggie across streams, and once across the Ocklawaha, when the water level was at the lowest I'd ever seen it during a drought.

"Eve," Max began as he dismounted. "I'm going to ride out there and see how deep it is. If I get to the point where Samson can't touch the bottom and he starts to get panicky, I'm getting off him so that he can swim across without my additional weight. Once we're across, I'll know what we're dealing with. I'm gonna go ahead and tie a mecate rein to Maggie. It's a long lead rope that attaches around her muzzle, and I'll take the other end of it across the river with me. If the river is too deep for the horses to walk across—and I'm sure it is—then once I'm on the other side, you ride Maggie on in but hang on like hell. You're small, so your weight won't matter to her, but she'll still be scared with the current running the way it is, and especially when she has to start swimming. When horses are spooked, there's no tellin' what they'll do, so you're going to have to hang on to her as best you can. I'll be pulling her to keep her headed in the right direction. But if you should fall off, or you throw yourself off because she's goin' wild, I'm letting go of that lead rope and swimming out to you. I know you're a good swimmer, but it's going to be a real tricky current. You come before Maggie. I'm not going to shout any directions to you from the other bank. If anyone's within earshot, they'll hear me. As soon as I get to the other side, you come on."

Untying a leather bag that was attached to his saddle, he withdrew a wound-up rope, stashed his boots and my moccasins in its place to keep them dry, and slung the bag across his chest. Then he tied the mecate rein on Maggie. Finally, Max climbed onto Sampson, and walked him down the bank and into the river. Even his well-trained horse hesitated for a moment when he first felt the current, but under Max's expert handling, he stayed calm enough. They went no farther, though, and Max turned to me.

"Eve, I need you to get into the water, too. Just stay right there at the edge. I need to brush away our tracks leading into the river."

I did as I was told, but Maggie was already nervous just standing in ankle-deep water. Sampson, however, remained in the spot where Max dismounted from him. Knowing he needed to hurry, Max quickly washed away our tracks, then returned, and remounted his horse. "Stay exactly where you are," he said as he gently kicked Sampson's sides to urge him into the river. As they rode away from us, Max let the long line feed out behind him.

I watched as the water rose up Sampson's legs, and then Max's, until the horse was submerged up to its belly. From the change in the way the horse moved, I could tell that it was no longer touching bottom but was swimming instead. Its head repeatedly jutted forward as its powerful chest and shoulders worked in unison with its legs to propel itself across the river, fighting the current as it did so. But the horse remained manageable, and Max was able to stay on him. About three-quarters of the way across, Sampson's movements changed again when his feet had obviously connected with the sludgy bottom. Within a minute's time, both he and Max were standing on the opposite bank. Now, it was my turn.

I guided Maggie into the water, but instead of hesitating slightly as Sampson had done, she backed up and tried to turn around. Jerking the reins back to correct her, I forcefully kicked my heels against her and urged her ahead. She became more skittish as the water deepened, and once she started to lose the bottom, she began to thrash around wildly.

"Get off her!" Max shouted, less concerned with alerting someone to our whereabouts than he was with the possibility of my drowning. Using the saddle horn, I pulled myself up slightly, got my right knee beneath me, and then pushed myself off as hard as I could. The murky green-brown river engulfed me. I tried to swim away from Maggie and was almost clear of her, but her back left foot just caught the right side of my head, stunning me. For a moment, it was hard to see or think clearly. Confused as to which way was up or down, I started to panic, and as I did, I sucked in a breath of river water. All sound started echoing and as my panic rose, so did any chance of thinking clearly. I inhaled more water, and my lungs felt as if they were about to explode. Trashing my arms and legs to try to find the bottom, or the surface, I suddenly felt like letting go. *It's an easy thing to do,* I thought. *Just let the water take me. All I need to do is stop fighting it, stop moving and—*

Suddenly, something took hold of the back of my shirt and yanked me up and out of the darkness into a place of light and air, blessed air…and Max.

He hooked his right arm around my ribcage, just under my breasts, so that he could keep my upper half above water. Then, using his free arm, he made strong strokes through the water, until he was able to stand again and drag me up onto the bank. Lying there, I alternated between throwing up water and trying to catch my breath. It took me a couple of minutes before I could actually fill my lungs to their full capacity and several minutes more before I could actually breathe normally again. As I recovered, Max untied the end of Maggie's mecate rein from the tree he had hurriedly tied it to so that he could help me, and guided my horse onto the bank.

Returning to me, he helped me stand up. "We can't stay here. We're out in the open. We need to move closer to the woods."

Max took the horses by their reins, and holding on to one of my arms to support me, we moved away from the river. When we were just inside the tree line, he told me to sit and wait for him while he got rid of the tracks from our exit up the bank. He started to walk away but turned around and looked at me.

"You did good, Eve. Real good." Softly chuckling, he added, "You truly are *hadcho*—crazy brave—that's for sure."

Chapter 26
The Dangerous Unknown

We paralleled the river, staying close to the tree line, following a trail of broken twigs and grasses until late into the day. Fortunately, the sun broke through the heavy gray skies, allowing us to dry out and warm up. Even after changing into fresh clothing after the crossing, I was chilled to the bone. Max said that the scare of almost drowning probably had something to do with it, but no matter what had caused my chill, I didn't feel warm again until the sun had baked me for a while. It also dried the land around us, which made sleeping in a makeshift shelter far more comfortable.

"We'll ride for another fifteen minutes or so," Max said after the sun dipped below the pines, leaving us in tree-filtered fading light. "We'll set up—"

Suddenly, he pulled back on Sampson's reins as something on the ground got his attention. All day he'd ridden or walked, watching the ground ahead of us for assurances that we were going in the right direction. But something had just gotten his attention.

"They turned here. Look," he said as he dismounted, then squatted, and pointed to an area on the ground to the left of the trail we'd been following. I dismounted, too, and squatted down by him. "You see that matted grass there?" He pointed but did not touch it. When I said that I did, he continued. "Let me walk ahead several yards and check, but I bet there aren't any more tracks to the south. They're heading east now." We both stood.

"What does that mean?" I asked. "What's east?"

"I don't know, and maybe they don't either. But I know they're hoping it leads to some kind of freedom—either that or they're trying to throw us off, and they're zigzagging."

"Well," I looked up from the tracks, off toward the east, and back at Max. "Then we'll do some zigzagging, too," I firmly stated.

Max smiled. "Ah, little *kaccv hokte*, you're not just crazy brave; you're a crazy, brave tiger woman." His broad smile faded to a softer one as he took a small lock of my bright auburn hair between his fingers and rolled it back and forth as though testing the feel of it. "And the fire that burns inside of you burns all the way to the outside, too. Your hair is the color of flames," he said, looking at the lock in his fingers and then at my face.

Neither of us said anything as we looked at each other. I started to walk away, to break the moment between us, but Max grabbed my arm to stop me. Gently pulling me back to him, he cupped the right side of my face in his hand and said something in Muscogee, the language spoken by the Creeks. I didn't understand the words, but I understood what was in his eyes. He must have seen the same in mine, for he pulled me to him and watched my eyes as he leaned in and kissed my lips.

I wrapped my arms around his neck, and when I did, he covered my mouth with his so that we could taste each other in the most sacred and beautiful way. I wanted to keep going, to continue down this path he was leading me on, but I knew I couldn't. Somehow, it felt like a betrayal of Ivy and the promise I'd made to myself not to fail her again. And it most definitely was a betrayal of David, who didn't deserve it. It had to stop. *I* had to stop. After unwrapping my arms from around Max's neck, I placed my hands against his chest and gently pushed him away. Covering my mouth with the back of my hand, I whispered, "I can't." I shook my head to emphasize my refusal and repeated, "I can't. I'm sorry." He let me walk away from him, but not before I saw the look in his eyes shift from want to anger and hurt as I rejected him. But there was no denying to myself that while my words said one thing, my heart was beginning to say another. And just like Ivy on the eastbound trail, I was afraid I was heading into the dangerous unknown.

Chapter 27
The Soul of Souls

We spent the night in a quickly built lean-to and ate some of the fish from breakfast while avoiding each other's eyes and any conversation for the remainder of the evening. The uncomfortable silence between us was deafening.

I knew I should apologize to him for allowing this to happen. If I'd been totally honest with him about the depth of my relationship with David, then Max would have known I was betrothed. I mentally kicked myself for the deception, but in my soul of souls, I knew that it had been a deliberate omission. The question I asked myself over and over again as I tossed and turned in the sweltering humidity of the endless night was why.

Why had I left out that very important fact? Finally, that little voice in my soul answered me: I was starting to feel something for Max Harjo that I'd never felt for anyone before—including David. It was an unsettling thought for it was an impossible situation. This was a relationship that was entirely built on raw emotions that were part of unusual circumstances, and once those circumstances changed, the feelings would likely fade, leaving nothing in their place but regret. It was a stressful time, a time when I was grateful to have the help and wisdom of someone as capable as Max, and I was confusing feelings of desire with feelings of deep gratitude. With that realization, my world righted itself once more and blessed sleep finally came.

The next morning, I knew I had to say something to Max. We needed to keep our minds on finding Ivy, not on each other. As we prepared to leave once it was just light enough to see, I spoke the words I'd been rehearsing in my mind.

"Max, I need to talk to you about yesterday afternoon," I said as I threw my saddle over Maggie. Max was in the midst of removing the blanket we'd used on the roof of the lean-to. After the slightest hesitation in his movements, he continued pulling it off the frame but said nothing. "I shouldn't have let that happen between us," I continued, "and I'm sorry. This is my fault. What you didn't know, and what I should have told you, is that David and I are engaged to be married." There was no indication that he heard me. He showed no emotion, and there was no hesitation as he continued to gather up our few things from the lean-to. "Anyway, I'm sorry. I should have been more forthcoming about the seriousness of my relationship with David."

Max barely glanced at me as he walked by. I mounted Maggie and waited for him. He finished loading his items onto Sampson, mounted him and then rode up next to me. "I know about you and David," he said, looking me square in the eyes. "Ivy talks to me, remember?" He made a clucking sound to get Samson moving and immediately started watching the ground for the eastbound tracks. I fell in behind him.

"Then why did you let it happen?"

He turned slightly in his saddle so that I was looking at his profile. The lines of his nose and chin were angular and strong. "Why did *I*? The question is, Why did *you*? I'm not the one engaged." That silenced me. Then, he said, "Eve, I kissed you because I wanted to, and if you're being honest—which you seem to have trouble with—then you'd agree you wanted to kiss me, too. But let's not make more out of this than it really is. It was only a kiss—a nice one, I admit, but nothing more. You're not the first woman I've ever kissed, and it's unlikely you'll be the last. And I'm sure the same can be said for you. I doubt David is the only one you've ever kissed, though it seems he'll be the last. And if that's what you want, then that's great, it's just wonderful. But stop kissing other men. It takes two, you know. Now, let's put it behind us so that we can find Ivy and Moses and then put this trip behind us. I have things to do that I've put on hold. I need to move on, and you need to get married. Let's just get this done."

"Fine," I replied testily. Neither of us said anything more as we rode toward the sunrise.

Chapter 28
Bad Company

The terrain changed as we rode farther inland. Subtropical land took on a more tropical feel. River-cooled breezes became a hot and dry wind, while scrawnier scrub pines and longleaf yellow pines filled the forests, replacing the luscious oak and magnolia trees. Grass poked up sporadically in the sandy soil, with sandspurs thriving far better in the desolate landscape. Gone were the crystal-clear blue-green springs; instead, there were countless deep sinkholes filled with water that was the color of dark molasses. Many of the sinkholes were deathtraps; the walls were nearly vertical and too slick from algae to climb out of. And water moccasins were still a threat wherever there was water, as were rattlesnakes.

The land mirrored my spirits. As we rode in virtual silence for a good part of the day, I started to have misgivings about continuing a journey that was beginning to feel more and more like a fool's errand. Though we were following tracks, how could we be certain that they were Ivy's and Moses's? Perhaps we were mistakenly following another pair of travelers. Max was sure we were on the correct track since one of the horse's hooves had a nick in it, but who was to say some stranger's hoof didn't have that damage to it, and we'd been following the wrong tracks all along?

Even if they were Ivy's and Moses' tracks, and we finally caught up to them, how would they react? That last thing I wanted was for any of us to get shot because Moses or Ivy thought we'd come to hogtie them and bring them home. I knew if I was feeling this low, they had to be feeling a hundredfold worse. I couldn't image the terror of feeling like the prize in a hunt.

As I was right in the middle of my depressing musings, Max swung his horse around so that Maggie and Sampson were nearly nose to nose. He'd been alerted to something behind me. "We have company," he grimly said as he reached for his rifle behind him then rested it in his lap. I quickly turned Maggie around to see what he'd spotted—or who.

Max moved Sampson slightly in front of me. "Son of a bitch! It's Tom Bigelow and Rayne Longwood. Now, what the hell do they want?"

As the riders got closer, sure enough, I could make out it was Tom and Rayne. They were the hunters I'd talked to outside of the store in Silver Springs. Between Tom and Rayne, Tom was by far the more talkative and uncouth. I'd always tried to stay out of his way, and though he and I had never had much interaction with each other, the little I'd heard from him was usually offensive in some way. On the other hand, Rayne was quiet and never had much to say about anything, which had always unnerved me. I preferred knowing what someone was thinking, even though I might not like it, instead of having to guess whether someone should be considered a friend or foe.

Tom and Rayne were riding hard, obviously try to catch up with us, so we waited as they crossed the desolate landscape. Finally, they reined in their overheated horses. The poor animals looked on the verge of collapse as they panted and snorted, trying hard to catch their breath. There was so much lather around their mouths that both animals looked rabid.

"Rayne, Tom." Max nodded at them. "How many horses do you all kill in a year's time?" Clearly, Max didn't like them.

Tom let the jab slide, or was simply too thick-witted to have caught it in the first place. Instead, he laughed. "Well, I get tired of the same ol' ride. I like tradin' 'em in pretty often."

"Trading them in, Tom, or *doing* them in?" Max's eyes were shooting shards of broken glass at him. If looks could kill, Tom would have been cut to smithereens.

Tom was starting to feel uncomfortable. He laughed, but it came out like a sharp bark. "You're a funny man, Max. Real funny. I always heard injuns didn't have no sense of humor. Always serious-like, you know? Well, I think you're proving 'em wrong."

Max ignored the insult. "What do ya want? What brings you all the way out here? I know it wasn't to discuss the many ways you know how to mishandle a horse. It's hot as hell, and I need to take a piss, so talk to me."

"Miss Stewart's pa sent us. He's put a bounty on that Hailey boy. Said he wants him dead, and for us to just bring back a little souvenir to prove he's crossed the Jordon River, so to speak."

I closed my eyes, stunned that my father could be so cruel. "What about my sister?" My mouth was dry, making my words sound thick.

"Oh, he wants us to bring his little girl home in one piece," Tom answered. "Said he'd take care of that issue. Hap had planned on findin' them himself—with Kite along for the ride, too. And they'd actually started followin' tracks, but that didn't last a full day." Tom turned his attention to me. "It goes without sayin' that your daddy ain't quite the man he used to be since that accident 'n all. Just ain't quite got the same giddy-up and go, and not as many body parts to giddy-up and go with."

He roared with laughter, and it took everything I had not to grab my own rifle and shoot him in the mouth. I looked over at Max and could see that his finger was resting on his trigger. He was trying to hang on to his self-control, but I knew it wouldn't take much more to push him across the line. He knew that Tom and Rayne were a threat, and not just to Ivy and Moses but to us, as well, if we tried to get in their way.

"So, that's the gist of it," Tom said, looking smug and relaxed. "And that's why we're here and why you don't need to be here anymore. We're takin' care of it."

"So, let me get this straight, Tom," Max said. "Hap started to track us, but when he couldn't keep up, he put you and Rayne on the trail? What happened to Kite?"

"Kite didn't relish goin' in the first place. Tol' Hap the last time he kilt a man was a Yankee during the war. Didn't much like doin' it then and really didn't want to start doin' it again. But he feels a real loyalty to Hap, I guess. When Hap couldn't go on, that was fine 'n dandy with Kite. He wanted out, too."

"So Hap got you and Rayne instead," Max finished, "with the grand prize being Moses for the bounty money and a little somethin' extra for you boys for the safe return of Ivy."

"Well, a safe return for her if she's willin' to come on home. But he said that if she's real headstrong about stayin' with that boy, or tries to get in the way of us takin' care of him, then it wouldn't be our fault if things ended up not goin' the way he's hoping. The main thing is Hap don't want no darkie grandbaby. If we can get her home, he said he'll send her up to some family in Georgia, until she has the little bastard. She'll be comin' back home alone, though."

"And what happens to the baby?" I was afraid to ask.

"Why, Miss Stewart, those Georgia folks don't like darkies any more than we do. I imagine your pap is gonna pay 'em whatever it takes to make sure that Ivy's well taken care of, and that her baby is, too, but in a different way." He grinned at his own sick humor. "There're lots of empty wells and sinkholes around them parts, not to mention woods as thick as the hair on a bear's ass. Them folks been hidin' things in those places since time began."

"Dear God!" I said softly, though Tom heard me.

"Listen, Miss Stewart, that Hailey boy took advantage of a poor white girl! God A'mighty! She's your *sister*! He deserves to be whipped, tarred and feathered, and *then* hung, if you ask me!"

"No one did," Max said grimly. "But I do want to ask you one more thing: If you started tracking Moses and Ivy only after Hap got back and then hired you to bring in the bounty, how the hell did you find us so quickly? Tracking isn't a fast-moving sport."

"Sure ain't!" Tom agreed. "But Emmitt was real helpful—talks good when he's encouraged to."

"What do you mean?" It was another question I was afraid to ask. Despite the heat of the day, I was ice cold.

"Well, first, we tried to be real nice to Emmitt and the missus about it. Said that all we wanted to do was find that son of theirs and warn him never to come back to these parts, and that we were gonna bring Ivy on home. But they didn't seem too convinced. Emmitt's wife starts cryin' and says she knows we're gonna hurt her boy. Then neither of them would say a word as to his whereabouts. So, we had to change tactics. And you know what I found out? Emmitt likes his wife pretty good—especially if someone is holdin' a hammer over those bent fingers of hers. Damn, she's got some bad arthritis in 'em, too. I asked her if they hurt a lot, and she said they did. And I told her that if she or Emmitt didn't tell us where that son of hers was, I was gonna make 'em hurt a lot worse. She said she didn't know, but Emmitt started talkin' when I started poundin' away. Lord, God, but that woman tried to hold it in! But smashing a thumb to pieces makes a difference.

"Emmitt tells us about them headin' south to Green Swamp. But I had a feeling he wasn't tellin' us the whole story. And I also got the feelin' that he might try leadin' us on a wild-goose chase. So, I told him that if he didn't tell us where they'd gone, I was gonna start on another of his wife's fingers. And if he didn't tell us the truth, and we ended up running from hither to yon without finding her boy and Ivy, we were gonna come back and find Emmitt and his wife. And they'd find out that smashin' fingers with a hammer was an easy thing to tolerate compared to what we'd put 'em through if they lied.

"That was all it took. Emmitt started tellin' us about an old fishin' cabin he's used on the river, and if someone crossed there and then headed straight east, they'd come to a huge old indigo plantation about twenty miles inland. Said they might be there if they were havin' trouble movin' south, or if they decided to just lay low until things simmered down around here. I asked Emmitt how he knew about that old plantation, if he'd been some overseer's whippin' post before the war, and he said that's where he was born. Lord have *mercy*, but that wife of his was madder 'n hell that he'd gone and tol' us the whole thing. Said he should have let her be smashed to bits before tellin'. Emmitt started sobbin' like a baby. I kinda felt sorry for the poor ol' fella, to tell ya the truth. But not so bad that I didn't give him a little smack on my way out the door, warning him that if he was lyin' about all this and then tried to hide somewheres with his wife, I'd make it my life's mission to find 'em and put 'em through hell."

"You son of a bitch!" I flew off Maggie and headed straight for Tom, but Max blocked my way by sticking his rifle out in front of me.

"Take it easy, Eve," Max said in a low voice. Then he turned back to Tom. "We'll bring Ivy and Moses back."

"Hell, no!" Tom shouted, while Rayne moved a little off to the left of Max. "And then y'all get the bounty?" Tom was furious. "Hell, no! There ain't a chance of that happenin'!"

"We'll give you the money. We don't want it," Max said, remaining calm. "We just want to make sure Ivy gets back safely, and Moses is dealt with fairly, and that his name is cleared. Moses didn't do anything that Ivy didn't agree to. And if Hap told you different, then he's not telling you the truth."

As much as I hated hearing the disparaging remarks about my family, I knew that what Max said was true. Ivy and Papa were each responsible for their actions and what resulted because of them. And if that meant that their reputations were badly tarnished, if not utterly destroyed, then it would be their responsibility to find their way back into society's good graces, too.

"You're a lyin' thief," Tom said, moving his horse a little to Max's right. "You really think we believe you'd give us that money?" His voice rose in pitch. He was clearly losing control.

Rayne and Tom were now positioned to each side of Max, making it hard for him to watch them both at the same time, and I mentally kicked myself again for not getting my own rifle out before Tom and Rayne rode up. Suddenly, a sharp blast broke the quiet of the morning. Crows, sitting on the edge of a sinkhole nearby, cawed frantically to each other as they took flight en mass, while other sounds from unseen animals created an eerie melody.

I snapped my head around to see where the shot had come from and immediately saw the small pistol, still smoking, in Rayne's hand. He'd kept it well concealed somewhere but within easy reach. I immediately looked over at Max. He was white as a sheet, in sharp contrast to the bright red blotch that was expanding quickly across his denim shirt, on the left side of his chest, near his heart.

"Max!" I screamed, and as I did, he slumped forward in his saddle as if bowing farewell to an audience.

Chapter 29
The Virtue of Being Stubborn

Rayne leaned out from his horse and took hold of Sampson's reins. The shot had startled the animal, and without Max keeping him in check, the horse started to nervously dance around. Then Rayne, the man of few words, looked over at me.

"Now, Miss Stewart, you have two choices: One, you can head back home by yourself. Or, two, you can come with us and try to talk Ivy into coming back with us real peaceful-like. Like Tom said, your daddy's main concern is having Moses taken care of permanently. He really doesn't want to see Ivy killed, but…things happen. If you're with us, it might make things go easier for everyone. So, which way is it gonna be?"

"I'll go home, and I'll take Max back with me," I said, remounting Maggie. I wasn't sure if he was dead or alive. If he was still alive, it wouldn't be for long unless I could stop the bleeding.

"We wouldn't want Max to slow you down, would we, Tom?" Rayne smiled.

"Why, no," Tom shook his head, grinning.

"Throw him in that sinkhole, Tom." Rayne's smile was completely gone. "I never did like him much. And I don't want to take the chance of him surviving and coming back to even things up with us."

"Us?" Tom didn't like being included in that scenario. "Hell, I'm not the one who shot him!"

"Yeah, but you're gonna be the one throwin' him in the sinkhole. Now, do it!"

It was clear who was in charge. Immediately, Tom dismounted and took Sampson's reins from Rayne and led both horse and rider over to the sinkhole. Max still hadn't moved a muscle, and Tom had to keep a hand on him to prevent him from falling out of the saddle, so I figured he was either dead or unconscious. But, even if he was still alive, he wouldn't be for long once he was dumped into the dark water of the sinkhole. And he'd never be found.

Tom stopped a couple of feet from the edge of the sink then pushed Max out of the saddle. Max landed half in and half out of the hole. Cursing, Tom walked around Sampson and rolled Max in. I counted the seconds until I heard the heavy splash and figured it was about two. I was glad I couldn't see him. To watch his face slip beneath the surface and quickly fade like a ghost in the murkiness of the black abyss would haunt me forever.

"We gotta get," Tom said as he led Sampson back to us. "You sure you want to leave her behind? I say we either make her go with us, or we toss her in the sink, too."

"There are a couple of things I don't like doing in this world," Rayne said. "The first thing is I don't like sitting with my back to the room in a poker game. The second thing is I don't like killing women."

"Yeah, but you're willing to kill that Ivy girl," Tom corrected him.

"I said I don't *like* to. I didn't say I wouldn't. Besides, I might just let you have the honor. Now, if you want to get a little target practice in, you can pull the trigger on this one here, or you can just let her go on home. I don't believe she's going to cause any trouble for us, so I think we ought to just let her be."

"How do you know that, Rayne? How do you know that she won't get mouthy about what we did to ol' Max, there?"

"You really think anyone's going to give two damns? Folks around these parts hate injuns just about as much as they do the coloreds! Now, let's get movin'. But, ya know…" He stopped as if he'd just thought of something, then turned, and looked at Sampson. "I'm gonna take this good-looking horse. Lord, he's a strong son of a bitch." He reached across his own horse to stroke Sampson's muzzle. "And he's a lot fresher than my horse is," he said quietly, as though he was remembering what Max had said about riding their horses into the ground. He straightened and dismounted. "Switch with the girl if you want to. I'm sure she won't mind, would ya?"

Rayne grinned at me and he looked evil. I'd never noticed the dark countenance of the man over the years, but it was all too clear now, and I wondered how I could have missed it. This was a cruel man, and he seemed to immensely enjoy being so.

I didn't want them taking Maggie. Maggie was part of my family. I wanted to keep both horses, though I knew there wasn't a chance of that happening. But I had to try to hold on to Maggie, at least.

"Mr. Longwood, please, let me keep Maggie. I raised her." I automatically backed Maggie up, putting a few more feet between us and the men. "Besides," I continued, backing up a few more feet, "she can't be run hard 'cause she was bitten on her leg by a moccasin when she was just a year old. We thought we'd have to put her down, but she recovered. Still, that leg isn't the strongest. We use her for pullin' the wagon to town and that's about it. It's all she's really good for."

"Then why'd ya ride her all the way out here?"

"There weren't any other horses at my house when I had to leave."

"Keep your damn horse, then," Rayne said then spat. "But I'm taking the big guy, here. Tom, stay on the one you've got. You'll do better on him than on one that's been snake bit."

Suddenly, I thought of something I might need. Though there was the slimmest of possibilities that I would, if I *did* need it but didn't have it, then nothing more could be done. The question was how to go about getting it. I had to do this just right or they might catch on to what I was thinking, and then there wouldn't be a chance of this working at all.

"Mr. Longwood," I called as I climbed down from Maggie. "Before you take Sampson, please let me get some of my clothes. Max was carrying my dirty clothes for me." Holding my breath, hoping that Rayne wouldn't object or be suspicious, I walked over to the leather bag attached to Sampson's saddle. Rayne had dismounted from his own horse and was standing there by Sampson, holding his reins. I was terrified he'd see what I was pulling out of the bag, but he started examining Sampson's teeth instead.

"Good-lookin' horse," he said under his breath. Then he began attaching a rope from his own horse to Sampson. He wasn't going to leave his own horse behind.

While he connected the two animals, I quickly lifted the flap on the leather bag and pulled out a huge armload of clothing. Able to feel through the wad of material that I'd gotten exactly what I was after, I hurried back to Maggie.

"You head on home now," Rayne said as he mounted Sampson, and then he and Tom turned their horses to the east. "It's not good for a female to travel alone in these parts. Ya never know what scoundrels you might meet along the way." He smiled that cruel smile again, then slapped the end of the reins hard against poor Sampson's haunch, and the two men rode off.

I stood there holding the load of clothes in my arms as I watched them ride away. Finally, when I couldn't see any more dust being kicked up by the horses, I dropped my load. There, among the clothing, which were actually only Max's, was what I'd really been after: the rope he'd used in the mecate rein. Snatching it up, I ran as hard as I could over to the sinkhole, praying the whole way. As I neared the edge of it, I hesitated for the slightest second, terrified of what I might see, then threw myself onto my stomach, and peered over the edge. There, about ten feet down, looking half dead but still alive, was Max, hanging on to a small crevice that was just deep enough to get his hand into. His left arm hung down below the waterline, and his face was turned up to the light, though his eyes were closed. He didn't know I was there.

"Max? Max! Can you hear me? It's Eve! Max!" Though he wasn't dead at the moment, I wondered how weak he was. If he couldn't continue to hang on…Suddenly, he opened his eyes, and focused them on me.

"Eve." He spoke softly, but I could still hear the relief in his voice. "I kind of dug myself into a hole, didn't I?"

He tried to smile at his joke but grimaced instead. He was clearly in terrible pain. His lucidity was a good sign, though I knew his strength couldn't hold out forever. The walls of the sink were covered with slime and algae, so even if he'd had two good arms, it was going to be difficult getting him out. The fact that he had just the one arm to help himself was going to make a bad situation even worse. But getting him out was just the first of our problems. He had a life-threatening injury, and without proper treatment, his chances of surviving were quickly diminishing.

"Hold on, Max! Hold on! I have your rope. I'm going to drop one end of it down to you, then tie the other to Maggie. This time, she's going pull you out of the water!" I smiled, trying to reassure him.

"Good," he whispered. "Good girl."

"Can you manage with the end of the rope? Should I jump in so that I can tie it around you? I can climb back up on it."

"No!" he said with a louder voice than he'd used before. "Don't jump in! I'll wrap the end of the rope around my wrist and then hang on to it."

Wasting no more time, I dropped one end of the rope to Max and tied the other to Maggie's saddle horn. As she backed up, I watched the rope pull taut as it took on Max's weight. Maggie hesitated, unsure as to what was stopping her, but I kept urging her on. She struggled with the unusual task and Max's weight, but, finally, I saw a hand, forearm, and elbow rise above the top of the sink. "Keep going, Maggie! Back, back!" I ordered, watching Max's head, shoulders and torso appear, and he was finally dragged out of the sinkhole and onto the blessed ground.

Max lay there, exhausted. I rushed over to him and began brushing leaves and other debris off his face and out of his hair.

"What made you go back to the sink?" Max asked. "What made you think I'd still be there?"

I stopped cleaning him off and looked him in the eye. "Because you're the most stubborn man I know, Max Harjo." Then I pulled another twig out of his hair.

Smiling, he closed his eyes.

Chapter 30
The Day of Reckoning

We found Tom Bigelow's body about nine miles east. He'd been shot in the back of the head and left to bake on the ground in the broiling midsummer sun. Ants had already begun crawling over the carnage, while vultures circled in the sky above as if they were drawing a target over the bull's-eye below. Just from the location of the bullet hole, we figured Tom didn't know what hit him. And considering that Rayne was nowhere to be seen, Max guessed that he was the killer, but I couldn't understand why. Why would Rayne have traveled all this way with Tom, only to kill him when they'd gotten this close to their catch?

Max shifted around in the saddle behind me on Maggie. He was obviously in pain. But, thankfully, the bullet had spared his heart, entering the area just above it, though it had torn through muscle and had caused a significant amount of bleeding. Other than wrapping the wound in strips of material to staunch the blood flow, there wasn't much more that could be done until we were someplace where the bullet could be removed, and the wound thoroughly cleaned and sutured. But Max was beginning to get glassy-eyed, and I was afraid a fever was setting in. God only knew what was in the water of that sinkhole. Undoubtedly, it had been the unsuspecting grave for creatures of all kinds, and the water was fetid because of it.

"Rayne wants that bounty money all to himself," Max reasoned.

I gently slapped the reins against Maggie, leaving Tom's body behind. We couldn't take the time to bury it. And, in truth, we didn't feel any obligation to respectfully dispose of his remains after he'd tried to kill Max.

"Why not just kill Tom early on? Why wait until now?" I asked.

"Why not?" Max asked. "Why *not* wait until now? It's safer for two people to travel together than one. And we're probably pretty close to that plantation now, and to Ivy and Moses, so this is as good a time as any. There aren't any witnesses, and as far as Rayne's story will go, he'll say something like they were ambushed by thieves and Tom got killed. Or, he might even say that Moses shot Tom when they were trying to apprehend him."

"But Ivy would say differently."

"Maybe Ivy would, if she could. But if she doesn't see what happened, then she's not a witness. Besides, who's to say Rayne has any intention of taking Ivy home alive? You heard Tom. Your father's main objective is to make sure that Moses is taken care of and that Ivy doesn't have that baby. Still lips can't spill secrets. Rayne won't have to split the money and no one will be the wiser as to what really happened if there aren't any witnesses. There was no love lost between Rayne and Tom. He caught Tom trying to cheat him in a game of seven-card stud up in Tallahassee some years ago. Rayne pulled a knife on Tom and sliced off part of his left ear."

We rode on just a little farther and saw Tom's bedraggled horse. The poor animal was just wandering around, most likely looking for water considering the intense heat.

"Do we have any water left in that skin?" I knew the horse wouldn't be long for this world if he wasn't given a drink. God only knew the last time the poor animal had had one.

"Unfortunately, that water skin is on Sampson. But we can't be very far from the plantation. We'll take him with us. We might be able to use him. But if not, then at least we've gotten the horse closer to a river. Every plantation is near one—or some kind of water—and where there's water, there're people. Somebody'll find the horse and take him. I'm going to ride him." Max started to dismount.

"Wait, Max! You can't ride by yourself. You're too weak!"

"It'll actually be more comfortable for me," he said and, gritting his teeth, slid off Maggie. Then he pulled his rifle out from behind me. He was lucky to still have it after dropping it when he'd been shot. But I'd been able to retrieve it after Rayne and Tom rode off. "Not that I'm not grateful for your help," Max continued, "but every time you slow down, I have to keep myself from bumping into you. It doesn't feel too good."

He attempted to smile, but I knew that if he admitted it was painful, it was agony. Before he turned to walk away from me, I could see that he'd bled through the makeshift bandages, and the bloody stain had expanded well beyond the edges of the bindings. We needed to get somewhere quickly to tend to him, or the number of deaths resulting from this trip would continue to grow. I hated to think what those numbers might increase to once we got to the plantation, where, undoubtedly, Rayne would be arriving shortly.

We had only traveled about fifteen minutes more when we came to a marshy area, and immediately beyond that was a large lake.

"Look," Max said, pointing off to our right. "I bet that's it."

About a quarter of a mile from us, sitting a safe distance back from the bank of the lake, was a weather-beaten old home. A couple of large oak trees stood on each side of the house. Out front, bordering a small section of shoreline, was a very small coastal hammock. On the other side of the house, opposite from us, was where a crop had obviously been grown, for many acres had been cleared.

Behind the house were several outbuildings, including a summer kitchen, as well as a smokehouse and barn. All along the back of the property was a much larger hammock. There had probably been one enormous hammock before the plantation was built, but much of it had been cleared away, leaving just a small section in front of the house and the much larger portion in back. At the moment, we could see no signs of life.

"We're not approaching from here," Max said. "We're way too visible." He was getting paler and paler, and his voice seemed to fade along with his color. "We've got to get out of here," he said, wheeling the horse around. "We'll come up behind the house through the hammock. We'll be able to get a closer look from there."

As we backtracked, I could see how badly he slumped in the saddle. Max was usually as straight as a ramrod, but not now. I knew it was a stupid question, but I had to ask. "How're you holding up?"

"I've had better days. But we can't worry about that now."

He was right. There was nothing I could do to help him at the moment, and both of us knew that seconds mattered when it came to Rayne, Ivy, and Moses.

We backtracked until we were out of sight and then headed into the hammock. It was blessedly cool beneath the dense canopy of live oaks, cabbage palms, and red bay. It was also the perfect place to watch the goings on around the plantation without being seen…and, apparently, Rayne thought so, too, for there, tethered to a large oak were Sampson and Rayne's horses.

"He's here," Max said flatly. "Now, the question is whether or not Ivy and Moses are, too." *And dead or alive*, both of us thought but neither of us said. "I'm going over to take a look inside that house." Max dismounted, but his knees buckled when his feet hit the ground, and he had to grab the horse's back to stay upright.

"No, you're not," I said as I grabbed my rifle from behind me and dismounted, too. He started to argue with me. "Listen, Max, the truth of the matter is you're badly hurt. You can barely stand up much less make it over to that house. Now, you're going to stay here and cover me as best you can."

Without giving him a chance to argue any further, I ran out from the cover of the hammock. Keeping low and cradling my rifle in front of me, I ran up to the back of the smokehouse, which was the building farthest from the main house.

I took a minute to collect myself for I was shaking like a leaf, and then I took a deep breath and peered out from the corner of the building. From that vantage point, I could see some of the back of the house, but the barn and smokehouse prevented me from having an unobstructed view. The white "I"-styled house was modest for a plantation and certainly not huge when compared to the lavish ones farther north, like back in Georgia. This plantation was made of wood, instead of stucco or brick, and it was long and rectangular. It had only two stories with a redbrick chimney at each end. There was no porch on the back, though I knew that there was one on the front for I'd seen it from a distance when Max and I first arrived. In the back of the home were several windows, and I wanted to look into each one of them. For the moment, there was no one in the yard, and no one in the neglected fields to my right, so I ran out from behind the smokehouse and up to the back of the barn. The doors were slightly ajar, allowing air to ventilate the building, but no one was inside. However, Moses's and Ivy's horses were.

Looking out from the back of the barn, I still couldn't see any movement, so I hurried up to the summer kitchen. I was more vulnerable there because it was an open-air building. Food could be prepared more comfortably during the hot months while not increasing the already-oppressive heat within the main house.

Hiding as best I could behind one of the thick brick columns supporting the roof, I quickly poked my head out and could look into the house's back windows. I didn't see anyone, but I needed to get to the side of the house and look into those rooms, as well. Saying a quick prayer, I ran up to the back-left corner of the house. Then I worked my way down the bank of windows, standing on tiptoe to quickly peer in each, before crouching back down and moving on to the next.

I looked into the dining room, where only odds and ends remained. What had once been a lovely room for large gatherings was now just a ruin.

Thankfully, there was no one in sight. I moved on to the next window, to what looked like a man's study, and saw no one in there either. Reaching the last window on that side, I peeked in at the old parlor, and finding that empty, too, I moved toward the front corner of the house, and the end of the porch. Carefully, I started to crane my neck to see around the corner, to make sure all was clear, but I was suddenly yanked up onto the porch by the front of my shirt. Cold steel was immediately pressed hard against the middle of my forehead.

"You should have gone home, Miss Stewart," Rayne Longwood said, holding me so close to him that we were nearly nose to nose. "Now, drop that rifle."

But instead of dropping it down by me, I tossed it out behind me off the porch, praying that Max would see it and know something was wrong. As close as Rayne and I were, I could smell and feel his warm, rotten breath on my face.

"You're a bad little thing, you know that?" He smiled that wicked grin I'd become all too familiar with. "Now, here I thought I was being real nice, letting you go, when ol' Tom wanted to blow your insides out. Like I told him, I don't like shooting ladies, but that doesn't mean I won't. Now, you're gonna tell me where that sister of yours is and her little ni—"

"Eve!"

My head snapped to the left at the sound of my name. Coming out of the small hammock in front of the house was Ivy, with Moses close behind.

At the same time, Rayne let go of the front of my shirt and swung his pistol around at them. Knowing I only had a second, I grabbed Rayne's arm and yanked hard. I fell backward off the end of the porch, pulling Rayne down on top of me; his weight knocked every bit of air out of my lungs. Cursing, Rayne pushed himself up and straddled me, and then he balled his hand into a fist and drew it back. As I braced myself for the shattering blow, a rifle shot exploded. Blood spurted out of the right side of Rayne's head at the same time a good-sized hole appeared on the left.

The look of shock on his face was as frozen as his body in that paralyzing fraction of a second between life and death. I pushed him over and he landed beside me with a thud. Turning over onto my stomach, I searched the tree line behind me. Max came stumbling out of the hammock with his rifle still in his hand. Off to the right, my name was being called, and I turned my head and saw Ivy running toward me. Then I laid my head down on the grass. I was still trying to breathe normally again, but the deep sobbing that started made it nearly impossible to do.

Chapter 31
The Salvation of Indigo

Ivy fell to her knees beside me. She helped me sit up, and we hung on to each other, saying nothing for several minutes, letting tears take the place of words, while Moses ran over to Max. "We gotta get you inside, Max!" he said, half holding and half carrying Max. "You've been hit!"

"Help him, Ivy!" I sobbed. "Please! He's hurt real bad."

Ivy and Moses got him into the house, then took him straight back to the kitchen. Ivy laid Max down on a long oak table and began to carefully cut away his blood-soaked bandages and shirt. Within seconds of his wound being exposed, I could see, as well as smell, the deadly telltale sign of infection. There was an enormous amount of dried blood on Max's chest, but there was also a small stream of it oozing out of the wound. Red lines radiated out from it.

"Eve, throw some wood into that stove," Ivy instructed. "And get that fire built up. Then fill that pot with water—the one sitting on the back of the stove there—and get that to boiling. I need you to cut some cloth into strips for bandages and I'm gonna need plenty of 'em. Take clothes—or anything else you can find—and start rippin' 'em up."

"Moses," she turned to him. "I need needles and thread, the heaviest thread you can find. Fishin' line, if you can't find thread. And I need some whiskey. I doubt there's any left around here, so check Rayne; he may have brought some." I told Moses to check the saddlebags on the horses tied up in the large hammock behind the house.

"How close is he to dyin', Ivy?" I asked as I rummaged through the kitchen cabinets looking for any kind of cloth. Max was slipping in and out of consciousness, and his face had paled to a chalky white, making the deep purple veins in his neck and face stand out, as well as the spidery red lines spreading out from his wound.

"Close, Eve. Real close. Here, help me sit him up so I can take a look at his back. I think the bullet exited but I want to double-check." I joined her at the table but stood across from her, and then we each carefully slipped an arm beneath him and raised him up. Max groaned in pain. Quickly, Ivy examined his back. "That's good. It's out. Okay, let's lay him down again. That's one less thing to worry about, but we've got an even bigger problem on our hands. That infection is really bad. Hopefully, it hasn't already gone to his heart, but if we don't get it stopped—and soon—it will."

Suddenly, my sister went completely still, as though she was listening to some inner voice guiding her; then she quickly turned toward the window. "Eve, you see that old field out there?" she asked as she turned to look at me. "That's indigo. The slaves called it 'the devil's blue dye.' I need you to go out there and pull up a mess of it up—roots 'n all. That little devil plant might end up being Max's salvation. If anything can stop this infection, indigo can."

I hurried out to the field and gathered up an armload of the wildly growing blue-flowered plant and quickly took it back in to Ivy.

"Set it on the counter," she said, handing me a knife. "That water's boilin' now. Cut those roots off and throw all of 'em in that water. We're gonna make a tincture out of them so we can clean Max from the inside out. And we're gonna cut those blue flowers off and make a paste out of them. I'll be damned if y'all rode all this way to have him die on me."

There were times when our mother had said that my sister's stubborn determination was the thing most likely to kill her. At the moment, though, it was the one thing that might keep Max alive.

Chapter 32
Fraction of a Fraction

For three days, Max's infection looked like it would be the victor. He drifted in and out of consciousness and was delirious at times, which was probably the most frightening thing of all. He yelled out in anger at ghosts that only he could see or moaned in pain, though I wasn't sure if it was physical or emotional. Saddest of all, though, was the night he cried out people's names—including his mother's and siblings', as well as others I did not know. He never opened his eyes during that bout of feverish ramblings, although tears slowly trailed down his cheeks. When he finally fell asleep, he was restless. Ivy and I took turns watching him, trying to keep him as still and quiet as we could for fear he'd rip open his stitches and start bleeding all over again. But the morning after, he became still and quiet, so much so that I brought my cheek down to his mouth several times just to see if I could still feel his breath on my skin. Finally, at the end of three days, his fever broke, and his eyes seem to refocus on the present, leaving the past, and the ghosts that haunted him, behind.

I walked toward the back bedroom on the main floor. It was early morning, and I was carrying a fresh pitcher of water to refill the empty one on the nightstand by Max's bed. As the fever had raged on, so had his thirst, and we gave him as much water as he could drink. It was vital in helping to flush out the toxins in his body.

I knocked softly on the door, and Max told me to come in. The night before was the first night neither Ivy nor I had slept on the floor next to him, and I was happy to see that he was awake, sitting up in bed and that more of his color had returned. "I was afraid I might wake you," I said as I walked to the nightstand and poured the water into his pitcher. "Are you hungry?"

"You know, I believe I am." Using his good hand, he adjusted the pillow behind himself and sat up a little higher. "Good Lord, I'm sore!" he said as he moved his left arm slightly, testing it.

"That's good! That means you're alive. Do you want to try eating in the kitchen, or do you want me to bring some breakfast to you?"

"No, I'll come to the kitchen. Let me ask you something, Eve. How long have we been here?"

"This is the start of the fourth full day—though five if you include the afternoon we got here."

"Are Ivy and Moses around?" I told him they were finishing up their breakfast. "Good. Make sure they don't head out somewhere. As soon as I can get a cup of coffee in me, we've got to talk about getting out of here. When Tom and Rayne don't show up back in Silver Springs, your father's bound to send someone after them to figure out what's going on, or he might just try making the trip himself. We want to put a whole lot of ground between us and whoever comes lookin'."

"Okay, I'll tell Ivy and Moses. We have a pan of biscuits but only molasses to put on 'em, I'm afraid. The pickin's are pretty slim around here." I turned and moved toward the door.

"Biscuits and molasses sound real good."

"I think you're on the road to recovery." I smiled.

"I've got to be 'cause we need to get out of here."

"Couldn't you give yourself a couple more days to rest?"

"We all might have an eternity of it if we don't get a move on. Your father isn't going to wait until I'm all better to start the hunt again."

"I'll pour your coffee," I said, closing the door to give him some privacy.

Max joined us in the kitchen a few minutes later. Other than moving a little slower than usual and not standing quite as straight as he normally did, he looked good—far, far better than he had several nights before.

"Morning," Max addressed Ivy and Moses.

"Good to have you with us, Max." Ivy looked so pleased. "The other night, we weren't quite sure you'd be around to see another sunrise."

"Well, thanks to all of you, I will, and I aim to for a long while to come." He poured molasses over several biscuits and dug in. After washing a bite down with a swig of coffee, he got right down to business. "Okay, we need to figure out what y'all want to do and then get down to doin' it. I wish we could've gotten a good start a few days ago, but we didn't, so we've got to make some serious tracks now—that is, if you're still planning on headin' south." Ivy and Moses assured him they were. "Okay, but I have a couple of questions for y'all. How come you didn't just keep going instead of making a detour? What happened?"

"Ivy was feelin' real poorly," Moses explained. "She had that mornin' sickness, and it got so bad she could barely stay on her horse. Said she felt better walkin' than ridin', and, o' course, that was slowin' us way down."

Ivy jumped in. "I knew if anybody was lookin' for us, at the rate we were going, they'd catch up to us in no time. I was so sick that the only thing we could do was head over here and let me rest for a few days."

"Ivy, I'm sure Eve has already told you that your father wants to do more than just catch up with you, right?"

Ivy's eyes immediately filled with tears. Choked up, she looked down at the table and merely nodded.

Max reached across the table and placed his hand over hers. "I'm sorry." A minute of heavy silence followed while each of us was lost in our own sorrow or anger or regrets.

Ivy got up from the table and looked out the kitchen window. After a moment, she inhaled deeply, as though to fortify herself. Then she grabbed the coffeepot and refilled Max's cup.

"We still want to go south, Max. We want to get as far away from here as we can. Emmitt mentioned Seminole country down in the Everglades. Do you know anything about that place, and those people?"

"I do." Max nodded. "There're just a small group of Seminoles left down there. About two hundred, I guess. Most of the Seminoles were forced to go to Oklahoma, but some just refused to give up their home and ventured deeper into the 'Glades. The white soldiers weren't too keen on following them, so they left them alone. Figured they couldn't do much harm there. And the likelihood that they'd be killed off by gators or snakes before too long made the army just let 'em go. But they survived, and some of those who did were my family. I don't know if they're still there, though, or even alive, for that matter."

"Who are they?" Moses asked.

"My mother's brother. Some cousins, maybe. I'm not sure. The last time I was there was several years ago. Folks move on. And speaking of which, we better get a move on." He pushed his chair back from the table and stood. "Gather up anything y'all need. We'll take what food we can, and then we're heading out."

"Let me ask you one thing, Max." Moses looked deeply worried. "How do we know those Seminoles will take us in? What if they tell us to go back where we came from?"

"They're not going to because we're gonna make it worth their while to let y'all stay. We're gonna give the chief ol' Tom's and Rayne's horses. And just to make sure that deal is sweet enough, we're gonna give him their guns, too. Somehow, I think they'll find it in their hearts to let you stay." He smiled.

We all got busy packing up. As I gathered up the few things I had, I kept thinking about the fact that we were going into unknown territory and would meet a group of people I knew nothing about, not their ways, language, or customs. Nor did I know how they felt about white people, though I could pretty well figure that they had no great love for them. But Max had family there, which was both surprising to me, as well as encouraging. Hopefully, they'd be more willing to accept my sister and Moses because of their connection to Max, especially if we gifted them with the horses and guns. According to Max, that would nearly guarantee that Ivy and Moses would be permitted to stay. But I was not nearly as confident that they *should* stay—especially Ivy. I worried that she wouldn't be treated as an equal, that she would be used, even abused, or perhaps neglected because she was white. How the tables had turned in my familiar and perfectly boxed-up black-and-white world, I thought. Suddenly, I felt a fraction of a fraction of what the black man and the red man had felt for hundreds of years, and that tiniest taste of empathy made me terrified for my sister.

Chapter 33
Where the Smoke Spirals

We traveled southwest for a couple of days and then headed south, stopping at any body of water where we could water our horses and catch fish, frogs, or turtles. Because of Ivy's condition, and Max's injury, we were forced to go slower than we would have liked, but to move any faster would have risked the lives of both Ivy and her baby and reopened Max's wound. But our slower pace allowed each of us time to think, and I thought a lot about what all had transpired in the last couple of weeks and what might lie ahead.

For the most part, my thoughts were grim, and I quietly worried about how drastically our lives could change in the blink of an eye, or the firing of a gun. Though we didn't think anyone was following us at that point, there was always the threat that trackers could show up at any time. I tried not to dwell on that possibility for too long for it served no purpose, but the threat was constantly with us and never far from my mind, nor anyone else's. I tried to stay focused on what we needed to be doing next, whether that was looking for food, fixing a meal or finding a safe enough looking spot to spend the night.

The farther south we went, the more the terrain changed. Bromeliads and wild orchids clung to the trees like babies holding tight to their mothers. While much of the vegetation also grew in Silver Springs, some did not. The plants I'd never encountered before seemed more primitive and wild than any I had ever seen in central Florida.

One of the most pleasant surprises was the abundance of wild fruits, dispelling all fears about food being scarce or difficult and dangerous to obtain. We ate with relish, which did more than just help to build Max's and Ivy's strength; it helped to lift our spirits, as well. So very little had been easy for any of us since we'd left Silver Springs that we welcomed the gift of abundant food with grateful hearts and big appetites.

The land became as flat as a board. Gone were the gentle hills of central Florida, replaced, instead, with soggy marshes and large swamps—vast pockmarks in a seemingly endless river of grass. The air was heavy with humidity, and to say it was oppressively hot was like saying cotton candy was sweet. It was so hot that our horses' sweat seeped through our clothing.

Late on the third day of traveling, Max, who rode several yards ahead of us and had done so much of the way, held up his hand, signaling for us to stop. "There," he said, pointing to thin spires of smoke in the distance that were barely visible against the pink and orange colors of the fading day. "We're here."

No one said a word as we took in this new land. The apprehension of what lay ahead held each of us in place.

"We must go," Max finally said as he kicked his heels against Sampson. "We don't want to enter the village in the dark. Let's give them a chance to welcome us before killing us."

He smiled, though it was tight and unsure. Seeing that tiny crack in his confidence made me question our decisions. I thought about turning around and begging Moses and Ivy to come with me, but instead, I kicked my heels against Maggie and fell in behind Max. The odds were that what lay ahead was far better than what we'd left behind.

We slowly wound our way through endless thickets of palmetto bushes, and other prickly, piercing plants. Aside from wanting to approach the village while there was still light, we also wanted to get there before we were forced to play Russian roulette in the dark with fat rattlesnakes and vicious water moccasins. Even a place as foreign as the Seminole village seemed like the safer choice.

As we approached the village, we saw women sweeping out their raised homes. Each dwelling, or *chickee*, as Max called them, was built on stilts, raising it off the ground by several feet so that flooding would never be an issue. The roofs were thatched with palmetto fiber attached to rafters, and there were no walls. As sweltering as the heat and humidity were, the likelihood of death by heatstroke would have been quite high if their homes had been enclosed. What the people lacked in privacy, they gained in cross breezes.

The women were totally engrossed in their vigorous cleaning. They wore long, layered patchwork skirts with short blouses and many layers of beads. Except for the younger children, all the women wore their hair in topknots, and their skin colors ranged from a light reddish-bronze to the deepest mahogany; there was a sprinkling of colored women among them.

Off to my left, men were busy throwing pottery, furnishings, and clothing into a pile, which would soon be set ablaze. A man holding a torch stood in the background, looking as though he was patiently waiting for the last items to be included. Finally, a bench was heaped on top, and the man with the torch walked up to the pile and began to light the mound at its base.

"The Green Corn Festival," Max said so softly that I had to ask him to repeat it. "It's the festival that honors the ripening of the corn. It's a time of renewal and a time of cleansing and for giving thanks. They're burning old items that are no longer needed—like pottery and old food—and replacing them with new things as a symbol of a fresh start. The men will fast and take ceremonial baths, and some will drink the black drink, which will make them purge everything in their system, just as they've purged much from their homes."

"And do the women take part in this black drink?" I asked. I was beginning to think we'd arrived at a very bad time.

Max smiled knowingly. "Only if they want to, *kaccv hokte*. Only if they want to."

"Max! Max!" The shouting came from one of the men tending the bonfire. He hurried over to the four of us. He was short, squat, and the color of burnished caramel. His smile seemed to take up the entire lower half of his face, and when I looked over at Max, I saw that he was smiling just as broadly. He quickly dismounted and hurried over to the man. They reached out with their right hands and clasped each other's forearms, while resting their free hands on each other's shoulders. They began speaking in the Muskogean language but switched over to English, which Max had obviously asked the man to do.

"Ah, Max, I've prayed so often to the Great Spirit that you would come back to us, and here you are!" He pumped Max's arm enthusiastically. "And right at the Green Corn Festival! Now, if that isn't the Spirit's hand at work, I don't know what is!"

Max chuckled. "Ah, Uncle Jay, it's good to be with you again. It's been—what, five years?"

"Seems like more!" Uncle Jay said before turning his attention to us. "Welcome, welcome! If you've come with Max, then you're family, and you're welcome here for as long as you choose to stay."

"Thank you," Ivy, Moses, and I said softy and almost in unison. Though we were all a bit overwhelmed and unsure of our footing in this unfamiliar culture, I knew I was humbly grateful that this man had welcomed us so warmly and without question; I knew that Ivy and Moses had to be feeling the same relief. I let out a long breath and loosened my grip on Maggie's reins. From the looks of the red crescent-shaped marks imprinted in my skin, I realized that I'd been holding the reins tightly for some time. Maggie was my comfort and a means of escape. I prayed there'd be no reason for any of us to feel as if we had to escape again, and I prayed that the rest of the tribe would be as welcoming as Uncle Jay.

Chapter 34
Into the Inner Circle

Immediately upon our arrival, the chief was informed, and we were summoned to a long *chickee*. Uncle Jay accompanied us, and we were brought before Chief Kitisci Haasi, which, I was told, meant Red Sun. His tribal council was gathered around him, and they watched us through waves of thick smoke emanating from several pipes. They showed very little expression but listened intently as both Jay and Max spoke in the low, guttural-sounding Muskogean language.

Finally, Moses was told to step forward. In broken English, Chief Red Sun asked him his ancestors' clan's name.

"My great-grandmother was a member of the Turtle Clan," he softly declared, though his jutting chin gave away the pride that he obviously felt in his heritage.

The chief responded in his own language and everyone laughed. Max chuckled too, then nodded at the chief and turned to Moses. "He wants to know if it is your wish to stay. If it is, the Seminole Tribe will gladly welcome a brother of one of their own, as well as your woman. He said, 'Tell the Black Seminole that he is permitted to stay. And so is his woman with skin as white as an alligator's belly.'"

Moses bowed slightly to the chief and confirmed it was their wish to stay and thanked him; then Max translated for him. The chief spoke for several minutes with Max, but their conversation was not translated for us. Finally, Max told us everything had been settled and it was time to leave. We softly and humbly thanked the chief and bid everyone a good night. We were immediately fed and then shown to the *chickees* where we would be staying. As we walked, I saw Max leading Tom's and Rayne's horses over to the chief's long house, and I knew that a deal had been made.

While we stayed in the village for the better part of the next three days, I became caught up in the various activities, games, dances, and meals of the Green Corn Festival. I realized that taking part in these rituals was a great privilege, which reassured me about Ivy staying and made me more than grateful to the Seminoles for accepting my sister and Moses.

The women were in the midst of preparing an elaborate feast to break a day of fasting for the men, and Ivy was helping. A couple of the women knew English, and they patiently explained what food was being served and how to prepare it. It was important that Ivy start learning the Seminoles' ways. She seemed willing and eager to learn, and the women seemed just as eager to teach her. They were excited to learn that she was a very capable medicine woman and had saved Max's life. The knowledge and skill that Ivy possessed made her an invaluable asset to the community, and without question, her status among the people would be high.

Ivy was engrossed in making a vegetable soup, so I took the opportunity to slip away and get a bath. I had wanted to earlier in the day, but the men had been taking their ceremonial one. This was the final step in the cleansing process after fasting and drinking the purgative "black drink." Max had taken part in the ceremony, and I hadn't seen him since yesterday afternoon.

The creek ran parallel to the village. In the midafternoon sun, the dark blue water sparkled and shimmered as a breeze ruffled its surface. Though most of the men had returned to the village, there were still a few who lingered, enjoying every last minute of a day that was intended to restore the body, both inside and out. Among the stragglers was Max. The upper half of his body was out of the creek as he lay back against its bank, supported by his arms, which were outstretched to either side of him. His head was tilted back and his eyes were closed as he raised his face toward the sun. A young man swam by and intentionally splashed him. Max said something to the young man, though I couldn't hear what it was. It made the young man laugh and swim away. As he did, he spotted me above the bank and said something to Max. Max looked toward me. Embarrassed at being there when there were no other women around, I quickly raised my hand and started to walk away, but as I did, I heard Max call my name. I turned to see him lift himself onto the bank and then walk toward me.

He wore nothing but a breechcloth, and his hair was loose and damp. As he got closer, I could see the water droplets on his body reflected by the sun as they made slow trails down his bronze skin, working their way around his well-muscled chest and arms and on down to his strong, defined stomach.

The wound on the upper part of Max's chest was healing beautifully. Gone were the red streaks that had spread out from the bullet hole when it was infected. What remained was the small clean line of Ivy's neat stitching. He was whole again and he looked wild in every sense of the word: free, strong, agile...and beautiful. He seemed pleased that I was watching him. About ten yards from me, he stopped at a tree and retrieved the long tunic he'd been wearing. We had all been given customary Seminole garb; I felt a little self-conscience in clothing so unfamiliar to me, but the layered patchwork skirt and lightweight short shirt I was dressed in were more comfortable than anything I'd ever worn. My hair had also been styled in the traditional Seminole topknot, which allowed a soft breeze to cool my neck and offered some relief from the heat of late July.

"Were you looking for me?" Max asked as he pulled his tunic over his head. "Or did you come to bathe?"

"Bathe."

"Come with me," he said, picking up the pace. "I know a spot where you'll have plenty of privacy."

Obviously, he knew this village well. "Max, you told Uncle Jay it'd been five years since you were last here. I thought you said you'd been to this part of Florida before—hunting or tracking, or something—but many of these people know you and were so happy to see you, like you're the prodigal son returning home."

Max nodded in understanding. "In a way I am. My mother's family were Creeks, and originally from Georgia," he explained. "After a while, some ended up in Alabama, and some came down here. My mother and Uncle Jay were brought here by their parents, but when their mother died, my mother went to live with her grandmother in Alabama, and Jay stayed here. I know it's confusing, but so is the Seminole history. The Seminoles were actually formed from an alliance between the Creeks, the Miccosukees, and several others. After I lost my family, I spent a lot of time down here. They were the only family I had left—well, the only family I knew, anyway. So I came and I went. And each time I left, they wished me well and welcomed me home when I returned."

"They're good people, Max."

"Yes."

We came to a place on the creek where a sandbar had actually created a natural bridge from bank to bank, but the middle of the bar had been dug out to allow the water to freely flow through. However, if one took a long enough leap, a person could jump from one side of the bar to the other.

"I'm going to jump across and then you follow." Without giving me a second to object, he took off at a run across the bar, then leaped high into the air, and made a clean landing on the other half of the bar. "Now you," he yelled.

Laughing, I hiked my skirt up and took off running. I jumped at just the right moment and landed on the other side, and then I followed him away from the creek and up through a thin line of pines. When we came out on the other side, I saw a small crystal-clear spring. The clarity and color of the spring reminded me of those back home.

"Your bath awaits." Max bowed.

"No gators? No snakes?" I asked, looking around and feeling quite vulnerable.

"I'll guard you with my life," he declared, and sat on the grass, where he immediately removed his tunic, lay back, closed his eyes, and allowed the sun to finish drying him.

"You'll be asleep in two minutes." I laughed. "I'm going to strip down to my underclothes, so close your eyes until I get in."

"They're already closed," He laughed.

I hurriedly disrobed down to my chemise and drawers, and then I sat down on the edge of the natural pool. I tested the water by first sticking my feet into it, and finding that it was refreshingly cool, I eagerly shoved myself off the bank. The spring was only about twelve feet deep, with a white sandy bottom and ribbons of seagrass floating like banners in a parade.

Suddenly, I heard a muffled splash and saw a mass of white bubbles as Max shot down into the water. Facing me near the bottom, he reached out and took my hands, and then we kicked our way to the surface. Laughing, we swam around the perfect little pool, playfully splashing each other, diving down into the cool depths, and talking about pleasant things for a change. There was no more talk about how to outfox trackers or how to go about finding my sister and what to do if and when we did. The place was perfect, as was the day, and all too quickly the time came when I needed to get back to the village to help set out the meal.

Swimming over to the edge and climbing out, I suddenly realized that my soaked cotton underclothes left nothing to the imagination. I quickly knelt in the grass to gather up my clothes. Max's hands came to rest on the tops of my shoulders. He had knelt behind me. Max leaned in and kissed my bare neck and then licked my skin. The heat of his tongue against my cooled skin caused me to shiver. It made me want more of him, and Max knew it.

Gently, he laid me back on the grass, and then he lay down beside me. Bringing his face just inches from mine, Max began speaking in his native language, and though I couldn't understand the words he whispered against my lips in his low, deep voice, the look in his dark blue eyes was explanation enough. I'd seen that fire before, when we were tracking Ivy and Moses, and we'd kissed. Now there was a deeper longing, a greater intensity, but also some vulnerability.

He brushed back my hair as he gazed at my face, smiling softly as he did, as if he was pleased with what he saw. Finally, Max covered my mouth with his, tasting me deeply and hungrily with his tongue, speaking in a language that every soul is intrinsically familiar with. And I answered.

Chapter 35
Unbreakable Bonds

We didn't stay much longer at the spring. Things were getting out of control—*we* were getting out of control—and I knew I needed to stop it. I told him that I needed to get back to help the women with the feast, but we both knew it was far more than that. As we walked back to the village, I brought up the subject that had been in the back of my mind since we'd arrived.

"Max, when were you thinking we could leave for home?"

There was silence for several seconds before he answered, and I wasn't sure if it was because he was giving the question some thought or if he was angry that this was utmost on my mind. But he had to realize that this surreal existence which we'd been thrust into was temporary.

There was no doubt that I had deep feelings for Max—deeper than I wanted to even think about—and if I didn't return to Jacksonville in a hurry, I was afraid things would spin out of control. The life I'd been living for several days was not permanent as it was for Ivy. Nor was Max the man I was committed to sharing my life with. I would honor the promises I'd made. I felt guilty that I had such intense feelings for Max. They were totally inappropriate, and so was my behavior. I needed to get back to David, to the newspaper, to the world that I belonged to. This one belonged to Ivy and Moses now—and to Max.

Suddenly, I felt very alone. I just hoped that feeling would evaporate once I was steaming down the St. Johns, with Jacksonville visible in the distance, and David standing at the harbor awaiting my return. I *hoped* he was waiting for my return. I knew that David would be upset once he found out that I'd taken off after Ivy. But I prayed that he would understand how dire the situation was and that I'd had no other choice than to try to intervene before my sister and Moses were destroyed.

"We'll leave after breakfast in the morning," Max said as he picked up the pace. "Have your things packed, and we'll go as soon as we've eaten." He was all business, and I was a little taken aback by his matter-of-factness. Both of our moods had changed as soon as the word *home* was mentioned. Max was once again the hunter and trader standing by the racks at the general store in Silver Springs.

"All right." I nodded. "That'll give me a chance to talk to Ivy and tell her good-bye." I started to tear up but fought back my emotions. They were flooding to the surface as I faced the harsh reality of saying good-bye to my twin sister. Unlike my leaving home to go to Jacksonville, this Seminole settlement was a place where I'd probably never return to. And whether Ivy would ever be able to return home remained to be seen. I knew there wasn't a chance of it happening while my father was alive, and he was not an old man yet. However, if he kept drinking, his demise would come sooner rather than later. The sad truth was that either way it worked out, there was no winning.

The village was quiet. There were a few women working at a long table that had been set up in the cleared area in the center of the settlement. They were decorating it with various flowers, greenery, and raw ears of corn; it was obvious that this would be the table of honor for the enormous meal that would take place as one of the final events of the Green Corn Festival. There were smaller tables, and they were decorated, too, but not as elaborately.

"Where is everyone?" I asked.

"It's nearly time for the feast, so the women are preparing the food while everyone else is either resting or dressing. After we eat, there will be a final dance, and the chief will thank the Great Spirit for another fine harvest of corn. Any others who care to speak can, and then the festival will end."

"I'm going to see if I can find Ivy. Will I see you for dinner?"

"Yes," Max said as he turned off in the direction of his uncle's chickee.

When I entered the small chickee where Ivy and I had been staying, I found her slipping into a beautiful red-and-white multilayered skirt. It wasn't the usual one that she'd been wearing, and I commented on how lovely it looked on her. Then, before I took the time to get dressed, I asked her if we could talk. She laughed and said she was about to ask me the same thing. Hiking up our skirts, we sat cross-legged on the bed, just as we had as children.

Ivy smiled as I took her hands. "You go first."

I got right to the point. "Max and I are leaving tomorrow."

My sister's smile faded. "I knew it'd be soon, Eve, but I just wouldn't let myself think about it." Her voice cracked, and she looked down at the bed as her eyes filled, and I pulled her to me.

"You're going to be fine, Ivy." My eyes were as full as hers were. "You're a survivor. Besides, I've never known you to want to live the same kind of life as everyone else." I lifted her chin up so that I could look her in the eye. "I think you'll be happy with these people, or I wouldn't leave you here."

"Where would you take me?" She laughed, wiping tears away. "Our old home isn't my home anymore."

"Well then, we would just make ourselves a new one somewhere, wouldn't we? But, I think you've found that special 'home' place here. A home is not so much about where it is as much as it's about feeling wanted and appreciated, and I believe you've found exactly that among these good people, don't you?"

"Yes," she said, squeezing my hands. "I honestly do."

"Ivy, I haven't been fair to you these last few years, and I'm sorry."

My sister looked confused. "What do you mean?"

"I should have been more supportive about your choice of work as a healer. I should have encouraged you and helped you more."

Ivy scoffed. "You never did anything to try to stop me or to make me feel like I was making a poor choice, Eve. That's ridiculous."

"That's just it!" I enthusiastically said. "I never did *anything*! I just stood by for the most part, keeping my mouth shut and trying to keep peace in the family. Sometimes raising a little ruckus is called for, ya know." I smiled. Then I placed my right hand against her left cheek. "I should have defended you when Papa was so critical about what you were doing—especially given the fact that you helped Mayoma save his life when he lost his arm. He should have—*we* should have—told you how fine a job you did and how important your work was to so many people, including your own family. I'm so sorry, Ivy. I'm truly sorry."

"And I'm sorry I put you in such an awkward position when you found Moses and me…together."

"It's over and done with, Ivy. We both need to look to the future now."

"And that's exactly what I wanted to talk to you about, Eve! Moses and I are going to be married tonight after dinner, as part of the Green Corn Festival!"

I was so startled I couldn't say anything for a moment. But as I looked at her, I saw the joy and excitement on my sister's face, and I knew beyond a shadow of a doubt that Moses and Ivy truly and deeply loved each other.

They loved each other to the point that they would forego their own families and homes to search for a new home to make their own family. What they had together was good and solid and right.

I pulled Ivy to me and held her hard. "You and Moses build that life you want, Ivy, and don't you ever look back." I kissed her cheek and tasted her tears. I knew that no matter how many miles might separate us because of people's prejudices and fears, our bond could never be broken by anyone or anything—ever.

Chapter 36
An Ill Wind Blows

I finished dressing for dinner and walked over to the cooking area to find Ivy. She'd left before I was ready so that she could help with the last of the food preparations.

"Here," Ivy said, handing me a very large bowl. "Pour that stew in that bowl and then carry it out to the main table. There's a—"

Suddenly, the sound of thundering hooves made everyone stop their tasks as a group of people rode into the village in a cloud of dust kicked up by their horses.

"Who are they?" I asked in awe as a group of seven riders, all majestically outfitted in dyed leather, beads, and feathers, pulled their horses to a stop in the center of the settlement.

"I don't know," Ivy said, "but from the looks of 'em, I'd say they're pretty important."

As I walked away from the cooking area, all the villagers came pouring out of their chickees to greet the new arrivals, who reached down to them from their horses, clasping hands and arms. A distinguished-looking middle-aged man was obviously the leader, for his horse stood in front of the others, and the tone and strength of his voice left no doubt as to who was in charge. But it was the young woman behind him, the only female among the group, who demanded everyone's attention.

The woman was strikingly beautiful and regal looking. She sat atop her solid-white horse ramrod straight, dressed in light peach-dyed suede. She wore strand after strand of beads, which hung down to the middle of her chest, and her tan legs were bare, though she wore a pair of beautifully beaded moccasins. Her hair had been styled into two long braids, and one hung down over each of her shoulders, showing off her long, slender neck. Her cheeks were prominent, and her nose was straight and perfectly proportioned to the rest of her face, which looked as though it had been sculpted by the finest craftsman. When she turned to look my way, I saw that her eyes were shaped like huge dark almonds, but then something got her attention, and her gaze immediately shifted to someone behind me. Looking over my shoulder, I saw Max. He had walked up behind me, and the young woman's eyes were now locked on him. She smiled broadly, but Max's face showed no emotion though his eyes remained glued on her. There was no doubt about it: They knew each other, and from the way they looked at each other, it was obvious that they knew each other quite well.

Max's Uncle Jay stood beside me. "Who is she?" I quietly asked.

"Naomi from the Wind Clan!" he answered excitedly. "She's beautiful, no? She was Max's wife, and she's come for every Corn Festival, hoping he'll be here."

"His wife?" I whispered, confused. "When was she...were they...?"

But before I could ask the hundred questions running through my mind, Jay hurried over to the guests to greet them. Stunned, I looked behind me to see if Max was still there, but I'd lost him in the crowd.

Chapter 37
A Festival of Forevers

I looked around for Ivy but couldn't find her either. When I saw the widowed woman whose chickee we were staying in. I asked, "Becca, have you seen my sister?"

"No, miss, but no time to find girl now," she insisted in her broken English. "We eat big food now, yes?" she asked, as though that would straighten it all out for me, and actually, it did. Ivy was very involved with the food. "Must come now," Becca insisted. "Hurry! Chief no like slow foots," she laughed, and I could see the many gaps where teeth had once been.

"Yes, okay," I relented, letting her drag me by the hand over to a table.

"Here, sit," Becca said, practically pushing me down onto a bench. I did as I was told, but once I was seated, I looked around for Ivy and spotted her spooning something out of a bowl onto the plate for one of the elders sitting at the main table. I needed to catch her eye, but she was focused on her task and moved down the table, filling bowl after bowl. Looking around, I saw that Uncle Jay was seated several people down from me on the other side of the table. Just then, he caught sight of Max and hailed him over. As Max walked toward Jay, he saw me and slowed for a second as if considering whether to come over, but he continued on toward Jay and sat down.

"Where you been, boy?" I could clearly hear Jay's booming voice, especially since he sat facing me. "Three different woman tried to sit here," he continued, "but I chased them all off and told them I was saving this place for you!"

I tried to hear Max's response, but because he was facing away from me, I couldn't make out any of what he said.

"What? And have the other two crazy jealous!" Jay responded. "No, no, Max. Tonight, you sit by me and save me from their wrath." Suddenly, his face lit up with excitement. "Did you see Naomi's here?"

Max said something in reply.

"She looks beautiful, no?" Jay beamed.

I saw Max nod but still couldn't make out what he said over the din of noise around us. Apparently, though, whatever Max said was not what Jay was looking for and the older man suddenly sounded slightly exasperated. "When are you going to come together with Naomi, Max? You know it's something she's prayed to the Great One for over many, many moons. She looks for you at every Corn Festival, and now you're finally here. It's destiny! This is something that my soul feels certain both of your hearts truly need—and *want*!"

Though I couldn't hear what Max said, I saw him cover his uncle's hand with his own, then lean in closer to his ear, and say something. I watched Jay's reaction to his words, and whatever Max said caused the older man's eyes to light up and then well up. Apparently, Max's response confirmed that Jay's soul had been correct all along.

All through dinner, I tried to keep my eyes averted from both Max and Naomi, but every time Chief Red Sun stood up to say something—none of which I could understand—I looked in Naomi's direction. Several times, I caught her looking at Max, and when I looked down the table at him, I saw that he was looking toward her. I caught him watching me once, but I quickly turned away.

The feast seemed to go on forever, especially since I didn't have anyone to talk to. The woman sitting to my right spoke very little English, while the one to my left spoke none at all. Making matters worse, Ivy was sitting at a different table with Moses, though she was up and down much of the time, attending to the guests at the chief's table. Finally, after what seemed like hours, Chief Red Sun stood and made some announcement, which quickly caused everyone to rise and move the tables out of the way.

Now that we were free to move about, I started to go find Ivy, but then the thought occurred to me that if I tried to talk to her about Max right now, to ask her what she might know about him being married to Naomi, I'd be taking away from the joy of this very special night for her and Moses. She needed to give her attention to Moses, not to me, so I kept to myself, stood among the villagers, and watched the festival unfold.

The chief, as well as the elders and special guests, sat on the edge of the cleared circle, where the lighting of a pipe commenced. The chief inhaled the pungent smelling herbs or tobacco, I wasn't sure which it was, and then he passed the pipe to his right and it continued from there. Soon, the deep, rhythmic beating of a half-dozen drums began to reverberate through the village. The central fire was built up as several men threw more wood onto it. As sparks and flames shot up to the darkened sky, elaborately dressed dancers appeared.

I watched, mesmerized, like the rest of the crowd, as they stomped and sang in perfect rhythm to the drums. There was an array of dances that changed along with the drums' rhythm. I didn't understand their meanings but guessed that one honored their bountiful harvest as ears of corn were used in the dance. It seemed as though the dancers, happy that their storage baskets were full for more seasons to come, used as much energy as they could muster while giving thanks to their Great Spirit.

During this dance I saw Max. He stood diagonally across the circle from me. I looked to see if I could find Naomi in the crowd, and sure enough, she was standing directly across from Max. I watched them, trying to gauge what they might be thinking, but their expressions gave nothing away.

Finally, the corn dance was over, and the chief walked out into the middle of the circle. He spoke in his native tongue, and the crowd murmured in response to something he said. Then he called for Moses and Ivy, and I saw them appear and move into the circle in front of the chief. Ivy looked around at the people, and I raised my hand so that she would know where I was and that I was supporting her. When she saw me, she smiled and mouthed the words *I love you*, and I mouthed the same words back to her.

She was dressed in the same way she had been when she'd left the chickee, but now a wreath of small, bright orange orchids encircled her head. Ivy turned toward Moses, and he took her hands. Then the chief asked them something in the Muskogean language. A man standing just behind the chief stepped forward and translated for them, and he did so loud enough that everyone could hear.

"Chief Kitisci Haasi asks whether it is the intention of this man to have this woman for his wife." He looked at Moses.

"I intend that, yes," Moses nervously responded to the chief; then he turned and smiled at Ivy.

The chief spoke again and the translator posed the same question to Ivy.

"Yes, that's my intention." Her voice was strong and sure.

The chief raised his hand and said something, and then the translator spoke. "Chief Kitisci Haasi has blessed this union and has asked that the

Great Spirit bless it too, by giving this man and woman many strong children to care for them in their old age, and a good and bountiful life together."

Regardless of whether it was the custom of the Seminole people or not, Moses leaned in and gently kissed Ivy on the lips, and that was it. The ceremony was over in a matter of minutes. It was beautiful, simple, and perfect, and I couldn't help but compare it to the elaborate wedding David and I were planning on having. Suddenly, all the extravagance seemed so pretentious and unnecessary.

But, David's family was from old money, and expected all the pomp and circumstance that went along with a high society wedding. Whether or not I agreed with it, I could understand it. Yet I was sure my sister's wedding had been just as lovely as mine would be, if not more so, for it was a simple celebration and a moving declaration of their love for each other.

My sister and Moses left the circle and made their way through the crowd to parts unknown. I was hoping to see her after the ceremony, but this was a night meant for her and her new husband alone, and I would probably not see her again until the morning came. There'd be time enough to say a final farewell to each other then.

Just as I turned to leave so that I could go to the chickee to pack up and get some rest before the long trip ahead, the chief spoke loudly to get everyone's attention. He said something in his language, and the crowd gave a small collective gasp. Then there was excited chatter among them. Curious, I stayed a moment longer to see what was about to take place.

The chief held up his hand as if to silence everyone. Once they were quiet, he beckoned to his right, and Max stepped into the circle to stand before the chief. He spoke to Max, and there was no need for a translator. Max nodded to the chief, and then he stepped up to the crowd. Reaching out, he took Naomi's hand and gently brought her into the circle; then they stood before the chief. I could clearly see both of their profiles as they turned to face each other. Smiling, Max took both of her hands in his, and the young woman's beautiful face lit up.

In a soft but husky voice, Max spoke to her. His words were obviously poignant for her eyes filled with tears as she listened. Then she spoke back to him in a voice that was just as emotion-filled. She rested her hand against the side of his face and smiled the most beautiful smile I'd ever seen until I saw the smile that Max gave her. I was witness to an immensely important and intimate moment between them. Every sound in the village ceased; everyone was as mesmerized by the scene as I was. Finally, Max tilted Naomi's chin up and tenderly and softly kissed her lips. They stayed that way for a couple of seconds; then Naomi laid her head against his chest and wrapped her arms around his midsection. He wrapped his arms around her as well, and when she raised her face to look up at him, he bestowed that glorious smile on her once again.

I couldn't stay for another second. I pushed my way through the crowd, and as I did, a tremendous cheer erupted from the people. It was obvious that they greatly approved of what had just taken place.

In the chickee, I lay on the bed and cried. I stayed there long after the crying stopped, just staring at the thatched ceiling. It was going to take a long time to sort things out. My feelings confused me. Seeing Max with Naomi had made the Seminole people happy, so why had it upset me so? As I'd confessed to myself earlier, I had feelings for Max—there was no doubt about that. But I also realized that what I felt for Max—and what I thought he probably felt for me—was something that would never last. Max came from a whole other world, and the life that he lived was very different from the one David and I planned to build together.

This momentary detour that we had taken to protect Ivy had thrust us into a set of circumstances that was beyond unusual, and those circumstances had brought us together emotionally because we'd depended on each other so much. I respected him and would be forever grateful to him for nearly forfeiting his life to save my sister's and Moses's. But being grateful was a world away from loving someone, and I needed to keep reminding myself not to confuse the two. Once I got back to Silver Springs, I would get on a northbound steamboat to Jacksonville, and David, and would never look back.

A thought startled me: Who was going to Silver Springs with me? Would Naomi be with us, ready to start a new life with Max there? Or would he take me by himself and then return to the Everglades? Perhaps he would find someone else to take me back. Though I would prefer it, I knew that he and Ivy wouldn't let me go by myself. It was dangerous country for a lone traveler, especially a lone female traveler. Even if I left in the middle of the night, Max or his replacement could easily catch up to me once it was daylight. No, the best thing to do was to get some much-needed sleep and be on my way in the morning with whoever was going with me. The sooner the morning came, the faster I could leave, even though that meant saying good-bye to Ivy. That was going to happen though, no matter who I was riding with. I rubbed my hands over my wet eyes, took a deep breath, then pushed myself up from the bed, and began to pack. The journey home had just begun.

Chapter 38
The Road behind Us

We left at daybreak. When Max and I saddled up our horses, the village was quiet and there were only a few people awake to bid us good-bye. Ivy and Moses were with us. I hugged Moses first, telling him to take good care of Ivy and their family, and that I was proud of him. Then it was time to say a final good-bye to my sister. We held each other hard and told each other how much we loved each other; then, not wanting to prolong the inevitable, I quickly mounted Maggie, and Max and I rode out of the village. I only looked back once, blowing a kiss to my sister, and then I set my sights on the trail that lay ahead of us.

The weather was good, which allowed us to travel fast and hard. We stopped throughout the day but only long enough to rest, water the horses, stretch our legs, and eat something before we rode on. We said little to each other, but I preferred it that way. I was too involved with the endless thoughts in my head to try to communicate with Max. He seemed to be lost in his own thoughts as well.

Finally, as the sun was getting lower on the horizon, Max said it was time to find shelter for the night. Fortunately, with the clear skies, a quickly erected lean-to was sufficient, and supper was easy enough to prepare because of the enormous amount of food that the generous Seminole people had sent along with us. Because there was no reason for us to travel as covertly as we had before, we were free to light a fire, and as soon as it was burning, I set on a pot of coffee.

We were tired and yawned as we ate fish and corn. We talked about superficial things, like how far north we would ride before coming to a certain lake or tiny settlement and how many miles we would travel each day if the weather held. Finally, after our conversation had run out, along with the last of our energy, we crawled into the lean-to. Max covered his face with his black hat and fell asleep almost immediately. I rolled onto my side, facing away from him, but sleep did not come as easily for me, even though I was exhausted.

On the second day of traveling, we ran into some rain, though it wasn't until late in the afternoon, so it didn't impede our travel much. As we watched lightning streak across thick, dark clouds to the north, Max decided it was time to stop and make a better shelter than the one we'd built the night before. After making the frame for the lean-to, we got busy weaving branches and greenery into the structure's roof until it was as waterproof as it could possibly be. We'd just finished warming up some food and coffee when the heavens opened. Taking our cups and the coffeepot into the shelter with us, we settled in for what looked to be a wet night.

We were tired, but the traveling had been good, allowing us to put many more miles behind us. We sipped our coffee as we discussed the day's journey and made plans for the next. We made small talk to stave off the impending deafening silence that threatened to take over. When the conversation hit an uncomfortable lull, Max stretched out, put his hat over his face, and said good night.

I quietly left the shelter to throw out the remainder of the coffee and double-checked that the fire had been doused by the rain. Looking up, I saw that the clouds had cleared, leaving a purple and orange sky. Because it was summer, the sun wouldn't completely set until well into the evening, which made falling asleep hard.

I went back into the lean-to and lay there, staring at the dark and dripping foliage above me. As tired as I was, I was restless, and I rolled from one side to the other. My mind raced with a thousand questions, until I couldn't hold them inside any longer. Rolling onto my back, I asked Max if he was still awake.

"Barely," he mumbled. "What is it?"

"Why didn't Naomi come with us? She could have, you know. Or you could have stayed there, and I would have paid someone else to accompany me home."

Slowly, Max lowered his hat from his face and looked over at me. "What are you talking about, Eve?"

"Naomi. I just wondered…" I didn't know exactly what to say. "You know…"

"No, I don't know." Max looked confused but slightly amused, too. "Tell me." He rolled onto his side to face me and sat up slightly, leaning on his forearm. Then he repeated, "Tell me."

"Well, at the Corn Festival, when you and Naomi stood in front of the chief, and..."

"You have no idea what we said, do you, Eve?"

"Nobody translated. I just assumed since Ivy and Moses had just gotten married, and then you and Na—"

"You just assumed we got married?"

"Well, ...yes. And you kissed her, so I just assumed..."

"Yes, but I didn't kiss her the way I kissed you, did I?" Suddenly, he didn't look quite so amused. "You think that I would kiss you in the afternoon and marry another in the evening? Is that what you think of me? That I would be such a *cetto*—such a snake? I'm going to sleep now, and I suggest you do the same." He rolled over, turning his back to me. "We have many more miles to go before we can put this road behind us."

The night seemed endless and neither of us slept much. We both tossed and turned, and it felt as though the new day would never come. When it finally did, the sky broke into magnificent shades of pink, peach, and blue. The fat white clouds reminded me of dumplings.

Both of us were quiet as we hurried through breakfast. It was obvious that we were more comfortable riding than forcing conversation. About midmorning, we came upon a small creek.

"Eve," Max called over to me as he slowed Sampson. "This is a good place to stop. We'll take a few minutes to let the horses drink while you and I stretch our legs. I want to talk to you."

We reined our horses in and dismounted. Both of us knelt on the bank, drank from our cupped hands, and splashed the tepid water over our faces and necks. Even at this early hour, the sun baked everything, especially at this time of year.

Max wiped away the water on his face, set his hat back on his head, then stood up. "Let's walk."

We quietly walked along the creek for several minutes until Max pointed out a massive oak tree. Sitting down with my back against the trunk, I waited as Max settled down next to me.

He didn't say anything for a moment, as if he was trying to decide how to start, but he finally spoke. "Like I told you before, when my mother, sister, and brother died, I spent some time with Uncle Jay. My father was lost without my mother, so he spent most of his time on long hunting and trading trips."

"Did you ever go with him?"

"No. My father just kept moving. I guess the pain was easier to tolerate if he did. But he wanted me to have some stability and some family around, so I went down to the Everglades.

"As I told you before, the Seminoles are a combination of several different tribes, and my mother's people were Creeks, just as Naomi's are. My mother's people were part of the Otter Clan, and Naomi is from the Wind Clan.

"Her people lived in Georgia, and most of them were forced to go to Oklahoma. But a few of them were able to avoid being captured, and they either married into the white world or scattered deep into swamps or thick woods in the middle of nowhere. And those people created tiny settlements, oftentimes with members of other tribes. They became the Seminole people—'the runaways.'

"Naomi's grandparents and a few others were able to avoid being caught. They traveled at night and hid out during the day, all the way down to the Everglades. Naomi's mother was born in the 'Glades but returned to Georgia with her parents and eventually married another Creek up there. However, she would come back to the 'Glades to visit family and friends, and she'd bring Naomi with her. That's how I met her.

"Jay was a good friend of Naomi's people; because Naomi and I were both Creeks, and from different clans, a marriage was arranged. Jay felt I was too alone in the world, and Naomi was of marrying age, and her family approved. So, eight years ago we were married in front of the Seminole tribe just as Ivy and Moses were. We were both nineteen. And we stayed with the Seminoles part of the time but also went to Georgia and Alabama on hunting trips.

"At the end of our first year of marriage, Naomi gave birth to our daughter. We named her Ivy." Max saw the startled look on my face. "That's what first made me notice your sister, her name. Ivy and I got along well from the start, and the little I knew about herbs and plants that my people used for medicine, I told her about."

"Where's your daughter now, Max?"

"She died when she was just a year old."

"Oh, Max!" I laid my hand on his. "What happened?"

"We were in the 'Glades, and we had our first cold snap of the winter, so Naomi wrapped Ivy up in blankets on her tiny bed. During the night, Ivy let out a sharp little cry, and Naomi checked on her. The baby kept crying so Naomi picked her up, and a coral snake fell out of her blankets. The snake must have crawled into Ivy's bed to stay warm, and Ivy disturbed the snake and was bitten. The coral snake's poison is very strong, so she was dead within thirty minutes."

"Oh, my God, Max. Oh, my God…I d-don't know what to say." And I didn't. I was stunned and deeply shaken. Max was fighting back tears and his mouth was tight as if he was working at keeping his emotions contained.

"I should have known better," he cried, slamming a fist down on the ground. "I'd heard of that happening before. And I should have been more careful. I should have protected my daughter better!" Tears spilled from his eyes. He turned his face away from me and quickly wiped them away with the back of his sleeve.

"Max, how many thousands of nights have thousands of children gone to sleep and been safe and secure in their beds? The odds of something happening to your daughter while she slept were so slim that there was no reason for you to do anything differently to protect her that night. I know you well enough to know that you were a good and loving father. Sometimes terrible things happen, things that we'll never be able to make sense of, and losing a child has to be the most terrible of them. I can't imagine anything worse!"

"I can," Max said, instantly silencing me. "Losing your child and *then* losing your wife."

"How do you mean?"

"Ivy's death broke us both in a way. Naomi wanted to go back to Georgia, but I didn't want to settle down in one place for too long. So I'd leave her there while I went off on long hunting and trapping trips. I just felt like I had to keep going—the same way my father did. That maybe I could outrun the grief. And Naomi ran, too, right into the arms Jess Armistead."

"Jess Armistead? Was he Creek, too?"

"No, he was white. He was a hunter and a trapper, too, and I'd often see him in Georgia. He'd even been a guest at our small settlement a time or two when the weather turned really bad. Even though hunters are competitors, there's also a kind of brotherhood among them, and most of them know each other. Some get real territorial, but most of 'em respect each other and know where each other's traps are and leave them alone."

"How did you find out about Naomi and Jess?"

"I came back to Georgia early from a hunting trip. I hadn't bathed in days so I went to a hidden swimming hole that Naomi and I used and found them there. I started to beat Jess pretty good. I guess I was taking all the pain of losing Naomi *and* Ivy out on him. The only thing that kept me from killing him was that Naomi tried to put herself between us. I didn't want to accidentally kill her. Oh, don't get me wrong. I felt like killing her, but feeling like it and doing it are two different things. Anyway, the son of a bitch grabbed his clothes and got the hell out of there, and I dragged Naomi back to the village and divorced her on the spot."

"How do you mean, like in front of some judge, or…what? I don't understand."

"Eve, under Creek law, all it takes to divorce someone is to say, 'I divorce you.' And so that there was no misunderstanding about it, I told her that I divorced her in front of a lot of witnesses in the village. And that was it. It was finished—well, as far as I was concerned, anyway."

"What do you mean?"

"Adultery is a major offense in the eyes of the Creek people. They wanted to cut off her hair and her ears, but I said no. I asked them to have mercy on her because of losing Ivy, and so they didn't hurt her. But she was disgraced and would remain so until I forgave her in front of witnesses. And that's what happened at the festival the other night."

"You forgave her?"

Max nodded. "The Corn Festival is far more than just a festival thanking the Great Spirit for another bountiful harvest. It's a time for renewal and forgiveness. It's a time to forgive the debts of others and a time to forgive wrongdoings. Apparently, Naomi has been coming to the festival for the last five years, since I divorced her, hoping I'd be there so that I could forgive her. And that's what I finally did the other night. I took all blame away from her and said that it was time for us to move forward with renewed spirits. I also said that she would forever be a part of my life because she was the mother of my child; she had been a good and kind mother, and Ivy's spirit connects us forever. I also wished her joy through her life, and that was pretty much it."

"And there was no way you and she could have worked it out—after the affair, I mean? Couldn't you have tried to understand that maybe she needed someone to turn to after Ivy died, but you were never there? You said yourself that you were hunting all the time, trying to run away from the pain. What about Naomi's pain? Couldn't you two have tried to ease each other's hurt?"

"She never asked me to stay home with her. Now I know why."

"Why? So that she could be with Jess?"

"Yes."

"Things might have been different if you'd just talked to each other more, tried to help each other, and *been there* for each other."

"Eve, what Naomi and I had was doomed from the start."

"Why, Max?"

"Because I never loved her."

"Then why the hell did you marry her!?"

"Because it was encouraged, and I was lonely. I thought that maybe I could learn to love her."

"And how did she feel about you, Max? Did you ever bother to ask her?"

"Let's get going." He started to get up, but I put my hand on his arm, stopping him.

"I want to finish this conversation, Max. I'm curious about something."

"About what?"

"When you decided that your marriage to Naomi couldn't be salvaged, you virtually said to everyone, 'I'm done. We're through.' One, two, three, that's it? It's all as easy as that, Max? There are no binding certificates or legal documents to say you're married? And then there's no document declaring that you're now divorced?"

"No." Max's face was hard.

"That's all well and good if things stay wonderful and lovely," I continued, "but what if someone gets really, really mad one night and says 'I divorce you,' but really just said it in the heat of the moment and feels bad about it the next day? Is it too late? Those three little words have already been said and there's no taking them back?"

Max smiled sarcastically and shrugged a shoulder. "Yep. That's about it."

"Well, that's about as ridiculous a thing as I've ever heard! You Creek people sure have flimsy relationships!" I got up and started back toward Maggie.

Max caught up and grabbed my arm to stop me. "Must I remind you that almost every single legal document and most every promise ever made by the white man to the red man has been broken? Paper and pen mean nothing to your people, Eve! *Absolutely nothing!* Talk about flimsy! I'd take the word of a red man over a hundred of the white man's legal documents. As far as I'm concerned, all those are good for is to wipe your as—"

"I'm not gonna listen to your vulgarities!" I yanked my arm free and started walking toward Maggie again. "We're from two very different worlds, Max, two *very* different worlds. And, if you don't mind, I'd like to get back to the one I belong in."

We mounted our horses, and just as I pulled Maggie's reins to turn her to the north, Max grabbed hold of them, stopping us. "You know, Eve—" His voice was calm again, but his eyes were dark and intense. "I thought I was falling in love with you. I thought you were something *special*. I see now that I was very wrong, and that you are absolutely right: You belong to one world, and I'm a universe away." Then he rode out ahead of me to return me to the world I knew.

Chapter 39
Crossroads

We traveled for two more days, only speaking to each other when absolutely necessary and riding as hard as we could without abusing our horses. Those long, quiet hours gave me plenty of time to think about the life I was headed back to and the people involved in it.

I was very happy to be going back to David. David represented security and normalcy, excitement and opportunity, and a world I understood and was comfortable living in. But the one thing that concerned me greatly was whether David would be as understanding about my sudden and lengthy flight south as I hoped he would be. I'd been gone far longer than expected, but I hoped that David would respect the fact that I'd made the journey to save my sister. In truth, I'd only seen a kind and patient side of him, and to conjure up and worry about some other side that I'd yet to see served no purpose at all, so I tried to push those thoughts out of my mind.

I also hoped and prayed that Mr. Jones would be forgiving of my lengthy absence and that my desk was still waiting for me. But I also knew that my boss had a business to run and needed people that he could count on to be there. I just hoped he found enough value in my work to allow me to return.

The one thing I dreaded was seeing my parents, and the fact that I felt that way broke my heart. I wondered what shape I would find my father in, and my poor mother, for that matter, too. I dreaded seeing their reaction when I told them about Ivy's decision to marry Moses, and raise their child among the Seminole people. I knew beyond a shadow of a doubt that it would shatter my mother, though I was curious to know what she felt Ivy's other options might have been. What frightened me more than every one of my fears bundled together was what Papa might try to do. If he had been almost unreachable before, the news about my sister could push him beyond all logic and reason, and God only knew what he'd attempt to do then.

Max and I finally reached the point where we needed to head east for the last miles home. Oddly enough, instead of staying out in front of me, he reined Sampson in so that we were riding side by side. I felt as though he wanted to say something to me, and I understood; there was so much I wanted to say to Max. But it seemed as though each of us was having trouble getting the first words out.

During the last two days of our journey, I did more than think about David, my job at the paper, and my family. I also thought a lot about Max. Perhaps it was because we had spent so much time together, just the two of us. Without any doubt, there had been many times that were terrifyingly intense, but it was the intimate moments that kept running through my mind. We had counted on each other, trusted each other, and learned to respect and care for each other. The only trouble was I cared for him a great deal more than I would ever admit to him. I'd had trouble enough admitting it to myself, so telling him was out of the question. As we both agreed, we belonged to two different worlds, and it was past time that we each return to them.

"Max, this is where the journey ends for me," I said as I pulled Maggie to a stop. We had literally reached the crossroads of our own separate worlds.

"I'm going to stop off and see the Haileys before heading back to my folks' house. I'm sure Emmitt and Mayoma have aged twenty years in these last few weeks, wondering whether their son stills walks this Earth," I said with a weak smile.

"Then you'll go to your parents' house. For how long?" His voice was flat, but his eyes were intense. All his emotions were evident there, and they bored into me at the moment.

"I'll stay with my parents just as long as it takes to catch the next steamer north. I need to get back to Jacksonville—to my job."

"And to David," he added.

"Yes, to David, too," I confirmed.

"Well…Eve, I wish you much happiness." He smiled but it was forced. "I hope to see your name on the byline of the *New York Times* someday."

"Thanks, Max." I smiled. He started to urge Sampson forward.

"Max!" There was urgency in my voice that surprised even me, and it certainly did Max for he abruptly pulled the reins in and turned around to look at me, waiting. "Max…I d-don't even know how to begin, much less what exactly to say to let you know how grateful I am to you for saving Ivy's and Moses's lives. They wouldn't have made it to the village without you."

"Yes, they would have," he said, confidently nodding. "Love conquers all, you know. At least that's what they say," he added softly. "You'd better get a move on, Eve. You have a boat to catch." Without saying another thing, he turned Sampson around and started to move out.

"Wait!" I shouted though I had no idea what I wanted to say.

He once again pulled Sampson to a stop, and turned around to face me. "What is it, Eve?" He sighed rather impatiently.

"You once said you had put things on hold to track Ivy and Moses down. What are your plans now, Max? What are you gonna do?"

"I'm heading down around Lake Weir. I bought a larger grove there."

I was surprised. Max had never mentioned anything about it. "Oh, I-I hadn't heard."

"It's time to move on, Eve." He started to leave but hesitated. "You take care of yourself."

It felt like he was looking right through me, as though he knew what was in my heart but also knew that I was too frightened to admit it. Finally, he tipped his hat and rode off. As I watched him go, I wanted to call out to him, to make him turn around again, but I just let him go. I just had to let him go.

Chapter 40
Sins of the Father

When I approached the Haileys' cabin, I saw Emmitt up on a ladder working on some siding. There was no way of letting him know I was there without startling him, but I stopped a distance from him and called out. "Hellooo, Emmitt!" He nearly fell from the ladder, but he grabbed a rung in time. With a mouthful of nails, he looked over his shoulder, and seeing that it was me, he dropped his hammer and hurried down.

He pulled the nails from his mouth as he walked toward me. "Moses?" he said, and even at the distance I was from him, I could see the terrible fear in his eyes.

"He's fine, Emmitt. He's just fine. He's safe, and he's married to Ivy. They're in South Florida, at the Seminole village."

Emmitt dropped the nails and fell to his knees, clasping his hands together. Closing his eyes, he raised his face toward the heavens. "Thank you, sweet Jesus! Thank you, Lord!" He began sobbing.

"Oh, Emmitt! Emmitt!" I dismounted from Maggie and hurried over to him. Kneeling in front of him, I pulled him to me, and the man, who was the same age as my father, cried like a baby in my arms.

Suddenly, I heard the banging of a screen door, and Mayoma walked outside with a look of absolute terror on her face. With Emmitt crying in my arms, she could only imagine the worst had come to pass, and she slowly and woodenly walked toward us as she wiped her hands on her apron. "It's Moses, isn't it?"

I went to her. "Moses is fine, Mayoma. He's fine, and he's safe. He and Ivy are living with the Seminoles in the 'Glades. They were married some days ago."

"Oh God, oh Jesus!" she said as her knees buckled and she fell onto the grass. Emmitt knelt in front of her, and the two held each other and rocked as they cried and uttered their thanks to the heavens.

There was nothing more I needed to say, so I quietly rode Maggie out of the yard, and as I did, I heard Mayoma shout to the Lord to always bless me and protect me. And I prayed that he heard her loud and clear and that her request would be effective immediately, for my next stop was at the old homeplace.

I was nearly out of the yard when I saw discarded pieces of charred siding. I almost made myself keep going. I really didn't want to know, but I had to. So reining Maggie around, I headed back to Emmitt and Mayoma, who were helping each other up their front porch steps. "Emmitt, what happened to your house? Why are there charred planks over there?"

Emmitt looked at Mayoma as if silently asking her if he should tell me. She gave one curt nod, and he came back down the steps and over to me. "Miss Eve, your daddy done tried to burn us down," he answered honestly, though I could see that it pained him to do so.

"Oh, my God, Emmitt. Oh, my God. W-when? When did he do it?" I could feel my legs shaking against Maggie's sides.

"Right after y'all left. He come over that night when Mayoma and I was sleepin', and the only reason we knew something was goin' on was because Mayoma's hands were a' hurtin' her, and she wasn't able to sleep. She was sittin' in the kitchen, havin' a cup o' tea, when she started smellin' the smoke. She hollered for me to come quick, and we ran out the house. Your daddy had poured kerosene down 'round that part you saw me a' workin' on, and the flames was already startin' to climb the walls pretty good. I seen Hap just standin' back by the tree line starin'—frozen like."

"Who put it out?" My mouth was as dry as the desert.

"Me and the good Lord Hisself." He smiled. "I started throwing buckets o' water on the flames, but it wasn't helpin' enough, and then the skies opened up, dousin' that fire! Your daddy was still standin' there when it was doin' nothin' but smolderin', and I went over to him and said, 'Mr. Hap, why you doin' this to us? We didn't do nothin' to you! Moses and Ivy done did what they did, and Mayoma and I ain't got nothin' to do with it. And to tell ya the truth, Mr. Hap, we don't much like what they done neither.' Then that poor ol' Hap dropped the kerosene can, fell to his knees, raised his face toward the face o' God, and cried like a baby."

"Oh, Emmitt! I'm so very, very sorry! Here," I said, reaching into a small pouch hidden within Maggie's saddle. I pulled out three silver dollars and reached out to him with the coins. "Please, take this. It'll help pay for the wood."

"Miss Eve! I can't take your money!" Emmitt backed away with his hands out in front of him.

"Yes, you can, and you will, Emmitt! It's the least I can do. Please. If for no other reason than it will help me feel a little better." I reached my hand out to him as far as I could. "Here, take it. Please!" He reluctantly did as I asked.

"Thank you, Miss Eve."

"Emmitt, our family has put yours through enough. I want you to know that it stops now. I promise you that."

"Don't go doin' nothin' foolish, Miss Eve. There's been enough people actin' crazy 'round here lately. Don't you go actin' crazy, too."

"I won't, Emmitt. I promise. But I also promise that you and Mayoma can go to sleep without worryin' that you'll both be burned up in your beds. It's over, Emmitt." I turned Maggie toward home. "I have to go now. You take care of yourselves, ya hear me?"

"You say it like we ain't gonna see ya no more." Emmitt was no fool.

"I'm not sure you will, Emmitt. I'm gonna be married soon, and once I am, there won't be much of a reason for me to come back here. It's not home anymore." I took one last look around. "Well...I'd better go on. I'm gonna miss you and Mayoma a whole lot." I kicked my heels into Maggie to get her moving before he could see the tears in my eyes. There'd been enough crying around their place.

Chapter 41
The Homecoming

Papa was sitting in a rocker on the front porch when I rode into the yard. He was staring off into space, though I thought I saw him quickly glance at me before he continued to look off into nothingness. I put Maggie into the corral, and watching my father closely, I mounted the porch steps and walked over to him.

"Papa?" I said flatly. There was no response from him, and I tried again. "Papa, can you hear me?" When he still didn't answer, I walked through the screen door and called out to my mother. I didn't hear anything, so I went into the kitchen just as she was coming in the back door with an apron full of eggs she'd gathered from the coop. Seeing me startled her, and she nearly dropped them but recovered in time.

"Eve! Oh, Eve!" she said as she started for me but then realized she had to unload her eggs first. "Here, help me with these! Lord, God, thank you, thank you!" she said as I helped her put the eggs into the sink. When they were all safely out of her apron, she pulled me to her. "Thank God you're home! Is Ivy here, too?" When I told her that she wasn't, she held me away from her at arm's length. "Weren't you able to find her?"

"I found her, Mama, and she's fine. But before we get into all of that, tell me what's wrong with Papa."

"He's been that way for nearly three weeks now. Hardly says a word unless he has to, and then it's usually just one word—like *yes* or *no*, that kind of thing. Spends most of the day just starin' off into space. I got that doctor to come out when he passed through a few days ago, and he couldn't find a thing wrong with him, but when he asked if your father had been through a traumatic experience lately, I said that he had; the doctor thinks that's likely the problem. He said with a little time, he'd probably snap out of it. Then that man charged me a quarter and left."

"Does he eat, Mama?"

"Yeah, he still eats some but not like he used to."

"Well, Mama, I guess you're gonna have to do what the doctor said and give it some time." I felt unemotional about my father's condition. I knew he'd brought this on himself, and I didn't have a thimbleful of sympathy for him.

"Sit down, Eve. Sit down. Tell me about Ivy. Where is she and how is she? And where is Moses? Lord, you don't know how relieved I am to hear she's okay!" She grabbed the coffeepot and two cups and sat across from me at the kitchen table.

"It's a miracle they're okay, Mama, seeing as how Papa and Mr. Kite started out to track them down and then decided to let a couple of professionals do it. We ran into Rayne Longwood and Tom Bigelow." I watched her expression closely as I took a sip of coffee.

Her face lost some color, and she covered her mouth with her hand. "Oh, God. Where did you run into them? Was anyone hurt?"

"You know, Mama, I was out trailing after Ivy for a good long while, but I finally found her. And when I did, I made sure that she was safe and sound—and gonna stay that way. I had plenty of time to think about things. And you know what I kept askin' myself, 'Just how did Papa have the money to pay Tom and Rayne the kind of cash I'm sure they wanted for a job like that?' I had to wonder if Papa was making good enough money again to be able to afford them, even though he was only workin' about half the hours he used to. And if he wasn't making much money on the river, then I had to wonder if he made it by doing something else, or maybe he even got some of it from someone else."

"If you mean was he doin' somethin' like makin' whiskey, or somethin', I can tell you he wasn't, Eve. He wouldn't do such a thing!"

I scoffed at that last remark. "Lord, Mama, you make it sound like he's a highly moral, ethical man!" I leaned across the table toward her and said in a low voice; "Must I remind you that he threatened to kill his own daughter and Moses?"

"Oh, he didn't mean nothin' when he said he would kill Ivy. It was Moses who took advantage of *her.*"

"Stop it, Mama!" I said, slamming my hand down hard on the table and sloshing coffee out of my cup. "Just stop it! Rayne and Tom told us that Papa's instructions were to bring Ivy home if she was willing to come, but if she was determined to take off somewhere and have that baby, they were supposed to kill her. So stop lying! How did Papa have the money to pay Rayne and Tom? *Tell me!*" I shouted.

"I gave it to him," she said in a whisper that was hardly loud enough to hear.

"You gave those two men money to kill your own flesh and blood?" I said in a low, flat voice. "Say it again, Mama! I just want to make sure I heard it right! You gave Rayne and Tom the money to murder my sister. *Say it!*" I shouted.

"Yes, I gave them the money!" The words exploded from her. "But they weren't supposed to kill her—*only* if they had to," she tried to reason. "Your father wouldn't leave it alone. He just wouldn't let—"

I stood up and kicked the chair back from me, knocking it half way across the kitchen floor. "Mama," I hissed, "you're a pathetically weak, disgusting woman. And you know what makes you even worse than Papa? The fact that you pretend to be something you're not. You can't even use being crippled and bitter as an excuse!" I backed away from the table and my mother. "I will never step foot in this house again. And never, *ever* try to contact me for any reason whatsoever! The irony of it all, Mama, is that the daughter you wanted dead is alive, and *I'm* the daughter who is now dead to you."

I hurried upstairs to retrieve the suitcase I'd brought when David and I came for Papa's birthday. It seemed so very long ago; my parents seemed like strangers now.

Mama was coming up the stairs, as I brushed past her on my way down. "Good-bye, Mama."

"Wait, Eve, don't go! Wait!"

But I paid no attention to her as I walked out the screen door and onto the porch. I set my suitcase down and stood in front of my father. He didn't look at me but continued to stare vacantly at something in the distance instead. Placing my hands on the arms of his rocker, I leaned in close to him. "I know you can hear me, Papa, so hear this: If you *ever* try to hurt the Haileys again, or hire anyone to do the dirty work for you, I will personally go to the sheriff and turn you in. Then, I'll be the best damn star witness the prosecutor has ever had the pleasure of putting on the stand.

"And one more thing—and remember this well, because I'm not comin' back and this is the last thing I'm ever going to say to you. So listen good, Papa. You listen good!" I was just inches away from his face now. "If you *ever* try to hurt one hair on Ivy's head, or her baby, or Moses, as God as my witness, I will kill you! Do you understand me, Papa? I will shoot you down like a rabid dog! And I'm gonna make sure I'm lookin' you square in the eye when I do it!" I pushed myself away from his rocker, grabbed my suitcase, walked down the steps, and never looked back.

Chapter 42
What Lies Ahead

I gave up trying to keep a hat on my head as the ship steamed into Jacksonville Harbor. It felt good to be back, although I was both nervous and excited about seeing David again.

It felt like a lot of time had passed since I'd walked out of my parents' house, but it had just been the day before. I had gone straight to the general store to see if I could catch Mrs. Brody before closing time. She was just counting the money from the cash register, and the door was locked, but upon seeing me peering in through the window, she'd quickly let me in. After telling her I'd be right back and grabbing a pencil and paper from the counter, I hurriedly located a deckhand who had just come off one of the boats and paid him to take Maggie back to the Haileys' house for me. I scribbled a note to Emmitt, asking him to take care of her until I could decide what to do about her, and I included a silver dollar in with the note to help pay for some horse feed. Then I went back to talk with Mrs. Brody.

Without giving her too many details, I asked her if I could stay the night in the store's back room because the next boat leaving for the St. Johns wasn't until early the next day. However, the Brodys were now living in their new home directly behind the store, and she kindly invited me to spend the night there. I was grateful to be able to have a hot bath, a good meal, and a clean bed to sleep in. It seemed as though months had gone by since I'd had any of those small luxuries I'd always taken for granted. Before leaving the store to go over to the house, I sent David a wire, letting him know I'd be back the next day, and when Mrs. Brody came home a little bit later, she handed me a return wire:

Long meeting into tomorrow night. Meet at park Wed. at 11:00. D.P.

As soon as I read his message, I was somewhat relieved. At least he hadn't replied that it'd been nice knowing me but...

Throughout dinner, Mrs. Brody tried to question me about what had been going on over the last several weeks. In Silver Springs, gossip spread as fast as fire on dry grass, and oftentimes, Mrs. Brody was the one holding the match. She tried to pry as much information as she could from me, even though she already knew that Rayne and Tom had gone in search of Ivy and Moses. She'd also gotten wind that I had come looking for Max, and she'd put two and two together and figured we'd gone out looking for the runaways, too. I simply told Mrs. Brody that we hadn't been able to find them and had finally given up. She asked me if I'd seen the other two men, and I lied and said no. I figured that since none of this was her business anyway, deviating from the truth in the name of protecting the somewhat innocent was a forgivable offense.

The next order of gossip concerned David Perlow and our upcoming wedding. Mrs. Brody met him while he was waiting to catch the steamer out of Silver Springs and was very much smitten with him. Mama and I had heard all about how lovely and polite David had been to her the day we came into the store to order the material for my wedding gown. Now, as I sat there trying to enjoy her overcooked bass and lumpy mashed potatoes, she drilled me on more details about my upcoming nuptials, which included asking me if we'd set a wedding date. I told her that we planned it for October 16 and that we would be married in Jacksonville. She asked if Mama or I was going to post banns about it in any of the newspapers, and when I told her we hadn't thought about it, she scolded me, saying it was only proper etiquette for a young lady to have her marriage plans publicly announced.

"Well," she said, with an affected sniff, "at least I can put an announcement in the store's window letting the good people around here know." I smiled, told her that would be fine, and thanked her for thinking of it, and then I told her I'd help her with the dishes if she'd like. Kindly, she shooed me off to take my much-desired bath, so I bade her a good night and went upstairs.

I was exhausted, and I had a headache that made me feel as though my skull was about to burst. The shock and horrors of the day had totally blindsided me. Finding out that the Haileys had almost been murdered by my father and that my mother had paid to have Ivy tracked down and killed if need be had left my body and mind reeling. And my heart had been shattered in the process. I needed sleep—wonderful, peaceful, deep sleep that would allow me to float off into oblivion, if for only a short while.

I caught the steamboat, the *Tandy Lynn,* early the next morning. I was as exhausted as I'd been the night before, but once we were underway down the Ocklawaha, I felt my energy and spirits rising a little. I drank in the sights of the wild and beautiful landscape around me and was glad that there were only a few people on board. I didn't feel like talking to anyone. I needed time to think, to process all that had taken place in the last few months. Whatever small part of me had still been a naïve, starry-eyed young girl had been destroyed the night my father's arm had been ripped away from him.

I turned my attention to the future and my rendezvous with David the next morning. As I'd done a thousand times, I wondered what he would say to me about my abrupt departure to find Ivy. I needed to be ready to field a thousand questions about who Max was, what he'd had at stake to make him want to go with me in search of my sister, and what kind of sleeping arrangements we'd made when we stopped for the night. I was certain that David would be very interested in those details. I wondered how he'd react when I told him we'd spent nights together in a tiny lean-to or hunkered down in an empty cabin to wait out a stormy night. I prayed that he'd be more concerned about the well-being of my sister than the fact that his fiancée had strayed far from society's guidelines for the proper behavior and decorum expected from any young lady of good standing. And I hoped that he loved me enough to understand what I felt I'd had to do and that we could pick up where we'd left off in planning our future together.

I was happy that David and I weren't getting together right after I arrived. It would have been very late anyway. I wanted to get another good night's rest and look as bright and fresh as I could for him. I also wanted to dress especially well. David was always dressed so elegantly; I planned to take extra care in picking out what I would wear for our reunion. I couldn't help but wonder what he would have thought had he seen me in James's old pants and shirts that I wore on the trail when I was with Max.

Max.

He kept creeping into my mind at the oddest times. Small things I'd done in just the last couple of days brought him rushing back to me as clearly as if he was standing in the room. When I'd eaten the bass at Mrs. Brody's, I couldn't help thinking how much more delicious the fish that Max had netted were. And as the wind rode through my hair as I steamed down the Ocklawaha, the feeling of it reminded me of my hair streaming out behind me as I rode Maggie hard and fast beside Max and Sampson.

My time with Max had offered me the time to be free and wild and uninhibited. *He* was free and wild and uninhibited whereas David was anchored and refined, and represented security and opportunity for me and my future. I knew David expected me to be there to support his ambitions in all his endeavors, and I just prayed that my heart was as committed to that future as it needed to be. I knew I had to push Max Harjo as far from my mind as I could, so I kept telling myself that I was confusing love for the gratitude that I felt for him for helping me find Ivy. Given a little time, and a little distance from that chapter in my life, I was sure that those confusing feelings would simply fade.

I forced myself to stop thinking about Max, and went back to thinking about the outfit I would wear to see David. I decided on the light yellow suit with the brown trim. It was the most fashionable outfit I owned, and it held sentimental value—at least to me—for it was what I was wearing the day when we'd first met. Besides, it was an appropriate outfit for the meeting I hoped to have afterward at the *Florida Times-Union* with Mr. Jones about returning to work. I just hoped he would be tolerant enough to excuse my lengthy absence and allow me to resume my duties.

The steamboat's sharp whistle startled me back to the present, and I looked around at Jacksonville's large harbor. As I waited in line to debark, I studied the city's ever-changing skyline. One of the tallest buildings housed David's office, and another one was the *Florida Times-Union*. I expected our life together would grow and change just like the skyline. I only prayed that we grew in the same direction.

Chapter 43
The Hawk and the Tiger

"Oh, David, that's so exciting!" I said, reacting to his news that we would be spending a week in New York City before going on to Philadelphia so that he could show me his family's home and his old stomping grounds.

"I'm sorry we can't go to Europe for our honeymoon," David said with a sad smile, which made him look as though he was pouting. "I was hoping we could sail on the Cunard Line's newest addition, the RMS *Etruria*. Unfortunately, my time is going to be limited because I have to be back for some land acquisitions that Henry needs for more tracks, and for a hotel he hopes to build. He has great plans for St. Augustine—amazing ones, really."

As I sat across from him at a corner table in the upscale Golden Shell restaurant, on the beach in Jacksonville, I watched his eyes light up as he talked about the plans Henry Flagler had for St. Augustine.

It was amazing to think that in just six weeks I would become his wife, while just six weeks before I had been traversing the Florida wilderness looking for my sister. How quickly things changed and how quickly people could move on.

Fortunately, David had been more than understanding when we met in St. James Park, the morning after I returned from Silver Springs. Before I could say anything other than hello, he gathered me into his arms and rested his chin atop my head; then he softly whispered how glad he was that I was home unharmed. I held onto him tightly for a moment, which allowed my quickly beating heart to slow down and for me to breathe normally again as I realized that all was well with David.

Hand in hand, we'd walked over to one of the benches and sat there for a couple of hours while I told him about my hunt for Ivy and what the outcome had been. He had listened patiently and had only interrupted me every now and then to ask a question or two. But he didn't ask for a lot of details or question me about things that I only lightly covered or chose to entirely omit. Most important, he made me feel as though I hadn't compromised my relationship with him or done anything too terribly inappropriate.

Of course, we didn't plan on sharing the details of my trip with friends and acquaintances while sipping sherry in the salon of some elegant home or lavishly appointed hotel. Those times were for telling stories about visiting Europe, or building new cities. Hunting for my sister as she fled a murderous father while carrying an illegitimate Negro baby was not conversation for the upper crust, but I was terribly grateful that David was so understanding about the position I'd been put in and didn't judge me unfairly because of it.

The one thing that David asked of me was that I never speak of that time again. He wanted me to file it away as just another part of the past. I didn't ask him why. Maybe because I was so relieved that he'd accepted my actions, or perhaps, I was afraid of his answer. So I agreed to leave it behind me and to never revisit it aloud again.

However, that did not mean those memories didn't work their way into my thoughts. I figured that over time, I would begin to forget the small details of that journey; given more time, I would forget some of the larger ones, as well. But there was one thing that remained crystal clear: Max telling me that he had started to fall in love with me. I prayed that memory would fade faster than all the others, because I thought of it constantly.

"Do you want Baked Alaska, Eve, darling? Hello, Eve?" David laughed as he waved his hand in front of my face, trying to get my attention. "Where were you? You were staring off into space like you're a million miles away."

"Oh, I'm sorry." I blinked my eyes several times to refocus. David was right; I'd been a million miles away, or at least a hundred or so. "I'm sorry. What were you asking me?"

David looked a little concerned. "I wanted to know if you want Baked Alaska for dessert or something else. Are you feeling all right? Maybe you'd just rather go on home."

"I'm sorry, David, but would you mind terribly? I slept so badly last night, and between that and trying to make up some lost time with the newspaper by having three articles ready for Mr. Jones by the middle of next week, I'm feeling pretty worn out."

Just at that moment, the waiter arrived to take our dessert order. "No dessert tonight, Arthur. Just the check, please." David reached inside his jacket for his billfold as the waiter bowed slightly and moved away to tally the bill.

"What is it you're writing about now, Eve?"

"Well, the latest piece I'm working on is about some of the folks who came here to homestead and what they've done to eke out a living in the wilds of Florida." I smiled, then felt a yawn coming on, and tried to stifle it, but the yawn won. "I'm sorry I have to end the evening so early."

"Don't be silly," he said as the waiter put the bill down in front of him, and David laid fifty dollars on top of it. "But I expect you to be all bright-eyed and bushy-tailed tomorrow afternoon when we go pick out our wedding bands. I have one in mind for you, but I didn't dare buy it without your seeing it. It's something special, though. I will say that."

He was obviously anxious for me to see it, and I knew that I'd feel more excited about it after I got some much-needed sleep. "I can't wait to see it," I said as I worked at securing my dark green velvet hat in place, just in front of my bun. I still couldn't get used to hat pins and tiny, useless hats, but I'd been determined to wear it. I'd fallen in love with the hat as soon as I saw it in the millinery shop's window. The green color looked good on me, but what really drew me to it was the beautiful feather that was set at a jaunty angle on the left side, just above the rolled-up brim. I'd gone into the store to inquire about the price and asked the shopkeeper what kind of feather was on the hat. When she told me it was a hawk's feather, I pulled out the cash for it immediately. Even though it cost me a small fortune, I just had to have it.

After David dropped me back at the boardinghouse, I entered the hall as quietly as I could. There was no sound coming from any of the rooms, so I figured everyone was either asleep or out. In the foyer there was a narrow table that stood against the right wall where Mrs. Sikes would put each day's mail to be sorted through by the residents. I saw that there were two small packages, and both were addressed to me. If they were wedding gifts, which I assumed they must be, they were the first ones I'd received at the boarding house. All the gifts coming from David's family and friends were being sent to the apartment he was renting near his office downtown. Though David's place was lovely, it was small, and we'd talked about getting a home immediately. As I gathered up my packages, I decided I'd ask him if he could take some time away from work one afternoon so that we could go looking. He'd been so busy acquiring properties for Flagler that he had neglected to acquire one for us. I smiled and shook my head, thinking about my very ambitious fiancé.

I tiptoed up the stairs and quietly entered my room. It was empty, so I figured that the nurses I still shared it with must have night duty again. Before getting involved with anything else, I got ready for bed and then sat with my two packages. The first one was from Mama's sister, my aunt Emma Jean, in Lexington. Mama must have written her about my marriage. Thinking about Mama was crushingly painful. I kept telling myself that the feelings would fade with time, but what she had done had cut me so deeply that it was unlikely I would ever completely heal.

Pushing aside that fact, as well as the package's brown wrapping paper, I opened a small box to find a set of six very old silver baby spoons. Included was a note that said the spoons had been in the family for longer than my aunt could remember, and she thought this was the perfect time to pass them on to the next generation. She said that she could vaguely remember using them as a child, which meant that Mama had used them, too.

Sighing, I set aside the spoons and picked up the other box, which was even smaller. There was no return address, so I didn't have any idea who had sent it. I quickly removed the thick brown paper and a lovely handmade oak box was revealed. It was well-crafted and beautifully simple, and the wood glowed a deep gold from the lacquer that had been carefully applied to it. Lifting the lid, I found a pendant nestled inside. Carefully pulling it out, I examined it under the lamplight. It was made from mother of pearl, and the face of a tiger had been perfectly and exquisitely carved into it.

As I moved it this way and that in the light, the iridescence of the shell shifted in color from purplish-grey to pink and even to soft green. At the top of the piece, a perfect little hole had been made, which allowed a leather cord to be threaded through it. When I slipped the pendant over my head, it came to rest right at the top of my breasts. I gingerly rubbed it as I looked back in the box, and found a small note in the bottom. I unfolded it and began to read the unfamiliar handwriting:

Eve, there is an old Indian saying that even though marriage makes two into one, the happiest unions are those where each person respects the other as a unique and strong individual. Never let your own spirit wither away, kaccv hokte. May you live with much abundance and joy.
Max

"Max. I miss you, Max," I whispered. "I miss you."

I wondered how he'd known where to send the gift, and then I remembered Mrs. Brody: She said she was going to post my wedding banns in the window at the store, and she'd asked me for my Jacksonville address right before I'd left.

Holding both the pendant and note firmly against my chest, I got into bed and stared at the ceiling. Finally, I fell into a restless sleep, and I dreamed about a hawk flying above a tiger as it ran along the banks of a dark and winding river.

Chapter 44
Wither Not, My Soul

"I'm sorry I'm late," I said as I entered David's office. It was fifteen minutes before five, and I had told him I'd be there by four thirty.

"It's all right." He laughed as he stood up from his desk and then came around to kiss me. "I had to finish up some paperwork, so your timing is actually good."

"Perfect! What time did you say the jeweler closes?"

"Five thirty. But he's just up the street, so we should be fine. Besides, I'm sure he wouldn't mind staying open a little longer, if necessary, considering the occasion."

"And considering the customer," I teased him. I was beginning to believe that there wasn't a soul in Jacksonville who hadn't met David Perlow yet. He was a good business man, as well as outgoing, and I was sure he'd never met a stranger.

"Just give me a minute to go to the washroom," he said as he started for the door, "and then we'll go."

I sat down in one of two leather wing-back chairs in front of his desk. "Oh, I need a—" I was going to say *stamp*, but he'd already stepped out of the room. Moving around his desk, I pulled open his top left drawer, where I knew he kept them. I'd written a thank-you note to Aunt Emma Jean, though I'd held off writing one to Max. I wasn't quite sure what I wanted to say yet, other than thanking him for his beautiful gift. I was afraid I'd say too much and just as afraid that I'd say too little.

I found the stamps and set the note down so that I could stick one on it. When I did, I saw several tax lien certificates spread out across the desk. Quickly looking them over, I saw that two were for properties around the

St. Augustine area, and the others were for properties in the north-central part of the state. Just then, David opened the door and walked in.

"What are you searching for, Eve?" He looked a bit taken aback to find me in such an awkward situation. And I was quite sure I looked just as surprised to be caught in one.

"I-I needed a stamp," I stammered. "So I took one from your drawer. What are these, David?" I held one of the certificates out to him.

David quickly walked over to me and took it. "It's just business, Eve. Nothing you'd be interested in, I'm sure." He moved around the desk, and I moved away from it.

"Actually, I am. I'm interested in what you do. Tell me how these work, David."

He quickly gathered the certificates up and stuck them in a desk drawer. "Eve, the jeweler closes in less than an hour. Let's go and I'll tell you as we're walking."

"No. The jeweler will still be there tomorrow. I'm real curious why you'd have those. How do they fit in with what you're workin' on?"

"Good God, Eve! Must we really discuss this now? I told Byron Hoffman we'd be there, and I don't like standing someone up."

"I'm sure he'll understand. Just tell him I delayed you. So, please, tell me about these tax lien certificates. What are they exactly?" I had a sinking feeling I already knew. Working at the newspaper had enlightened me on quite a few subjects I hadn't known much about beforehand.

David impatiently sighed and sat. I sat across from him. "Eve, as I'm acquiring property for hotels, as well as for the expansion of the railroad, it's necessary to purchase properties that are sometimes owned by other people. Without that property, the building of the hotel can't be undertaken in the desired location, or, in the case of the railroad, the tracks have to deviate from a straight-line route. That adds a lot of hours, labor, and costs to projects, not to mention headaches. So, we try to buy these properties, and most of the time, people are willing to sell. But if they're not, and if they owe any back taxes, then we buy their tax liens."

"And you don't give them a chance to pay you before you call in the debt, is that it, David?"

"No, Eve! That is *not* it! Granted, we do charge a much higher interest rate than they originally paid, but if they've fallen into arrears, then whose fault is it really if they get into a bind and can't make payments?"

"And that bind would be paying you an exorbitant amount or you foreclose on the property. Right?"

"Eve, this is business! It's the way it's done. It's legal, and it's—"

"Heartless," I finished for him.

"Oh, for heaven's sake, Eve! If it were left to small-property owners to bring progress to this country, then a hundred years from now the landscape would look exactly the same. It would be a rough, snake-infested wasteland, with just a few antiquated steamboats huffing and puffing down the rivers, past a few pathetic weed-ridden gardens and rickety homesteads every now and then!"

"Is this what our life is going to be about, David? Seeing how fast we can bulldoze little nuisances out of our way so that we can get ahead of everyone else in order to have the biggest house or the best table at the country club?"

"What do you have against success, Eve?"

"What it takes for some folks to achieve it, David. I don't want to turn into one of them. I want to be able to look myself in the mirror and like the person looking back. If this is how we'll afford living the kind of life you have planned for us, it will make me want to smash every mirror in the house."

"Aren't you being overly dramatic, Eve?"

"Maybe from where you're standing, David, but not from where I am. I see a whole other side of it. I'll tell you what." I stood. "I'm going to forget about the jeweler's and dinner tonight and just head on back to the boardinghouse. I'm really not very hungry."

"You're being ridiculous, Eve!" David was standing now, too.

"Maybe so, but at least I know I'm not letting my own spirit wither away." I turned and walked toward the door.

"Excuse me? What the hell does that mean?"

"Never mind, David. It's just an old Indian expression." I walked out, closing the door behind me.

Chapter 45
On the River Again

"Are you sleeping standing up?" I heard a familiar voice ask. I opened my eyes to a glaring sun and immediately put my hand up to shade my eyes. Standing in front of me was my brother Joseph. "I didn't wake you, did I?" He moved around to stand beside me at the bow railing.

"No, no. I just closed my eyes for a minute. This breeze is wonderful, isn't it? I do believe there's a touch of fall in the air." I looked out at the St. Johns and watched a large anhinga break the water's surface with a fish in its mouth. His long neck gave him a snakelike appearance.

"Well, it is September, so it should be gettin' cooler. Nice, isn't it?"

"Mmmmm," I said as I lifted my face upward again. "Are you on a break?"

"Yeah. I'm gonna get some dinner. You want to eat with me?"

"Shoot! I just ate. If I'd known, I'd have waited."

"No problem. It wouldn't have been a leisurely dining experience anyway. I'll be shoveling it in so that I can get below deck to make sure the men are shoveling coal into the furnace," he quipped. "We'll be in Palatka in about thirty minutes. Do you know what boat you're taking from there?"

"I'm not sure. When I bought my tickets, the clerk wasn't sure which one was runnin' the Palatka-to-Lake Weir route. But whichever boat it is, I pray Papa isn't on it."

"I don't think you have to worry about that, Eve. From what I've heard, he never leaves the house anymore."

"Have you seen them at all since this thing happened with Ivy?"

"Just that one time I told you about. I got the last of my things out of the house and told them I wouldn't be coming back. Lord, God, but Mama wailed like I'd just died."

"Well, in a way you had—and James, too. I got a letter from him, you know, and he told me he'd written a letter saying he could never forgive them for what they'd tried to do to Ivy. He told me he was just going to stay in Athens instead of coming home for vacations. Said he had a nearly-full-time job now, and between that and his studies, he was pretty well stuck there. Said he probably would be until he graduates in a few years. And when he does, his plan is to go straight from the university to Atlanta or one of the bigger cities. Sad we had to cut all ties with our folks, Joseph." I sighed.

"They brought this on themselves, Eve. Hell, I wish I could go back home every now and then, too, but it's out of the question after what they did. Speaking of letters, have you heard anything from Ivy?"

"I've had one letter from her, and she said she's gettin' as big as a barn with the baby. Said it wouldn't surprise her if she had twins. Lord, I think one set in the family is plenty enough," I laughed. Though the truth was that if my sister had twins, I'd be tinkled pink—or blue, or both.

"Not to change the subject, Eve, but I wanted to ask you about your own plans; if you're planning on going back to Jacksonville, or what? And are you sure you don't want to see David again?"

"I'm not due back at the paper until Tuesday, so that gives me four days off. And as far as seeing David again, no, we said all we needed to say."

"I'm sorry y'all had to break off the engagement." Joseph hugged me hard. "I was really hoping this would work out for you."

"I know." I was touched by his brotherly concern. "But things always turn out for the best. David and I had a good talk, and we parted as friends. That was really important to both of us, I think. We just had to be really honest with each other—and ourselves. We were mismatched from the start. He wants one thing out of life, and I want another. He wants to reshape Florida into something glittery and gold, while I like the natural green- and blueness of it. I think we would have butted heads throughout our entire marriage, and he saw that, too. We had breakfast together yesterday, and it was nice to be able to say a proper good-bye to him. He's a good man, but he's far too aggressively ambitious for my liking. I'm sure he'll swoop some woman off her feet before too long, though."

"Probably," Joseph said. "And so, dear sister, you're headed for Lake Weir now?"

"Yes. That was part of being real honest with myself. You know I have to see Max, Joseph."

"I know," he said as he ran his hand down the hair on the back of my head. "I heard he bought a good-sized grove there, somethin' like twenty acres of orange and grapefruit trees. That's pretty nice," he said as he pushed himself away from the railing. "And I've heard he's still huntin' some and sellin' the meat at the dock. If he's not there when you get to Lake Weir, someone will know where to find him. Okay, I better go."

"I'll see you later," I said. Then I turned back to face the river and pray to whoever was up there listening that Max Harjo wanted to be found.

Chapter 46
Stepping through the Door

I always found that when I was faced with the unknown, it was a comfort seeing a familiar face. And such was the case when the *May Breeze* pulled into the dock at Palatka. I could see Emmitt Hailey's broad smile beaming at me from the pilot house. I don't think I'd ever been gladder to see him because as this final leg of the journey to Lake Weir was getting underway, I could feel my anxiety and uncertainty rising along with the tide.

After handing my satchel to the steward, who, I was relieved to see, was not my father, for safekeeping, I climbed the wooden steps up to the pilot house and poked my head through the open doorway. Captain Dial was down on deck, leaving Emmitt alone for the time being, and he stood and invited me in when I appeared.

"Well, Miss Eve, if you ain't a sight fo' sore eyes, I don't know who is!" He pumped my hand up and down as enthusiastically as if he was working the handle on the water pump of a nearly empty well. "Here, have a seat, have a seat!" He indicated the vacant chair next to his. "We ain't leavin' for another fifteen minutes or so. I want to hear what all you got goin' on and why I have the pleasure of havin' ya on board today!"

"Emmitt," I laughed as I sat. "*You're* the one who's a sight for sore eyes. I'm sure glad you're doin' the piloting today."

"So what brings ya all the way from Jacksonville?" He turned his chair toward me and sat.

"A fool's errand, I'm afraid," I said with a smile.

"Oh, pshaw, Miss Eve! I ain't never known ya to do a foolish thing in your life. I have a feelin' you're worryin' more about the outcome than about whether or not you should be doin' it. So, what is it you're a-doin'?"

"Goin' to see Max Harjo." I looked down at my blue-and-white paisley dress, not wanting to see the judgment in Emmitt's eyes.

"Well, I wondered when you'd get 'round to doin' that."

I looked up and saw that comforting, familiar smile of his, and his eyes weren't filled with judgment or disapproval, just a warmth and a kindness that I needed as badly as a drowning man needs air.

My eyes welled up. "Have you seen him?" I whispered.

"A few times," Emmitt softly replied, almost conspiratorially. If it was possible, the twinkle in his eyes seemed to grow even brighter. "When I seen him, he ain't had a whole lot to say. Been lookin' real serious-like. Maybe it's 'cause he's got a lot on his mind—like the new grove 'n all. Sometimes a man'll just throw hisself into his work to escape some other ghost a-ridin' his back. I seen many a man with that haunted look in his eyes, and it always comes down to one thing causin' it, and that'd be a woman." He beamed at me, as though he was just plum tickled with what was going on. "And the cure for that world-ain't-a-bit-o'-good look in his eyes is when that woman happens to come around again. Then it's like the good Lord washed away every problem that man had a-weighin' his poor ol' shoulders down. Just lifted 'em right off! Amazin' thing, really."

Just then, Captain Dial signaled to Emmitt from the deck below that it was time to depart. When he noticed me sitting next to his pilot, he smiled and made his way up the stairs to the house, and I stood to greet him.

"Stay where you are! Stay where you are," he insisted, though I remained standing. "How are ya, Eve? I swear. It's been too long! I'll tell ya one thing, you keep gettin' prettier every year!"

"Thank you, Captain Dial." I laughed. "It's surely been a while. It's good to see you."

"How's Hap doin'?" he asked, losing his smile.

"Honestly, Captain Dial, I couldn't say. Last time I was home, things weren't goin' so well."

"I bet," he said as he patted me on the back. "The dock's a small place," he went on apologetically. "People talk."

"I know, Captain, and it's okay. Probably most of what you heard was true anyway."

"Well," he said as he inhaled deeply, "we're sure glad you're on board today. And I hope it'll be more often."

"Thanks, Captain. Really…thank you."

"All righty then." He smiled broadly and looked over at Emmitt. "Let's start gettin' to where we're goin'. And you stay right where you're at, Eve.

I'm sick o' that ol' man's company, anyway." He chuckled. He stepped through the doorway and started down the steps.

"You 'bout ready to step through your own doorway, Miss Eve?"

"As ready as I'll ever be, Emmitt."

"That's plenty ready enough," he assured me.

We arrived at the Lake Weir landing several hours later, and the place looked just the way it had the last time I'd been there, which was much like Silver Springs, with its general store and busy docks. I scanned the area off to the right of the store, where some meat racks were set up, but saw no sign of Max. As if he was reading my mind, Emmitt told me not to worry. "If he ain't here, Miss Eve, we'll see about gettin' you a ride out to his—Wait, now," he said, interrupting himself and craning his neck over to the left. "Yeah, there he is!" He pointed.

I looked over to the left side of the general store, and sure enough, there was Max. He was leaning against the building with his left leg bent at the knee and his boot braced up against the wall behind him. His hat was pulled down low over his eyes, and he smoked a thin cigar. The way he looked at that moment reminded me of the day I bought the deer meat for Mama but was short on money.

Emmitt blew the steamboat's whistle to indicate he was pulling into the dock, and when he did, Max lifted his black felt hat ever so slightly to see which boat was coming in and then lowered it again.

"It's now or never, Miss Eve." Emmitt smiled encouragingly.

Wishing I felt half as confident as he looked, I took a deep breath and kissed him on the cheek. "Thank you, Emmitt—for everything."

He looked a little shocked at my open display of affection, but he looked pleased, just the same. "Why, you know you're welcome, honey. Anything. Anytime. You just let me know. Now, you go on and get out there. You got a future to start."

I started for the door but a thought stopped me. "You know, Emmitt," I said, turning to look at him. "With Ivy and Moses bein' married 'n all, and with the baby on its way, that makes you and me kin now." I smiled.

"You know," he said with a little awe in his voice, "I never thought about it like that, but that'd be 'bout right, wouldn't it?" He looked both amazed and pleased at the same time. "Well, now, ain't that somethin'?" he said. "Ain't that *somethin'*!"

Chapter 47
Our Two Worlds

I walked down the dock among a good many people who had just come off the *May Breeze* as well. Being surrounded by a small crowd gave me a chance to watch Max for a few moments without his realizing I was there. At one point, he tossed his cigar away, pushed his hat up a tad to see who was coming off the boats; then, spotting nothing of much interest, he drew it back down over his eyes.

Suddenly, his head snapped up, and he pushed his hat away from his eyes and immediately locked gazes with me. He watched me, without moving another muscle, until I got closer, and then he pushed himself away from the building and walked over to his racks to wait for me.

I stopped in front of him. "Hello, Max," I said as I awkwardly shifted my satchel from my right hand to my left.

"Eve," he said in his low, deep voice and then said nothing more.

I had known this wasn't going to be easy, but I hadn't realized how extremely difficult it would be. I didn't know what to say. I just knew what I felt. "I-I…um, I was…"

"Yes?" Max seemed a bit amused at my obvious discomfort and, from the looks of it, wasn't about to make things any easier for me. "You here for a visit?"

"Well, I guess…In a way." I was completely at a loss.

He suddenly sounded a little impatient. "Why are you here, Eve? What did you want to see me about?" There was no fooling him that I'd come for any other reason.

"I wanted to thank you for the tiger pendant," I blurted out as I lifted if up from the front of my dress to show him I was wearing it. My excuse sounded pathetic.

"You sure came a long way to thank me for a wedding present when you could have sent a note, especially since I know you never let yourself run out of stamps. Anyway, how'd the wedding go?"

"It didn't," I said, letting the pendant drop.

"And why's that?" Max asked flatly, though I could see in his eyes that my answer had sparked his interest.

"Because a person shouldn't marry someone they're... Oh, damn it!" I said, both tired and frustrated. "Never mind! I should never have come here. Just forget I did." I swung my whole body and satchel around to head back to the *May Breeze* for the return trip.

"Hold up, little *kaccv hokte*." Max laughed.

Out of everything that he could have done to irritate me, laughing at me one was the one thing that was sure to get my dander up like nothing else. "Never mind!" I shouted as I swung around again, nearly hitting him with my satchel.

"Here, give me that thing! You're dangerous with it!" Max snatched the bag out of my hand; then taking me firmly by my upper arm, he pulled me to the side of the general store. "Sit!" he said as he maneuvered me over to an old tree stump that had been polished by enough derrieres that the top was as smooth as glass. "Talk." He stood in front of me with his arms folded, watching me hard.

"I...I just miss you." I lowered my head so that my chin was nearly touching my chest, and though I bit my bottom lip hard trying to fight back the tears, I began to cry. Max rattled off a string of words, but because they were Muskogee, I had no clue what he was saying. And the fact that he was talking in a language that I couldn't understand—and perhaps berating me in it—frustrated me. I pushed myself up from the stump.

"You know what it took for me to come see you?" I took a step closer to him. "Do you, Max? *Do you?* Do you not realize that all the plans I've made have been squashed now? I've put my job on the line, and my life on hold, so that I could come see you face to face!" Angry, I was pointing a finger at him. "Everything that I have worked so hard for and had lined up for my future, I was willing to forfeit for you, Max. *For you!*" My voice rose in both pitch and volume. This man's smugness and arrogance made me damn mad.

"That may be so, Eve," he said, "but you haven't given me the first reason as to why you'd do that—give up all these things that you thought were so extremely important. What I want to know is why? *Why?*" All of a sudden, I felt totally drained and exhausted. In response, I let out a barely audible moan as I exhaled, and my shoulders sagged. "Because," I said in a resigned and utterly defeated voice. "Because I love you." I bowed my head and stared down at the tops of my black booties, watching as small clean spots appeared where the teardrops landed on the dusty leather.

Suddenly, large warm hands gently but firmly cupped my face and raised it up so that I was staring into a pair of intense dark blue eyes that seemed to look right through me. And below his eyes, his strong masculine mouth came down to whisper against my own mouth, "That's it, Eve. Yes, that's it." His voice was husky, filled with emotion as he ran his hands up from my face and into my hair.

"Do you think we can make our two different worlds work together, Max?" I whispered.

"Yes, little *kaccv hokte,*" his beautiful mouth whispered against mine. "I think you and I can do just about anything."

Then he covered my mouth with his, and as we stood there tasting and embracing each other, I heard the sharp blast of a steamboat's whistle. There was no need to interrupt our kiss to see who was blowing it, though. I knew that standing in the pilot house of the *May Breeze* was a wise and wonderful old friend, smiling his broad smile of approval.

Epilogue
Our Own Corner

Lake Weir
Ocklawaha, Florida
1885

Max ran his hand down my slightly rounded belly and lower, until he found the most sensitive spot on my body. Using his other hand to pull me over to him, he touched me firmly, more quickly, until he brought me to a perfect release in the clear, cool waters of the spring. Bringing his lips down to mine, he sealed the exquisite moment with his mouth and then started to climb out of the pool, but I pulled him back again and wrapped my legs around him, encouraging him to find the same beautiful release that I had just found.

As he moved within me, I saw the glint of my wedding band reflected in the bright morning sun as I gripped his large shoulders, and I marveled again at the fact that we had been married for nearly a year, with a child due in just a few short months. I held Max tightly as he moaned deeply and shuddered and then waited as his breathing slowed and returned to normal. We climbed out of the spring together and lay on the soft grass to allow our naked bodies to dry in the early September sun. Putting an arm beneath my head, I looked out at our vast citrus grove and saw that the small yellow and orange fruits were quickly ripening.

Much like the babe in my belly, I thought to myself. Max pulled me over to him, and as I snuggled against his side, I couldn't help but think about how happy I was.

Fortunately, I still wrote for the *Florida Times-Union*, but from afar and on a freelance basis. Charles Jones had been more than kind by keeping me on the staff and printed as many stories as I could send to him. I traveled as much as I could and as often as Max was able to leave the grove. He always accompanied me as I wandered around the state, taking advantage of the different areas for hunting while I gathered stories about the people and the places that made Florida an interesting amalgam of the past and the present.

Sadly, I hadn't spoken to my parents since the day I'd walked out of the house. And from what I'd been told by the very few who still knew anything about their day-to-day existence, Papa was still the same while my mother seemed to be quickly fading. Her health was poor, and she was unable to work anymore. Because I kept in touch with James and Joseph, I knew that they were sending money to get our parents by, but I still hadn't been able to bring myself to the point of reaching out to them.

Ivy and Moses were doing well with their baby, Charles Maxwell, otherwise known as "Charlie," and we were planning on visiting them within the month, before I got much bigger.

Ivy was becoming a well-respected and much-sought-after medicine woman in South Florida in just the relatively short time she'd been there. Because she was white, she was able to go back and forth between the Seminoles and the white world. Both groups of people had learned to trust her and count on her.

Moses had been fully embraced by the Seminole people because of his heritage and had learned their language quickly. He became instrumental to the negotiation of trades or sales between the Seminoles and the whites.

James and Joseph were following their dreams with great focus and determination. James continued his studies in structural engineering at the University of Georgia, and he was considering the southern part of the state as the place to begin his career upon graduation. Florida seemed to be in an ongoing state of change, and James realized that progress would continue south, where land was plentiful and opportunities awaited. It was inevitable that the trains would end up running the length of the state someday, and James seemed to have set his sights on helping to raise new towns and cities all along the rail lines. But while James looked toward the south for his future, Joseph was interested in all points of the compass as he continued working his way up the waterways of America.

My older brother signed on with the prestigious Anchor Line Company, in New Orleans in March of '85. The ship he'd been assigned to was the *City of New Orleans*, and it was nothing short of a floating palace. At two hundred ninety feet in length, the ship required five boilers, which Joseph expertly oversaw. The ship ran the New Orleans to St. Louis route, carrying passengers as well as large tonnages of cargo for trade. Working for the Anchor Line Company made it necessary for him to move to New Orleans, so as soon as the ink was dry on his contract, he moved with his wife Regina, and their son Matthew Wayne, to his new home port. Though I missed him, I was terribly proud of him for being considered one of the finest maritime engineers in the area. He had worked hard to achieve that reputation, and it was paying off handsomely for him.

Regardless that my siblings and I were scattered far from each other, we knew that nothing would ever come between us again.

Suddenly, I felt the baby moving and turned to Max to tell him but saw that he was sleeping. He looked so peaceful that I just let him be. As I watched him, I thanked God once again for this beautiful man with whom I shared such an intense yet gentle love. We had indeed created one world out of the two vastly different ones we'd come from, and though it was not a perfect world, it was ours, and our own special corner in Glory Land.

Don't miss the next novel in Janie DeVos's fascinating account of early Florida,

The Rising of Glory Land.

Preface

My world changed as I sat hidden within the branches of a wasted orange tree. I was playing hide-and-seek with my nearly nine-year-old brother, Dylan, and at the moment, he was "it." As I sat silently upon a limb, my mother appeared below me and, refusing to give away my hiding spot, I watched her look soundlessly at the devastation that surrounded us. Even at the age of seven, I knew that the amount of damage our citrus groves had suffered was enormous. Thousands of shriveled and pitted-skinned oranges covered the ground, and beyond what I could see were another hundred acres of the frozen remains of our tangerine and grapefruit trees. Nothing had been spared.

Mama squatted down and picked up a ruined orange, but the sound of a wagon rolling down the road that ran parallel to our grove got her attention, as well as mine, and she stood up and looked in that direction. Several rows of orange trees blocked our view for the moment, but just from the creaking, sluggish sound of the wagon plodding along, I figured it was heavily weighted down. When it cleared the trees, I could see that I'd been correct. The conveyance was piled high with belongings, and crowded in and among them all was Clyde Whitfield, along with his family. All five of his children, as well as his wife, Grace, looked as beaten down as our groves. But as Clyde turned toward Mama to touch the brim of his sweat-stained hat in greeting, I saw more than just defeat look on his face. I could see a terrible fear in his eyes that seemed to ask the question: *What now?*

When the first freeze slammed Florida on December 29, the temperature sank to nineteen degrees, and snow blanketed areas from Tampa across the state to Titusville. But even while Dylan and I were making our first snowballs, I couldn't stop thinking about the things I'd heard during the meeting at our church the night before. Another grove owner Bob Chapman started saying that Armageddon had begun, and since Reverend Short had preached about that very thing just a few weeks before, I knew what Mr. Chapman was talking about and it terrified me. Looking around at how unusually full the church pews were, I couldn't help but believe he might be right. We prayed together as "children of a mighty and merciful God" for hours that night, and at first it seemed as if our prayers might actually have been heard, for within the week small signs of life began shooting out in green buds on the sturdier older trees.

My parents, Max and Eve Harjo, knew that many of our younger trees wouldn't survive, but they felt that the older ones could, and Papa had said those that did were almost guaranteed to give us the sweetest fruit we'd ever tasted. But all hope was lost when the second freeze, on February 8, hit us even harder than the first one had. There was no snow this time, but after the temperatures stayed well below freezing for two straight days, there was nothing left of the trees but shriveled fruit and blown out bark when the sap froze in the trunks. Leaves and fruit fell from the branches, leaving our once beautiful groves a dying wasteland. My father said that if Mr. Chapman was right—that Armageddon had begun—then the Bible had gotten it wrong, after all. We wouldn't be consumed by fire and brimstone, he said, but by an icy grip instead.

Suddenly, I heard Papa calling Mama's name. "I'm in the third row," she shouted, and a moment later, he appeared through some of the trees about halfway down the row from us. I knew I should make my presence known, but there'd been too many hushed conversations between my parents lately, and I wanted an unfiltered version of what was going on, so I remained silent and still.

"Did you see the Whitfields?" he asked as he walked toward her.

"Yeah, but I didn't get a chance to talk to them. I just saw them ride by with what looked to be everything they own piled into that old wagon. Did you talk to Clyde?"

"Yes. They've had enough. Since losing most of what they had in the '86 freeze, they only had the fifteen acres of tangerines left, and most of those were younger trees. The grove's destroyed. They're heading back to Brunswick. You 'bout done here, Eve? We need to sit down and settle on what we're gonna do, and when."

"Still thinkin' about doing what we talked about last night, Max?" Mama asked.

"Yes," Papa confirmed.

"I figured you'd already made up your mind that's where we're headed." She smiled up at him. After ten years of marriage, it was obvious they knew each other pretty well. "James will be thrilled," she said, referring to her older brother.

I liked Uncle James. He always brought Dylan and me something when he came for a visit, and he looked a lot like Mama, with his dark red hair and brown eyes. He lived far away, south of us, in some tiny little placed named Miami. I'd heard him tell my parents more than once that we should move down there, too, but I wasn't so sure that was a good idea. I liked living among the orange groves and swimming in the blue springs, and I saw no reason to change any of that. I had to admit, though, Uncle James' enthusiasm was fairly contagious as he described the beauty of the place, and the different and exciting things to do, like swimming in an ocean of salty water. What a strange thing that would be!

"Well, I'm glad someone will be thrilled about it," Papa said, "'cause Miami's a pretty rough place. But, things will change fast once the railroad gets down there. It didn't freeze that far south – at least not to the extent and duration that it did here, and I'd be willing to bet that railroad man Flagler knows it, too. Even so, we don't have to have groves again, Eve, at least not as large as we have now. There're other ways to make a living, too, and after what we've just been through, I'm leanin' towards those other ways. There's the fishing industry, and, soon enough, there'll be a good tourist industry as more and more folks come down on the trains. James says he's gonna help build up Miami, and I have no doubt that he will. He'll prosper in a big way because of it, too. If we get down there while the place is still young, we can do the same, Eve."

"Still, Max, there's hardly anything there, or anyone either." Mama sounded a little uneasy. "Remember what James once told us? It's mostly dreamers of the hardiest kind or hard people of the most desperate kind that are there now, and we'd be settling our family among them. But I guess we're pretty desperate now, too," she said, forcing a smile.

I was reminded of a letter we'd received from Uncle James soon after he'd arrived in Miami six months before, when he'd gone down to help design and build a hotel. He'd written that the area had so many mosquitoes, horse flies and sand fleas that they were thicker 'n thieves at a blind men's convention and could suck a body dry in a matter of minutes. And if that wasn't enough to make one turn tail and run, there was the fact that the longtime homesteaders and Seminoles didn't take too kindly to a bunch of outsiders coming into their territory and rearranging things as they saw fit.

Though Mama had laughed and said that most of the letter was probably exaggerated, I figured there was some truth in it, too.

My thoughts of the future were quickly replaced by the present when I heard Mama say that it was nearly dinnertime and ask Papa if he was hungry.

"I could eat," he confirmed.

"Let's find Dylan and Eliza," she said as she bent down to look beneath the branches of the trees to see if she could spot our legs down one of the rows. "We need to let them know what's going on."

As they headed off toward home, I didn't move from my branch. I needed to think things over for a minute or two, to see how I felt about it, and to see how it felt to say the name of that strange new place out loud. "Miami," I whispered. I climbed down through the branches, shimmied down the trunk, and then started for home. "Miami!" I said a little louder. I decided I liked the name. *Maybe I'll decide I like the place, too*, I thought, *if the 'skeeters don't run us off before I have enough time to settle in.*

About the Author

Janie DeVos, a native of Coral Gables, Florida, first began working in the advertising industry in the late 1980s, but left the field in 2000 and turned her love for writing into a full time career. She is the author of the national-award winning poem *How High Can You Fly*, as well as acclaimed children's picture books and women's fiction novels

Ms. DeVos has made numerous appearances in schools and libraries as well as in bookstores including Barnes and Noble and Borders Books. She has been a keynote speaker, a selected author for special events for the Miami Book Fair International, and has served on various committees, including being the authors' liaison for the Reading Across Broward Festival in 2006. In the autumn of 2013, she was a highlighted author at the Carolina Literary Festival, outside of Asheville.

Janie DeVos continues work on her novels, while enjoying her not-so-quiet life with her husband and two howling Basset Hounds in a log cabin on the top of a mountain in North Carolina.